The Rostrum

By

W. T. Sanders

Written by: W.T. Sanders

Cover Design: Erica Starr

Publisher: The Script Mentor

Chapter I
Enter the Jackal

It was a sweltering afternoon on September 6, 1901, at the Pan-American Exposition in Buffalo, New York. The sprawling 350-acre tourist attraction was a World's Fair intended to showcase the progress of modern society and technology and as noted by its official slogan "promote the commercial wellbeing and good understanding among the American Republics." Unfortunately, the five-foot eight-inch-tall wireworker from Detroit who was entering the exposition grounds had other less benevolent intentions. As he purchased his ticket and entered the main gate, none of the exposition goers in the vicinity seemed to notice the slight bulge in the right pocket of his gray coat jacket. Not even the City of Buffalo police officer standing to his left who was trying to impress a young woman with the size of his billy-club took notice of the plain looking man with reddish brown hair as he passed by within arm's reach.

Like a nervous jackal avoiding the observation of a pride of lions, the man moved cautiously ever deeper into the venue until he saw it: the Exposition's Temple of Music. For a temporary construction intended to stand only for the seven months of the fair, the Temple of Music was one of the Exposition's most ornate and beautiful structures. It was located on the Esplanade near a cascading water fountain and was filled with the throaty melodies from a great pipe organ. But it wasn't the beauty of this structure or the lively music emanating from it that drew him to this setting. No, this jackal had a blood lust to fulfill, one that would change the course of destiny if he were successful. Standing across the road near a display of shrubbery, he reached into his pocket and withdrew a white handkerchief that concealed an object about the size of his hand. Being sure to conceal his treasure from prying eyes, he unfolded the corners of the handkerchief one by one to reveal a silver Iver Johnson revolver that glinted in the broken rays of sunlight that made it through the concealing fo-

liage.

Chapter II
The Prey

In a private room across the Exposition grounds, President William McKinley was freshening up and preparing to attend a public gathering. His personal secretary George Cortelyou, concerned about the potential security risks, commented to the nation's leader, "Mr. President, I really don't think it is a good idea to have you greet the general public in a reception line this evening."

With a look of disbelief, President McKinley responded, "Oh, nonsense, George! You worry about me more than Ida does."

"Well, the First Lady has good cause to worry about you these days. Mr. President, the reception line just makes you too vulnerable to a potential attack. It is difficult enough for your protection detail to control such a large crowd, but when they are so much closer to you, it is even harder," pleaded Cortelyou.

President McKinley cajoled, "Why shouldn't I go out there, George? After all, no one wants to hurt me!" Pointing to a slender, well dressed Secret Service agent who was just entering the room, he continued, "Besides, I have a detail of fine Secret Service men like Agent George Foster here, a group of Buffalo detectives, and a squad of Army troops to protect me. Who's going to get past all of that protection?"

"Well sir, I just don't feel right about this," Cortelyou said in an unsure voice.

"Everything this evening will be fine. The Exposition's Temple of Music is a splendid setting, and that magnificent pipe organ they have is going to fill the air with the great works of master composers. I just wish Ida felt like attending; she would very much enjoy this evening. By the way, I have requested that the organist play Schumann's *Traumerei*. As I recall you are as particularly fond of it as I am." Pausing for a minute, he added, "Don't worry George; Agent Foster will be there by my side to protect me every minute, won't you Foster?" President McKinley said, turning to the agent.

The efficient agent paused as he flipped through some papers, looked towards the President, and replied, "Yes sir, I'll be right there watching everything. You don't have to worry about anything, Mr. President." Looking quickly at his pocket watch and then placing it back into his vest pocket, he added, "Mr. President, it's 3:20. Shall we go, sir? The Exposition's president will be nervously waiting for you at the Temple's steps to escort you inside."

"Why yes! We must not be late," said President McKinley. Agent Foster opened the door and then escorted the President and Mr. Cortelyou to the awaiting carriage out front of the building.

Arriving at the Temple of Music at the appointed time, a fidgety John Milburn, the Exposition's president, greeted President McKinley on the front steps of the building and led him and his entourage into the ornate, Byzantine styled interior hall. Walking into the cavernous opening before them, President McKinley looked up, admiring the architecture, and commented to Milburn, "This place is magnificent, John. You have done a great job." As they continued into the great hall to take their positions in the reception line, the melodious sounds of the great pipe organ could be heard in the background. Once positioned in line, they began to greet the long procession of well- wishers and visitors eager to shake the President's hand. Positioned to the left of the President, Agent Foster was watchful for anyone in the reception line who looked suspicious. He scanned the faces of the throngs of people, looking for expressions and nervous twitches that would betray an assailant's malevolent intent. Spotting something he didn't like about a small- framed Italian man standing in the line of closely bunched well- wishers, Agent Foster swiftly stepped from his position, grabbed the man by the shoulders of his overcoat, and pulled him out of the line to the side of the chaotic reception area. In an instant, a couple of Foster's fellow agents quickly joined him and assisted in escorting the man away from the group of dignitaries. After a quick pat- down, Foster and his men found nothing, apologetically released the understandably shaken man, and allowed him to rejoin the reception line.

Before Agent Foster could return to his position next to President McKinley, another man approached the President with a handkerchief awkwardly wrapped around his right hand. As the President reached his hand out to greet the man, two shots were fired from the revolver concealed underneath the handkerchief. Fired at almost point-blank range, the first round struck a glancing blow on the President's chest, stripping a button off his vest, but the second round found its mark deep in his abdomen. Unsure of what had just occurred, the President remained standing but stumbled backwards a couple of steps in shock. Before Agent Foster or others could reach the man, a large black man directly behind the assailant struck the would-be assassin in the neck so hard that the small gun was knocked from his hand, skipping across the marble floor and coming to a spinning stop beneath a row of nearby chairs.

Agent Foster was the first of the startled protection detail to jump on the assailant and restrain him, neutralizing the threat. Foster excitedly yelled to others in the protection detail, "Get the gun, get the gun, get the gun!"

Realizing what had just happened, the surrounding crowd, incensed by the attack, quickly closed on the gunman, ripped him from Agent Foster's grasp, and began to savagely pummel the assailant. Seeing this unfold before him, President McKinley shouted to his protection detail, "Don't let the crowd hurt him, boys!"

Before the vengeful crowd could beat the subdued assailant to death, the responding squad of soldiers rushed in to pull the assailant from the melee, withdrew with him in their custody, and secured him in an adjacent room. Agent Foster hurried over to the President's side and looked around frantically for anyone with medical training or practice. Foster yelled, "Someone summon an ambulance! Is there a doctor here?" Assisting the President to a seated position, he said to him, "Mr. President, hold on; we'll get you to the hospital soon." Maintaining pressure on the President's abdominal wound, Foster turned to the other agents and said, "Help me get him outside to the street." By the time they were able to carry McKinley out the doors and down the steps, the Exposition's new electric ambulance pulled in front of the building, where the President was quickly loaded and transported to the local hospital. Before the ambulance pulled away, Agent Foster explained calmly, "Mr. President, Agent Ireland will go with you to the hospital. I'll join you at the hospital once I've cleared things up here. You're going to be fine sir, you're going to be just fine."

Returning to the scene of the assassination attempt, Agent Foster entered the back room where the assailant was being held by the Buffalo detectives and Army detachment. "Who is this guy?" he asked one of the detectives.

A tall, balding detective in a pinstriped gray suit leaned over the suspect and replied, "Apparently, his name is Leon Frank Czolgosz. He claims he is from Detroit and that 'he was just doing his duty.' That's all we have gotten out of him so far. Leave me alone with him for a few minutes and I will get more out of him."

"Not now, we can't keep him here any longer. That crowd outside is getting pretty ugly. Let's get him out of here and downtown to the jail so we can safely question him further," Agent Foster directed. "Get a doctor to look at him when you get there; he looks pretty bad. I'll be there in a little while. I've got someone to thank first."

Returning to the great hall, Agent Foster looked around the room and spotted the tall black man who had initially struck Czolgosz and prevented a third shot. He quickly walked over to the man and asked, "Sir, what's your name?"

"Well sir, my given name is James Benjamin Parker, but most people just call me Big Ben," replied the man.

Reaching out and firmly shaking his hand, Agent Foster said, "Mr. Parker, I want to thank you for what you did earlier. If you had not acted as you did, the President would be lying dead on the floor over there. This country owes you a debt of gratitude."

"It just wasn't right what he did to the President. I just did what anyone else would have done," Big Ben replied. "I hope he will be okay."

With a concerned smile, Agent Foster said, "So do I. Oh, so do I."

Chapter III
The Rostrum Project

In the present day, a tall, slightly overweight man dressed in a wrinkled dark- gray business suit walked into the auditorium of the FBI Field Office at #24 Shackleford West Boulevard in Little Rock, Arkansas. He was alone, as was usual for him at such official Bureau functions. FBI Agent Stan Thompson didn't have very many friends outside the Bureau, much less any at work, and those agents he did work with normally didn't care about spending too much time around him. No, Thompson was somewhat of a loner; an island to himself most of the time.

Annoyed at having to attend this dog and pony show to begin with, Thompson scanned the large room, looking for anyone of authority in the vicinity who he wanted to avoid. He spotted Special Agent in Charge (SAC) Brenner and some of his lackeys standing in the middle aisle towards the front, engaged in what appeared to be a serious conversation. Brenner and the tall blonde woman in the group looked up from their conversation and noticed Thompson standing at the back of the auditorium. Having unintentionally made eye contact ever so briefly with Thompson, both individuals quickly turned their attention back to the other members of their group, never acknowledging Thompson. Thompson figured correctly that they were talking about him and decided this was a group he wanted to keep his distance from at all costs. So, like a good Baptist, he quickly took the aisle seat in the back row and settled in for what he figured would be an uncomfortable, boring and long drawn-out presentation.

As was his normal tendency he was early, so to kill time as he sat he looked through the program he had been handed as he came through the door. He, along with every other agent in the Field Office, was instructed to attend today's big gathering. Since the Director of the Secret Service was coming into town to speak at the event, SAC Brenner wanted the auditorium filled to capacity. All the agents were told to be there or pay the consequences. Thompson had thought to himself that it was just like Brenner to try to suck up to the bigwigs. Never mind that all the agents were busy working cases, they all still had to attend, and if not, Brenner indicated that the only acceptable excuse for missing it was that they were in hospital hooked to a ventilator.

In the middle of reading his program, a young, stylishly dressed man wearing dark sunglasses paused in the aisle next to Thompson and asked, "Anyone sitting here?" and pointed to the seat next to him. Thompson, thinking it was quite obvious no one was sitting there said, "Why no, you are welcome to sit here. You must be thinking the same thing I am; these seats will make it easy for us to exit quickly when the agony is done."

With a grin, the young man replied, "No, actually I'm supposed to take down the names of all those who begin to nod off during the Director's presentation." Thompson squirmed a bit in his seat. Quickly, the younger of the two men held out his hand and added, "Just kidding. Hi, I'm Special Agent Matthew Foster with the Secret Service."

Relieved that he hadn't stuck his foot in his mouth as he normally did in such situations, Thompson shook his hand and said, "Stan Thompson with the FBI's Little Rock office."

As he took his seat next to Thompson, Foster said, "A local guy. You're one of the lucky ones that didn't have to fly halfway across the country to attend."

"They made you fly here to attend!" Thompson declared in disbelief. "I thought it was bad enough that all of us from the local office had to be here. So why do you Secret Service guys have to be here for this boondoggle?"

"You mean besides the usual bunch of staff managers that have their noses up the Director's butt?" responded Foster.

"Now that's funny. I think I'm gonna like you. By the way, that reminds me of an old joke. Do you know what the difference is between a brown noser and a shithead?" With a puzzled look Foster said, "Why no, I don't."

Thompson quickly answered in a slightly louder than acceptable level for the situation. "Depth perception. Get it? Depth perception!"

Foster uttered a short, muffled laugh and continued his explanation. "No, the only working agents who had to be here were those of us that are being assigned to the protection detail for the upcoming election. You see, they are going to unveil something they've been working on for a while that is made by a local company here in Little Rock. Whatever it is, it's supposed to revolutionize our protection programs for the future."

"Do you like the election protection details?" asked Thompson.

"I don't know, this is the first time I've been assigned to one. Happened all of a sudden, but I'm glad, you know?" Foster paused for a second to reflect. "You see, my great great grandfather, George Foster, was one of the Secret Service agents assigned to protect President William McKinley."

"Wait, didn't President McKinley die from an assassination attempt?" interjected Thompson.

"Well yes, that's what I was getting to. My full name is Matthew McKinley Foster. Even though it wasn't his fault, George Foster felt personally responsible for the failure and started a tradition of naming all firstborn male sons in the family with McKinley to honor the fallen president. I see it as my family duty to reclaim the Foster name, which is why I joined the Secret Service to begin with."

"Wow, brother, that's a heavy burden to bear for such a young agent," consoled Thompson. "You need to live your own life, not that of some distant dead relative you didn't even know."

"I know, but it has hung over the family for so long. I mean, I don't want to name my first son after McKinley. I want to break the cycle of tradition. It's just time."

"Well, I understand where you're coming from. Best of luck with that" added Thompson. Foster nodded in acknowledgement of Thompson's empathy and opened his program to check the agenda.

By now the auditorium was about full and the people stirring around down near the stage was a tell-tale sign to Thompson that things were about to kick off. He looked around and saw what he assumed were lots of political dignitaries and government officials towards the front. He recognized the governor, a senator and a handful of representatives from the great State of Arkansas, both directors from the FBI and Secret Service, and a horde of staffers from both agencies. But strangely there were no reporters or cameras recording this event for posterity. In the middle of the stage Thompson could see what appeared to be a podium covered by a red velvet drape that seemed to flow like a crimson waterfall onto the polished hardwood floor of the stage. Whatever it was, it emitted an air of elegance or maybe even a regal impression. The stage lights came up and the auditorium overhead lights dimmed a bit. The Director of the Secret Service walked up the short flight of steps along the right side of the stage, approached the draped object and paused beside it a second or two before speaking.

Beginning his official statement, the Director said, "Ladies and gentlemen, thank you for joining us today on this momentous occasion, for today we mark a milestone in our agency's service to protect members of our government's Executive Branch. Since 1894 our agency has a long and distinguished history in fulfilling its role and providing protective services for the Office of the

President of the United States and aspiring candidates for the oval office.

"I and my fellow members of the Secret Service take our responsibilities very seriously, and we are continually monitoring national and international events for potential new threats and attack methodologies that would- be assassins might employ. Based upon the recent success that terrorists have had in the use of suicide bomber attacks in other countries, we knew our agency had to do something to address this potential threat against government officials and political candidates in the U.S. A single individual wearing a vest packed with explosives and various forms of shrapnel, a suicide bomber, need only gain close proximity to their intended target to be relatively effective. Use of non- metallic shrapnel, powerful plastic explosives, and a separate battery source would make a cloth vest almost impossible to detect with metal detectors. Therefore, an assailant with a false pass carrying this lethal combination would be able to gain access to an inner protective perimeter with relative ease.

"To counter this potential threat, we at the Secret Service not only had to be creative in our detection capabilities, but we also had to be able to ensure the survivability of the principal should detection occur at the very last second. We have used bulletproof podiums, in varying degrees of bullet resistance capability, for many years. The first podiums we used were only designed to be effective against a handgun, the most concealable firearm available. Using a handgun required the assailant to get in relatively close to the target to initiate an assault. As the threats changed, our podiums were then designed to stop a round fired from a rifle, the longest-range firearm threat that could be used. A rifle allowed the assailant more standoff distance, but required them to have an unobstructed corridor to the target. Aimed bullets were very predictable, but what about explosives with multiple fragmentation projectiles and blast waves from the detonation of a suicide vest? Protection would take something more substantial but relatively portable that can travel to various venues. To address that risk, we conceived the Secret Service's Rostrum Project."

The Director continued, "In ancient Rome, a rostrum was a platform or stand for an orator in their senate. For our use, we envisioned a rostrum that would be constructed of special materials, capable of withstanding all of the effects of a moderate explosive blast within thirty or so feet. Our operational concept for the Rostrum was that, when an imminent threat is detected at the last minute, whether a firearm or explosive, the Secret Service agents positioned to the rear of a principal, behind the Rostrum, would move quickly to the principal, push him down behind the Rostrum, and shield the back of his body with theirs. Given proper material resistance, weight, and deflective surfaces, the explosive effects would pass over and around the Rostrum, providing a protective area for at least three personnel taking cover behind it."

"In preparation for this election season, we at the Secret Service conducted a competitive bidding process to select a vendor to manufacture one hundred of these podiums. Our plan is to pre-stage these safe-haven podiums in regional areas across the country, so that they are available when and where we need them. The

reason we have assembled here in Little Rock is because
a local company, Smithson Integrated Engineering,
Inc., was selected to produce, certify the protection
level of, and deliver all one hundred Rostrums. The decision by our source selection board was a no-brainer.
Smithson was not only the lowest bidder, but they also
added back-up battery power within the podium that
would support built-in infrared communications that
interface with remote speakers for a public address
system. In the opinion of our selection board, this was
an impressive innovation because we are beginning to
use electronic jamming devices similar to the U.S. military's Warlock System, used to prevent remote detonation of improvised explosive devices. Many of us
questioned how they could make a profit with such extra bells and whistles at such a low price. When asked,
Smithson responded that they weren't doing it for the
money, but out of a strong sense of patriotism, and that
it would give them nationwide recognition and promote positive public relations." As the director turned
toward the covered podium, he pulled the drape off and

announced with ceremonious fanfare, "Ladies and gentlemen, I give you the Rostrum."

Positioned just to the right of center stage, the Rostrum appeared sleek, polished, and substantial, but not imposing. The fine mahogany finish subtly glistened under the intense glare of the spotlights and gave it a quality of fine art. Though it was built for form and function, the craftsmanship made it a rare thing of beauty.

Pointing to the various features of the Rostrum, the Director explained, "Smithson's unique design of overlapping and angled ballistic panels uses a combination of advanced military- grade ceramic and Kevlar materials which we consider very innovative. Because it uses lightweight ceramics behind a polished wooden veneer, the ballistic panels are removable, to allow our agents to inspect and replace them if they are ever damaged by a bullet or accident of some kind. Smithson was an excellent choice to produce the Rostrums. As you can see, they are artisans of their craft. Besides, there are no cost overruns, and production is currently ahead of schedule. Now when was the last time that you heard of a government project that was on time and within the projected budget?" The crowd laughed and applauded at the comment. "We are very pleased with our selection and with the final product that Smithson has delivered. Ladies and gentlemen, that concludes my formal presentation, and I invite each of you to come down and examine this work of art for yourselves."

Responding to the Director's invitation, some attendees began to get up from their seats and walk forward to take a closer look at the Rostrum, while others remained seated and began to talk among themselves about the project.

Thompson stood and stretched a bit before turning to Foster. "Well, that didn't take as long as I expected it to."

"Yeah, I thought for sure we would get an added lecture about our behavior living up to the Service's expectations. That has been the norm since the guy didn't pay his hooker down in Columbia several years back."

"Whose protection detail are you being assigned to?" Thompson asked.

"Senator Jamal Jordan."

"That sounds like a good assignment. He seems to be kicking butt in the primaries for the Democrats. What can you tell me about him?" Thompson inquired.

"I've been reading up on his background getting ready for the details to start up. He's a first-term senator who seemingly came out of nowhere on the national stage. He was born in Detroit and raised by his grandmother. He got an Ivy League education and law degree, and after schooling, he returned to Detroit, set up a law practice, and caught the eye of the Democratic Party. They were desperate for a promising future contender, so the party got him into the state senate. Then before his term was up, the powers that be pushed to get him appointed to the U.S. House of Representatives to fill the seat of a long-term and influential Congressman who died while in office under suspicious circumstances. He then ran for U.S. Senate and was elected less than a year ago.

"The similarities to President Obama's race in 2008 are unmistakable. I guess the Dems are planning this race on a proven formula from the past. My assignment here is working white supremacists in the regional area. Because he is black, his rapid rise in politics has not gone unnoticed by the kooks I've been monitoring around here. They are not at all happy with the prospect of another black left-wing president, after they endured Obama's time in office," described Thompson.

"That's why I'm glad to be assigned to his detail. A controversial candidate always draws the nuts out of hiding. I want to be the one to stop an attempt. You know, to reclaim the Foster name."

"Oh yeah, still trying to compensate for that distant dead relative."

Trying to shrug off the comment, Foster asked, "You want to go down and check out that podium?"

"Nah, I'm just gonna slip out and head back to my office." While shaking Foster's hand he added, "It was good to meet you. Here's my card. Give me a call if you come back into town."

Foster took the card and gave Thompson one of his in exchange, saying, "Will do."

As Thompson began to walk away, he turned back to Foster and said, "Remember, depth perception." Foster grinned and headed down the steps to the stage.

Chapter IV
The Agent and Package

It was a late summer afternoon at the FBI Field Office at #24 Shackleford West Boulevard in Little Rock. SAC Frank Brenner, a tall, heavy-set man of African descent, had been with the Bureau for almost twenty years and had made all the right political moves during his career to become SAC and he wouldn't do anything that would jeopardize it. Brenner's office was well organized and was always kept in an immaculate manner that characterized his propensity for order and attention to detail. Three of the four walls of his office were neatly adorned with numerous plaques, awards, and pictures of himself with various political dignitaries from over the years. The fourth was a glass wall that looked out over the large bullpen of desks where he could see several more junior FBI agents working. As he stood behind his desk looking out the glass wall at a couple of his agents, his expression gave away his obvious agitation. Jackie Kerr, a thirty-something blonde, slender female walked into the office while she flipped through the thick personnel file she was carrying. As Assistant SAC, it was her job to maintain performance data on the agents assigned to the office and process all personnel actions such as requests for transfer.

Brenner looked towards her and asked, "Jackie, what is this with Agent Thompson out there? Does he ever do anything else besides put in request after request to be transferred to the Joint Terrorism Task Force? You would think after so many denials he would get the message and give it up. I mean, come on, give me a break."

Agent Kerr looked back out the glass office wall at one particularly disheveled agent who was sitting going over some notes from recent field interviews with his feet up on his desk. "Special Agent Stanley Arthur Thompson ...now there's a real piece of work," replied Kerr. "He has had a less than impressive career. He graduated at the bottom of his class from the academy, and he's never been involved with any high-profile cases. For the last several years he's been working with the skinheads and white supremacists around here. Hum ... it doesn't look like he's even taken a case to court for over two years."

After taking a sip from his FBI logoed coffee cup, Brenner set it back down on his desk on the brass and leather FBI logo coaster that accentuated the officious décor of his desk. "Well, it's a good thing the Oklahoma City bombing and Timothy McVeigh case was already wrapped up before he got involved. Since we cleaned up the big white supremacist organizations a while back it's been pretty quiet on that front, so I guess he can't screw that up too much." Brenner remarked.

Agent Kerr handed him the file. Brenner took one quick glance at it and handed it back. He took another sip of coffee and turned back to look in Thompson's direction. "Deny his request again. I'm not going to put my professional reputation on the line by recommending him for the task force."

Out in the bullpen Thompson, still with his feet on the desk, looked at a certificate on the wall in his cubicle and then looked over to continue talking to a fellow agent. "Ya know Danny," he said, "it's hard to believe it's only been fourteen years since I graduated from the academy. It sure seems longer than that!"

Agent Danny Danovich, a sharply dressed agent with neatly trimmed brown hair, replied, "Yeah, well that's what happens when you don't get much satisfaction out of what you do."

"Yeah, you're right, I get about as much satisfaction out of this job as I did from my failed marriage. Besides, Brenner reminds me of my mother-in-law," Thompson added.

"Man, I've seen pictures of your mother-in-law, and in comparison, Brenner makes her look hot." Danovich paused. "So, tell me Stan, how many times are you going to keep putting in for the Joint Terrorist Task Force and keep getting denied? You know you're just pissing in the wind on that."

"I don't know, Danny. I'm just tired of chasing all these home-grown malcontents, nuts, and reactionaries around here. Those numbskulls have pretty much fallen off the Bureau's radar screen because they don't have anything to do with radical Islamic extremism," said Thompson. "I envy those guys on the task force. They get to stretch the limits of the Patriot Act to get information I never could. Then they get the glory of executing a preemptive strike on some alleged Islamic terrorist cell. No, that's where the real action is, Danny. Yep, and I'm stuck here in Little stinking Rock, Arkansas dealing with the local yokels and chasing unorganized skin-heads who have no direction, money or support structure."

"Well, on the other hand, my friend, with the way this economy is going, you should probably be happy you have a job. Besides, it keeps a steady income going to support that nasty habit you have of eating and having a warm place to sleep at night," remarked Danovich with a brief laugh.

With a smile that recognized Danny's terse wit, Thompson said, "Yeah, that's especially true when you consider that more than half of my hard-earned federal pay goes to my wonderful ex-wife. And at the end of the month after everyone else had taken their toll, there's barely enough change left at the bottom of the till to keep a bottle of Jack in the cupboard of my shabby rundown apartment."

"To make things worse, gas is at an all-time high. It's to the point where I have to get a bank loan every time I fill up that gas guzzling monster of a broken-down SUV I've got," Danovich lamented. "To top it off, the evening news has nothing good to say either. Food prices have doubled; airlines are filing for bankruptcy left and right; the war against terrorism and COVID drained our military; and illegal immigrants continue to flood across the border unchecked. All this while our influence and reputation as a country around the world is falling faster than the dollar."

"Well, I don't mean to add to your woes, buddy, but we also have a new presidential election season revving up here. Soon the TV and radio waves will be filled with a relentless stream of sound bites and paid political ads. I just can't freaking wait!" exclaimed Thompson.

"So, tell me Stan, are you even going to bother to vote next November?" asked Danovich.

"If I do, it will very likely be that my write-in candidate will be either Jack Daniels or Evan Williams. Those guys are the only names that I trust. I take in-depth counseling from them on a frequent basis." Thompson looked back at his desk and began to scan his field notes.

"So, what are you working on now?" Danovich inquired.

Thompson looked up briefly and then back down at his notes. "On my last interview with one of my confidential informants, they mentioned something was coming down involving the gang and it was tied to some initials. Can't remember what they are right now. I've got it written down here somewhere."

With a big smile, Danny leaned back in his chair. "That CI wouldn't happen to be that classy white-trash high school prom queen gone astray, named Candy, would it?"

Slightly embarrassed, Thompson glanced back at Danny. "Well, yeah."

"Is she still the main squeeze of the local captain for that Aryan motorcycle gang the Copperheads? What's his name ...Jake?" asked Danovich.

"Yeah, that very same one," replied Thompson.

"Man, whether she has any real information or not you drop everything to go meet her," remarked Danovich.

In a slightly defensive tone, Thompson rebutted, "Well, can you blame me?" referring to her unrefined beauty. "As the redneck locals would poetically put it, her sultry southern charm is as intoxicating as moonshine under the Arkansas pines, beneath a moonless summer sky."

"Well, you better watch your ass with that one, buddy. If Jake or Brenner finds out about her, she and you will be royally screwed! By the way, why does she keep this CI relationship going with you?" asked Danovich.

With a distant gleam of hope in his eyes, Thompson looked back at Danovich. "Maybe she's attracted to me too. I sure wish I knew for sure."

"So, what was it she had for you last time?" asked Danovich.

Thompson looked back at his notes and flipped through a couple of pages. "Candy mentioned something about her low-life boyfriend Jake saying that there was something big coming, just what she wouldn't say. From past experience, I took that to mean just another drunken road trip and progressive party from town to town. This time she mentioned a new set of initials that I didn't recognize. I wrote them down somewhere in here."

Thompson continued to scan his notes until he found what he was looking for. "Here it is." Thompson then turned back to Danovich and asked, "Do the initials KGC mean anything to you, Danny?"

"They don't ring a bell right away. You sure she didn't say KFC like in Kentucky Fried Chicken? You know that's what the gang's main diet consists of." Danovich smiled, got up, slapped Thompson on the shoulder and began to walk away.

"This KGC means something, and I'm going to get to the bottom of it," Thompson declared.

Danovich shook his head and said under his breath, "Yeah, right, Sherlock." He then turned and continued to walk away.

Late that afternoon at the Port of San Francisco's cargo container ship terminal, a group of container transporters waited in line to be loaded with a group of cargo containers destined for transfer to a nearby warehouse. A dock foreman paced restlessly in front of a row of approximately thirty sealed twenty- foot cargo containers that had just been unloaded off a China Ocean Shipping Company cargo container vessel. Pacing nervously up and down the line of cargo containers, the burly dock foreman pulled out his hand- held radio from its holster and transmitted, "Does anyone see any sign of the Customs officer?"

Over the foreman's radio, a call came back out of the speaker. "Jack, I saw him come through the gate a few seconds ago. It looked like he was headed in your direction."

"Okay, then let's look alive, guys. We will need to get these containers moving quickly as soon as we are done with him," instructed the dock foreman over the radio.

As soon as he had given those instructions, a Ford Explorer with U.S. Customs Service markings on the doors drove up and stopped in front of the dock foreman. As he got out of his vehicle with a clipboard in his hand, the uniformed Customs officer put on his uniform hat and walked directly over to the dock foreman. He reached out his right hand to shake and said, "Brother Jack, how are you doing?"

The dock foreman replied, "I'm doing very well, Brother Frank. But I'll be better when we get these containers off this dock and into the cover of the warehouse where we'll get them ready for delivery. Did you fix all the paperwork for us to get them moving?"

The Customs officer responded, "Sure did Jack. I got all the authorizations, completed the Release of Shipment for Immediate Transportation forms, and logged out the inspection seals to put on the containers. After I spend enough time nosing around the containers to convince the crane operator up there that I've conducted the necessary inspections, you can help me get these seals on each of the containers and you can then get the crane to start loading them up on your transports over there."

Together the dock foreman and Customs officer opened a few of the cargo containers and went through

the motions as though the Customs officer was conducting an effective and official inspection as required
by U.S. Customs procedures. After they closed each
container, they affixed the seals across the door seams
of the container and then recorded the seal numbers on
the bills of lading. In addition, the dock foreman placed
high-security padlocks on the door latches to secure
them for their trip ahead. When the ruse of an inspection process was completed, the Customs officer sealed
the rest of the containers and finalized the paperwork
to release the shipment. He then handed the clipboard
over to the dock foreman and said, "Jack, I need you to
sign here to make it look official and we can get you out
of here. Oh yeah, press hard. There are five copies."

After he signed several copies of the forms, the dock
foreman handed the clipboard back to the Customs officer, laughed, and said, "The forms say these containers carry farm implements destined for several cities
across the country. They aren't suited for planting, but
they are well suited for reaping. Will this paperwork
exempt them from further search?" he asked the Customs officer.

"Yep, this paperwork and the U.S. Customs seals we just put on will get them through the state inspection weigh stations on the highways with no problems. There should be no reason for anyone to ask to open them," replied the Customs officer. "If anyone questions your guys along the way about anything, have them call me on my office cell phone and I'll clear the way."

"Will do," said the dock foreman. "It will be a great day when these so-called farm implements are put to their intended use and reap the harvest we planned for so long."

"It will be a great day indeed," replied the Customs officer as the two shook hands again. "I'll stick around until your guys are out of the terminal and on their way to the warehouse."

"Thanks, Brother. That will make me feel a lot better," said the dock foreman.

After the last container was loaded and on its way to a nearby warehouse, the dock foreman and Customs officer shook hands and went their separate ways. By early evening, the last of the thirty cargo containers had arrived inside the cargo warehouse of the Kensington Global Corporation, where the warehouse supervisor directed crews to prepare the containers for shipment to other cities. Overhead cranes and large forklifts were arranging them in order of the shipping destination in preparation for loading them on over-the-road haulers the next morning. In a hurry to finish up before shift change, one of the forklift operators misjudged the clearance and ran into one of the containers with his large forks, causing a large, gaping gash in the side of the container, partially exposing the secretive contents inside.

The warehouse supervisor ran up to the operator and said, "You dumb ass, watch what you're doing. You've really screwed up now, Bobby. This is going to come out of your paycheck at the end of this week. If you weren't my sister's husband, I'd fire you right now."

"I'm really sorry, Jimmy, I was just trying to get it done before we shut down for the night. I know the truckers will be here early in the morning to move them on to their customers," replied the forklift operator in an apologetic tone.

The warehouse supervisor responded, "Well, it's a good thing this particular container is staying here. It would have been a real problem if it were going to Atlanta, Little Rock or someplace else. We would have had to call our Customs contact to change out the containers and redo the Customs paperwork and seals. That would have made some people very unhappy ... and Bobby, believe me, we sure don't want them to be unhappy with us. We'll just have to unload the contents of this container sooner than we had planned. Get a tarp from the storage room and cover the gash up so no one can see what's inside until we can get a chance to unload it tomorrow after the others are loaded on the trucks and on their way."

"All right, Jimmy, I'll take care of it right now," said the forklift operator. He got off the forklift, found a large green tarp in the supply room and covered the side of the container with it so that the damage to the container wall was not readily visible.

Early the next morning, twenty over-the-road haulers with their diesel rigs showed up at the warehouse to be loaded, and forty to fifty members of the Copperheads motorcycle gang gathered around for their instructions. Once the containers were loaded on the trailers and the paperwork was provided to the truckers, one by one each of the trucks, escorted by two or more bikers, pulled out of the warehouse complex, and headed for their individually designated destinations.

Two days of haulage later in Little Rock, Arkansas, one of the trucks carrying the secretive load pulled off the highway and onto the service road while the biker escort continued to travel down the highway so that any observing law enforcement units wouldn't connect them with the truck as it neared its final delivery destination. Unexpectedly, the truck driver made a couple of abrupt turns to ensure that he wasn't being followed and then slowed and pulled up to a garage building in a run-down area of the Little Rock industrial district. The driver honked the horn, and the garage door began to open to let the truck pull inside. As soon as the truck had pulled all the way into the garage, the roll- up door with its windows painted over was closed behind it to conceal the truck's arrival from anyone outside.

While he got out of the truck, the driver was met by two men dressed as construction workers, both armed with sawed off shotguns. One of the men asked, "You sure you weren't followed?"

"Yep, I made a couple Crazy Ivans before I got close, and I monitored the police scanner to make sure there were no communications from any of their units in the vicinity," replied the trucker.

"Well, good job," the other man said as he shook his hand and gave him a slap on the back. "Welcome home, Brother. How was the trip?"

"Went off without a hitch, smooth sailing all the way home," he replied.

"You Navy SEAL boys like that sailing thing, don't cha?" kidded the other.

"Yeah, only because you Rangers are afraid of the water," he returned with a big shit- eating grin.

The former Ranger threw him a set of keys and said, "Your car's out back in the alley. Why don't you head home, get cleaned up and say hello to that sweet thang of yours for me, or did you blow your wad on a lot lizard at the truck stop on the way through Amarillo?"

Grabbing his own crotch with one hand like Michael Jackson would on a music video, the former Navy SEAL said, "I got your sweet thang right here, Brother!"

Responding to the vulgar gesture, the former Army Ranger said, "You Navy boys are all the same. Now get on home before I pull out my Ka-Bar and show you the other end of that thang." Pointing to the truck he continued, "Ben and I will provide fire-watch for this baby tonight. We'll keep the local crack whores and homeless out of here. Tomorrow we'll start unloading this cargo container when Jake and about six of our guys get in here at 0700 hours. By the way, for operational security's sake, Jake doesn't want anyone showing up on their bikes or wearing our colors here. Everyone is to wear construction gear and clothing as part of the front for this operation."

Early the next morning at 0646 hours, two paneled vans pulled up to an adjacent roll-up door at the garage and honked the horn twice. Ben went quickly to the door and hit the green control button to raise the door for the vans to enter. Closing the door behind the vans, Ben then walked up to the vans as Jake and the other Copperheads got out. "Morning, Jake, you're early," declared Ben, as though he had been caught off guard by their time of arrival.

"If you're on time you're late, and if you're early you're on time, is what my platoon sergeant always said," responded Jake.

"How's that fine little piece of ass sister of mine Candy doing ya?" Ben asked.

"To tell you the truth, I did her once just for you this morning, Ben," Jake replied. "She tells me that the only reason she was a virgin till I met her was because she could run faster than you. Is that right?"

"And you really thought she was a virgin before she met you," Ben laughed. "If I recall it correctly, I think she did the whole trailer park before she was 16 ...but you know, she could run pretty fast."

Walking over to the back of the cargo container still on the tractor trailer where it was parked overnight, Jake said, "Let's see what our comrades overseas have shipped us, shall we?" Jake pointed to a nearby toolbox and told Ben, "Hand me that hammer over there."

With the claw of the framing hammer that Ben had just handed him, Jake broke the U.S. Customs seal, pulled a dog tag chain from around his neck over his head and then used one of a set of three keys on the chain to unlock the high-security padlocks that the dock foreman had used to secure the doors. Stepping back, Jake allowed two other men to rotate the door latch levers up and outward, releasing the double doors, and watched as they swung open with a low-pitched, squeaking groan to reveal the anticipated contents inside. "Well, I don't read much Russian, fellas, but I do believe that box says AK-47 rifles right there, and that box says Semtex. Boys, it looks like we're in business," hollered Jake with an extremcly pleased expression on his face.

Ben responded by saying, "I'd prefer good old American M-4 carbines and C-4 explosives, but Russian AK's and Semtex will work just fine for our purposes."

Pointing to the doors of connecting rooms, Jake said, "Okay, we'll use that shower room over there as the storage room for the weapons still boxed in the crates and use these cleaning vats over here to get the packing grease out and clean them up ready for use. Once they've been function-checked and are duty ready, we'll use that large room over there with the big security door as our armory." Pausing for a moment to look around at all the other men, Jake directed, "Now let's get to work off loading this container and getting these guns ready for the range."

With a well-coordinated work plan, some of the men set to work on unloading the weapons crates into the storage room while others began to open the crates, remove the packing grease that protected them from potential corrosion during long-term storage and then visually inspect the weapons. Once cleaned and determined to be fully functional, the weapons were carefully leaned against the wall of the makeshift armory. Later that afternoon all of the approximately five hundred rifles had been cleaned, inspected, and stored in

the armory along with twenty rocket- propelled gre-
nade launchers, most often referred to as RPGs. In addition, two crates of Russian SA- 7 Grail shoulder- fired
heat seeking anti- aircraft missiles were also unboxed
and stored in the armory.

Pleased with the efficiency of the operation, Jake
came out of the armory and instructed two of the men,
"Load all the Semtex, blasting caps, det- cord, and RPG
rounds into those vans. We will take them directly out
to the quarry and cache them in the service mine shaft
this afternoon." Nodding in acknowledgement of
Jake's direction, the two men set off to complete the assigned task. Once the vans were loaded, Jake and four
others got into the van and headed out to the old, abandoned quarry located about thirty miles outside of town
that used to be operated by the Kendal Mining Company. Pulling up to a side gate entrance to the quarry,
two gang members on their bikes had arrived before the
vans and already had the gates standing open for them
to enter without having to stop. After the vans made
their way past the open gate, the bikers closed and secured the gate behind them and proceeded to follow the

vans down the windy gravel road down to the main quarry complex about another half mile in.

In the fading light of the late afternoon sun, the vans came to a stop in front of an opening in the face of a sheer rock surface that was closed off with a gray corrugated metal wall with a large industrial door in it for access. This remote mining tunnel had been used in the past to store heavy equipment when the Kendal Mine was still operational. The opening itself was hidden, tucked around the corner of a rocky outcropping that concealed it from view of the main quarry grounds. Jake got out of the van, unlocked the padlock that secured the large door, turned to the others, and said, "Stack the Semtex and RPG ammo in the very back and put the blasting caps and det- cord in that old office shack just inside the main door."

Jake stood in the sunlight and watched as the other men removed the crates from the vans, carried them over to the door and disappeared inside the dim lighted cavern. Once they had unloaded all of the items and secured them in the tunnel, Jake pointed to a tall rocky ledge across the lake formed by the quarry and said, "I want a covert sniper providing overwatch of this facility twenty-four seven, from the hide we prepared up there, to make sure that no one messes with our stuff. Because we don't get cell phone coverage out here, we have a hard-wired phone line set up in there to be able to report any activity here." Looking at Candy's brother, he continued, "Ben, you're in charge of posting the sniper detail and keeping them out of sight. I think a twenty-four-hour shift for each sniper will be sufficient and reduce the amount of transit in and out of here. I don't want any sign that we are here. Keep out of sight and report any unexpected activity to me by phone."

"Will do, boss," Ben responded. Turning and looking at one of the men, Ben instructed, "Brother Tom, you have first watch. Grab your gear, get set up and do a commo check with the main command post back in town before we leave."

Understanding his instructions, Tom responded, "I'm on it," then grabbed his rucksack and Russian Dragunov sniper rifle out of the van. Once he had all his equipment for the assignment, he then proceeded on foot to assume his position on the other side of the lake where he could observe all key terrain features, approaches, and other points of interest on the quarry property.

As Tom was walking away, Jake turned to the others and said, "Over the next couple of days we'll all rotate through here to sight in our assigned weapons and do a little preparation training for our upcoming op. We'll work on our tactics, techniques, and procedures for now, and then rehearse the operation once we know our target location and mission objectives. Now, let's get out of here and get a drink."

Across town in Little Rock, the Rostrum project was on track; Smithson Integrated Engineering Company had already begun cranking the Rostrums out one by one, each provided with a serialized identity number. Each time a group of five or more Rostrums were ready for delivery, the Secret Service would send a local agent over to inspect the panels and place a tamper-indicating seal over the panel seams. Once affixed to the panels, the serial number for each seal was recorded in a centralized database. If someone attempted to open the panels, the tamper-indicating seal would void itself by making the serial number appear opaque, thus providing a visual indicator that someone had tampered with the ballistic panels. By mid-November, Smithson had produced seventy, and number seventy-one was about to be born from the assembly line. Work on the aluminum frame of Rostrum #71, which was the skeleton upon which to form the body, began on November 15th. By the 17th, the panel wells that would contain the armor were formed and attached. On the 20th, the outer finish was applied and on the 23rd, just before the Thanksgiving holiday, the ballistic panels, electrical power, and infrared communications system, the heart of Rostrum #71, were connected and tested for the very first time. Like a slap to a newborn baby's butt, a flick of the switch brought Rostrum #71 to life. Rostrum #71 was a beautiful piece of art; its lines were subtle yet distinctive, and its finish was flawless. Though its predecessors were of identical craftsmanship, somehow Rostrum #71 took on its own character. Anyone who had the good fortune to stand behind it in a public address would somehow seem more stately and strong. Following the Thanksgiving holiday, a Secret Service agent from the local office arrived, inspected Rostrum #71, sealed its panel seams, and watched as it was crated in preparation for shipping. The shipping clerk filled out the shipping label with its new destination: the campaign headquarters of Senator Jamal Jordan in Detroit, Michigan.

Early the next morning, the crate containing Rostrum #71 was positioned on the loading dock with several other Rostrums waiting for the freight truck to arrive so they could be loaded and sent on their way to their final destinations. At about 9:30 a.m., a Roadway Trucking Company driver backed his tractor trailer up to the loading dock, exited the cab, and opened the doors in back. He looked around and found the shipping manager, handed him his copy of the pickup order, and said, "Here you go, Chief. I'm supposed to pick up five pieces of freight headed to cities somewhere north of here."

The shipping manager pointed to the crates and replied, "There they are right there. I'll get one of the warehouse crew to load them on there in order of their delivery."

The trucker looked at the bill of lading and asked, "Those bastards sure are awful heavy. What's in 'em?"

"Just something a future President of the United States is going to stand behind someday," replied the shipping manager.

With a puzzled look, the trucker just nodded his head and watched as the weight of each crated Rostrum caused the bed of the trailer to groan and creak as the forklift gingerly moved and positioned them in the trailer. Another warehouse worker used a series of heavy nylon straps to secure each crate to the floor and trailer walls to eliminate the possibility that they might shift during the trip. This cargo was far too important to allow them to become damaged in transport. Once loaded and secured, the trailer door was closed and latched in preparation for the drive to the first point of delivery.

Looking at the bill of lading, the shipping manager said, "Your first two drops will be Tennessee, Box # 67 in Memphis and Box # 68 in Nashville. Then Box # 69 will be delivered in Louisville, Kentucky, Box # 70 in Columbus, Ohio, and your final drop will be Box # 71 in Detroit, Michigan. Pay close attention and don't get them mixed up. If you do, you and I will both be looking for jobs, 'cause that's what'll happen if we piss off the U. S. Secret Service!"

"No sir, that definitely wouldn't be a good thing, would it?" replied the trucker. "I wouldn't want Federal agent men coming after me!"

Handing the paperwork over to the trucker, the shipping manager said, "You're loaded up and ready to go. Have a good trip."

"Thanks, Chief, we'll see you on the next run," replied the trucker. He then jumped off the loading dock, proceeded to get in the cab, and started the diesel engine of the tractor. With a quick wave out the window, the trucker put the truck in first gear, eased out of the lot, and merged into the traffic, on his way to make his deliveries.

Two days later, after having delivered the other four crates, the trucker arrived in Detroit and found his way to the campaign headquarters of Senator Jamal Jordan.

He backed the tractor trailer up to the loading dock and opened the doors. A young man in a suit and dark sunglasses stepped out of the building's door and said, "Can I see some identification, please?"

Seeing the butt of a semi-automatic handgun peeking out of the man's suit jacket, the trucker gladly reached in his rear pocket slowly and pulled out his wallet, which was attached to his belt with a long silver chain. Handing his driver's license to the man, the trucker said, "I have a delivery for you Secret Service guys. It's my last one of this trip, and I'd like to get it off-loaded so I can head back home. Momma misses me, and to tell you the truth I sure miss her, if you know what I mean."

The Secret Service agent handed the license back to the trucker and said, "I'll get them to open the roll-up door and unload the crate."

After the roll-up door was opened, both the trucker and the agent watched as the forklift drove onto the trailer, lifted the crate, and backed out with the load. Pulling the shipping receipt off the side of the crate, the agent looked at the bill of lading and checked the numbers to ensure that the paperwork and the item being delivered matched. Convinced that everything was correct, the agent signed to acknowledge that he had received the shipment. Looking at the paperwork, the trucker couldn't make out the name on the signature block and asked, "Sir I can't make out the signature, so if you don't mind me asking, what is your name?"

Pulling his dark sunglasses off his face, the agent looked at the trucker and said, "Special Agent Matthew Foster. Now if you wouldn't mind, please get directly in your vehicle and leave. We don't allow large trucks to be parked near this building when Senator Jordan is inside."

"Senator Jordan is inside? Can I meet him?" asked the trucker in an excited voice.

"No sir, that would not be possible. Now please move this truck immediately or I'll have to take you into custody and have it towed," replied Agent Foster.

"Well, I wasn't going to vote for him anyway," responded the trucker. He turned sharply, got back into the truck cab, started the engine, and departed.

Chapter V
The K.G.C.

Back in Little Rock, Agent Thompson was sitting at his desk doing some research on the computer, while Agent Danovich flipped through a *Guns and Ammo* magazine at his desk.

"You know, Danny, these initials KGC probably apply to a person," said Thompson in a questioning voice.

Without looking up from his magazine, Danovich responded, "Why don't you run the initials through the National Crime Information Center database and some of the local parallel systems?"

"That's a good idea! I'll give that a shot first," responded Thompson, as though he should have thought about it himself. Thompson turned back to his computer screen, typed some characters on his keyboard and waited for a response from the system.

Danovich quickly asked, still looking at his magazine, "Anything come up?"

"Well, there are several hits that I'm sorting through," replied Thompson as he scanned the search results on the computer screen. After opening one interesting result line, Thompson continued, "Hey, here's one that looks promising, Kenneth Günter Collins." Thompson read a little more on the computer screen before continuing. "Says here that Collins' father was one of several key Aryan Brotherhood leaders that were arrested not long after the McVeigh case. Those arrests accelerated the Brotherhood's demise just before I came to the Bureau."

A big smile came to Danovich's lips as he replied, "That's a while back, you old fart."

"Hey, I'm not that old," rebutted Thompson. "It says he was raised under his father's racially prejudicial views, graduated from the University of Mississippi, was commissioned under the Reserve Officers Training Corps program, and had begun a promising military career that ended prematurely due to several controversial command issues that identified his racial biases.

He was convicted of several hate crimes following his military discharge and has been in confinement for five years at the Big Sandy High Security Federal Penitentiary near Inez, Kentucky."

Danovich turned his head towards Thompson and said, "That's not too far from here for your Copperheads gang to be involved with."

"Yeah, you're right ... Now this is strange." Thompson said in a puzzled tone.

"What's that?" asked Danovich.

"When he entered prison, his middle name was James and a year ago he changed it to Günter. I wonder why?" asked Thompson.

In a flippant reply, Danovich said, "Maybe James wasn't Aryan sounding enough. You know you could call someone at the federal pen and see what they know."

"Another good idea, Danny."

Thompson moved the screen pointer and changed the computer screen by clicking his mouse over a federal phone directory icon located on his Windows

Desktop. He quickly picked up the phone, dialed a number and waited for a response. After hearing a couple of rings, Thompson was greeted by the prison operator, "Big Sandy Federal Penitentiary, how may I direct your call?"

"Yes, I'm with the FBI in Little Rock. I need to talk to someone who would have some information on an inmate there, Kenneth Günter Collins."

"Yes sir, one minute and I'll connect you," replied the operator.

After listening to recorded music on the phone handset for a few minutes, the melody was interrupted by, "Officer Johnson here. How can I help you?"

"Yes, this is Special Agent Thompson with the FBI Field Office in Little Rock. I'm tracking down some information about an inmate there, Kenneth Günter Collins."

"That prejudicial son of a bitch. What do you want to know?" asked Officer Johnson.

Thompson began his questioning. "In general, what can you tell me about him?"

"Well, he's a smart one, I'll give him that," replied Officer Johnson. "He's a natural leader even if he's misdirected. The members of the Aryan gang here just about worship him, and everyone else either respects or fears him, especially if they're not white. If he weren't so prejudiced, he would have made the General Officer ranks for sure ...that is, if he hadn't been dishonorably discharged from the Army."

Thompson continued, "I pulled up his service records, and I see in his history file he was discharged while in Yemen. What did he do over there to be court martialed and discharged while he was in a combat zone?"

Officer Johnson explained, "Though he got results in kicking the enemy's ass, there were several cases reported about him segregating his troops within his unit and ordering the minority troops in the front of his convoys where they would be in the most likely vehicles targeted by road- side bombs. And to top it off, he would handcuff suspected Yemeni insurgents to the exterior of the vehicles of the white soldiers to deter them from being targeted at all by the road- side bombers."

"I could see where the senior military commanders over there would have taken action, even if the units he commanded were effective in rooting out and clearing enemy strongholds. He isn't due for his next parole hearing for another two years, right?" Thompson asked.

"That's correct sir, especially after his last one," Officer Johnson laughed.

"What do you mean by that?" inquired Thompson.

Recounting the past parole board hearing, Officer Johnson described, "Well, you see, the parole board was made up of both black and white staff members. When that parole board asked him if he had rejected his white supremacist views, he calmly stood up in front of the table and said that as a rightful heir of the Knights of the Golden Circle, he could not be subjugated to the will of a board whose membership was compromised by inferior genetics."

"I guess he answered that question in no uncertain terms!" exclaimed Thompson. "So, I can see why the board will not consider parole for another two years."

"Yes sir, after that answer that board just closed their notebooks, stood up and walked out. There was no reason to ask any more questions," concluded Officer Johnson.

"So, what are the Knights of the Golden Circle?" asked Thompson.

"Hell, if I know" replied Officer Johnson. "We didn't care to find out, just closed the parole board and filed the case away for another two years."

Continuing his questions, Thompson asked, "So what has Collins been up to over the last couple of years?"

"Somehow Collins is still calling the shots on the outside with his Aryan gangs. We haven't figured out just yet how he's doing it, but he is still an active force in the white supremacist movement," the officer claimed. "His brother Dennis comes by for visitation every opportunity he gets, so we think that's his main means of unmonitored contact with the outside world."

Wrapping up his conversation with the prison officer, Thompson said, "Well, thanks for the information. If anything else comes to mind about him, let me know."

"Sure thing" replied Officer Johnson. "Give me your contact information and I'll let you know if something comes up."

"Okay thanks, the number here at the office is 505 221-9100," confirmed Thompson.

"Got it. Have a good one," closed Officer Johnson.

Thompson replied, "You too, bye." Looking back down at his notes, Thompson hung the phone up and said to himself, "So Collins is still active, I wonder what he is up to. What is this Knights of the Golden Circle thing?" He turned his desk chair towards Danovich and asked," Danny, have you ever heard of the Knights of the Golden Circle?"

"It doesn't ring a bell," answered Danovich. "Have you checked the Internet? You know, do a Google search? You can use the Internet to find more than just porn."

Annoyed with Danny's comment, Thompson turned back to his computer and responded, "Yeah, I know. I just haven't had time to look it up yet."

Thompson pulled up the Google search page on the screen, typed in Knights of the Golden Circle and hit the enter key. Immediately a long list of search results was displayed reflecting the Knights of the Golden Circle. Surprised at the number of results, Thompson said to Danovich, "Damn! Would you look at all this that came up?"

Danovich set his magazine down on his desk, got up from his chair and leaned over Thompson's shoulder to look at the computer screen.

"For a name I've never heard of," said Thompson, "there sure is a lot of shit on it. It says here that it was a northern pro- slavery group. They referred to it as the KGC. . . . . Hey maybe that's why Collins changed his middle name to Günter, to match the initials of the Knights of the Golden Circle."

With a skeptical look, Danovich said, "He must really believe in this organization to do that."

"Yeah, you're right." Thompson thought for a second then said, "I've got to go somewhere. I know a history professor who might be able to shed some light on this subject for me." Thompson grabbed his suit coat and quickly left the bullpen. Wanting the perspective of a learned scholar on the topic, Thompson left his office and drove across town to visit a history professor he knew at the University of Arkansas.

Within a few minutes, Thompson drove onto the campus of the University of Arkansas Little Rock and parked his government Chevy Tahoe in front of the building that was the home to the History Department. Walking down the long main hallway of the first floor, Thompson entered a small office and asked an older bearded gentleman sitting behind a desk stacked with books and folders, "Professor Edwards, how are you doing?"

Looking up from his work, he took a moment to recall Thompson's name. Professor Edwards replied, "Stanley, I am doing very well. How about you? You know, I haven't seen you in a long, long time. I think it was the last class you took from me back three or four

years ago. Did you finish your master's degree program?"

Looking down at his feet and feeling somewhat embarrassed, Thompson replied, "No sir, the job just
seems to always get in the way."

"Sorry to hear that! You always showed such potential in your classwork. So, what brings you down to see
me?" the professor asked.

"Well, I'm doing a little research into the Knights of
the Golden Circle," responded Thompson. "What can
you tell me about it?"

Professor Edwards turned towards a wall of shelves
filled with books of varying sizes and colors and used
his index finger to point at their titles as he scanned
them searching for the one he wanted. Having found
what he was looking for, he pulled an old book off the
middle shelf, opened it, and said, "As you can see from
the many entries in this book, there is a lot of information about the group. Some historians believe the
KGC to be the most significant subversive organization
in the history of the United States. The KGC was
founded in 1854 by George W. L. Bickley in Cincinnati,

Ohio, and as a group they supported the institution of slavery. One of their goals was to annex Mexico, parts of Central and South America, and Cuba as slave states to keep a cheap labor force available to the States. This annexation would have formed a circle around the Gulf of Mexico, thus the name Golden Circle. Membership was once documented in the northern states of Ohio, Indiana, Illinois, Iowa, Wisconsin, Kentucky, and Pennsylvania. Some historians estimate that the membership of the KGC may have reached as many as 300,000 at its height. During the Civil War, these northern sympathizers to the Confederacy were known as Copperheads and were said to have acted as a fifth column in the north that tried to destabilize the Union Army in its own home territory. These Copperheads frequently assisted Confederate troops who escaped from Union prison camps to get back home, and they were known to raise money and arms to aid Confederate forces."

Thompson asked, "Did they ever actively interfere with governmental politics in the U.S.?"

Professor Edwards responded to Thompson's question by saying, "Some historians speculate that President Lincoln's assassin, John Wilkes Booth, was a member and that the KGC was behind the plot to kill him just days after the Confederate surrender at Appomattox Court House. After the war was over, the KGC refused to acknowledge the Confederate surrender and continued to support annexation of Mexico. Do you know that there were documented cases where the KGC actually mounted unsuccessful incursions into Mexico from Texas? Some historians believe, and some evidence exists to support it, that the Ku Klux Klan, which was formed in 1866, was the military arm or enforcers of the KGC."

Thompson inquired further, "I know that clements of the KKK are still active in many parts of the U.S., but does the KGC still exist today in some other form?"

"In the many years after its formation, the KGC morphed into other organizations, such as the Order of American Knights and the Order of the Sons of Liberty. All references to these groups seemed to end around 1915 at a time when the KKK experienced a resurgence of power, which lasted until around 1944," replied Professor Edwards.

"I wonder..." speculated Thompson. "Did the KKK replace the KGC, or did the descendants of the KGC become a more covert and powerful force behind the scenes? Could the KGC have been behind the newfound strength of the KKK in 1915?"

"That's a good question," replied Professor Edwards. "It was said that the KGC had amassed a great treasure. On the Internet you can find numerous offerings of books and media for treasure hunters looking for their accumulated loot. Now mind you, many of the members in this group were not uneducated backwoods simpletons; they included wealthy political leaders and businessmen on the verge of the Industrial Revolution. If they existed beyond 1915, I doubt they would have buried their riches in some cave. They would need it to be readily available to finance their operations."

"That's true. If the KGC had accumulated great wealth, they would probably have invested it in that New York cavern called Wall Street instead of some dark damp cave. If they were politically connected back then and are still around today, could they still be behind the political scenes pulling strings that control the national agenda and direction of this country?" Thompson added.

"Now see there, you're using your brain to consider the possibilities!" replied Professor Edwards. "If you had used that level of curiosity towards your studies, you would have made an A in my class."

"To tell you the truth, Professor, it's been a long time since I've had something I was even curious about," Thompson confessed. "Thanks for your insights into this group, Professor, but I've got to go."

"Alright Stanley, it was good to see you again. Stop by any time," concluded the professor as he shook Thompson's hand.

Thompson left the campus and headed back to the office to follow up further on this information.

Later that month, in a large, stately mansion outside Cincinnati, Ohio, the birthplace of the KGC, a group of electronic security technicians were completing a sweep for eavesdropping bugs in preparation for a large dinner meeting scheduled for the great dinning hall. In the middle of the hall was a large mahogany table set with thirty place settings. The old-money wealth of the estate was evident because the hall was lined with expensive wood paneling and wainscoting, and a large crystal chandelier hung from the ornate ceiling. One of the technicians closed an equipment case and walked over to a large man in a tuxedo and reported, "Our team has completed its static sweep. There are no active devices in the dining hall."

The tuxedoed man asked, "What about dormant ones waiting for activation?"

"Well, there is nothing we can do about those right now. But during the evening's activities, our team will be set up in a room next door monitoring for electromagnetic signals, in case there are any," explained the technician.

"Good job," said the tuxedoed man. "Looks like we're just about ready. The guests are arriving as we speak. If anything comes up, let me know immediately."

"Will do," said the technician as he withdrew from the dining hall.

Later that evening, a group of about thirty wealthy businessmen, lawyers, and politicians sat around the long, dark mahogany table finishing dinner. After the wait staff cleared the table of fine china, silverware, and service platters, they withdrew from the great hall and secured the doors behind them with impressive efficiency. With grand precision, guards were posted at each entrance to the great hall to stand watch to assure that the party was not interrupted or that the surreptitious proceedings that were about to begin were not overheard by unauthorized personnel. Indeed, great care had been taken in preparing for this momentous event, and even greater care had been taken to make sure that only the initiated were participants. No one other than those within the hall would hear or see what was about to take place.

From the end of the table, the host of the gathering stood and said, "Knights of the Golden Circle, I propose a toast." With this, the guests stood, holding their brandy glasses close at hand.

"We are about to embark upon a new phase of our secretive existence," said the host. "Our forefathers laid the groundwork for us, and we are about to realize our destiny." As he lifted his glass, he toasted, "To the successful execution of our most ambitious endeavor yet."

That said, those around the table raised their glasses, replied, "To the Order of the KGC," then drank from the glasses and returned to their seats.

The host turned to the Sergeant at Arms and asked, "Are we assembled with all members accounted for?"

"Yes, sir," replied the Sergeant at Arms. "The roll has been taken and all are present."

"Then we will begin," stated the host. "Since its founding in 1854 by Brother Bickley, the KGC has gained great power both politically and economically, it did not; however, come without cost. In the early days when the existence of the KGC was widely known, our brothers met significant resistance, and some of their ranks were pursued and prosecuted by the government. To continue to operate in the light of day would have resulted in the extinction of the Order. So, over a number of years, we moved ever deeper into the background of society and eventually, like Satan, we convinced the

American public that we do not exist." The host added, "We have even been able to keep the existence of our forefathers out of the very history books from which our own children and grandchildren are taught in school."

After a short pause, the host continued, "This precious anonymity has enabled us to develop our economic base, broaden our reach, and expand our capabilities. As a result, this Order of the KGC has played a major role in the course of American history. Our Order was behind Brother John Wilkes Booth when he shot President Lincoln, and with Brother Leon Gzolgozs when he assassinated President McKinley, right in front of his own Secret Service detail. And in our own lifetimes, the Order facilitated the removal of President Kennedy when we co-opted an outsider, Lee Harvey Oswald, to provide cover for our main assassination team. When he was captured and it appeared that he would cooperate with the Dallas Police and the FBI, we used Brother Jack Ruby to silence him so the existence of the Order would remain secret. Our influence over the Warren Commission assured that our Order's existence remained unknown. And in 1968, we executed preemptive strikes on two evolving threats, Martin Luther King, and Robert F. Kennedy. These things the Order has done in the past to move the United States in a preordained and righteous direction. As your appointed leader for the last twenty years, I, Franklin Whittaker, have seen this group achieve many difficult milestones toward our eventual goal. This generation of the Order has been the most active and has achieved much in a short period of time."

Whittaker concluded his opening comments by saying, "Tomorrow, as the Lords of your respective Castles, you can go back and inform your subjects that the time is near, for we shall set into motion actions to cause the collapse of this decaying democracy we call the United States and to begin our reign under a modern-day feudal system." At this point, the guests around the table stood and applauded loudly.

"Gentlemen," Whittaker continued, "the stage is set. While we never overtly annexed Mexico, as envisioned by our predecessors, we have worked to keep their economy depressed and made them dependent upon us, thereby creating a low-cost workforce for us to exploit. Unknowingly they are enslaved to do our bidding for pennies on a dollar, and they voluntarily flow across the border to do so. The intelligence agencies of this administration are focused outwardly, and if they do look to the homeland, they are preoccupied with anything of Islamic origin. With the military forces of the current government overextended fighting in Jordan against Hezbollah and the Houthis in Yemen, and the remaining forces at home fatigued from lengthy overseas deployments, they have limited capability or will to react to internal disturbances. Economic conditions are the lowest since the Great Depression, gas prices continue to escalate, and the dollar is at an all-time low overseas. The general populace of the country has lost confidence in the government, is apathetic to their political processes, and has essentially abdicated their right to vote to the vast minority of the people that do vote. As a nation we are greatly divided, and our plans will capitalize on these divisions."

Whittaker paused for a briefly for the guests to absorb the gravity of the situation and the vast opportunity it presented to their cause.

"With this as the setting, the Democrats have provided us the kindling necessary to ignite a race war in the streets of the inner cities across America, and our subjects will be prepared to pour volatile fuel upon the flames as soon as the embers begin to glow!" exclaimed Whittaker. "Senator Jordan from Michigan has once again given the blacks and other inferior races their hope: hope that he can continue to make a change in this country by becoming the second black president and progressing the county towards Communism. Not many years ago, each of you personally witnessed what the police killing of an insignificant individual like George Floyd caused in Minneapolis and across the country. Imagine the possibilities of similar reactions nationwide from an event that brutally extinguishes that hope!" he added.

"Our ownership in Smithson Integrated Engineering has provided us the capability, and we have co-opted a motivated participant that will provide us the opportunity. Our Russian and Chinese brothers fulfilled their promise by providing the weapons and materials necessary for us to execute our plan. The Russians were more than eager to contribute the arms for our cause, and the Chinese used their great volume of exports to conceal the transfer of these vital military supplies into the States. In return, our foreign brothers are poised to forcefully annex their former states of Azerbaijan, Georgia, and Taiwan when we have done our job of destabilizing the current government's ability to respond," claimed Whittaker. "With the Federal government of the United States paralyzed from reacting to an internal crisis, they will be able to reclaim these disputed territories unchallenged." He concluded by stating, "We have one task left, and that is to liberate the commander of our forces to make final preparations, to mass his Aryan Alliance troops at key locations, and to lead them into history in our name. Soon we will free Kenneth Günter Collins and send an unambiguous message to federal law enforcement, and we will set this final phase into motion." With this said, the great hall erupted in a thunderous standing ovation.

Chapter VI
The Co-op

In a Congressional office in Washington, DC, two U.S. Congressman were preparing for their next meeting. Congressman Turner asked his fellow KGC brother, "So what do we know about Agent Foster?"

Congressman McClure replied, "His full name is Matthew McKinley Foster. He happens to be the great great grandson of George Foster, who was one of the Secret Service agents present when President William McKinley was shot. After President McKinley died from his wounds, Agent George Foster, feeling personally responsible for the failure, started a tradition of naming all firstborn male sons in the family with McKinley to honor the fallen president."

McClure added, "Agent Matthew Foster is new to the Secret Service, ambitious, wants to redeem the name of Foster within the Secret Service, and to say the very least is not a fan of Senator Jordan's candidacy for president. Since the Order of the KGC became aware of him, we staged a series of encounters that he thought were purely happenstance to test the waters, build a relationship and gain his trust. He knows nothing of the KGC, but thinks that we were moved by his family's story and that we want to assist him in erasing the blot on his family name. He is sure to aid us in our endeavor."

"What if he notifies his superiors in the Secret Service of our plan?" asked Turner.

"We have all his phones tapped, and his every move is under our surveillance. We will not hesitate to terminate a threat, if he poses one, but based upon our earlier discussions I am confident he will play out his part according to our plan," replied McClure.

Congressman McClure's administrative assistant used the intercom and announced, "Agent Foster is here to see you, sir."

McClure told her to see him in, and a moment later a smiling young Agent Foster stepped into the office and shook McClure's hand, saying, "Hello, Congressman, it's good to see you again. I hope all is well."

"Indeed, indeed," replied McClure, adding "I'd like you to meet a dear associate and fellow lawmaker, Congressman Turner."

Foster extended his hand and said, "It's good to meet you, Congressman." Foster was truly impressed that he was meeting with two prominent congressmen ...men who could be very influential in his career and life.

McClure said to them, "Please, gentlemen, let's sit and talk."

As they sat down in the thick, overstuffed leather chairs, Foster thought to himself, "I've made it now; my career is on the fast track. Having a couple of Congressmen in your corner can never be bad."

McClure began, "Agent Foster..." He paused. "Given our relationship, I feel that I can call you Matthew. Is that okay with you?"

Foster quickly responded, saying, "By all means, sir, and you, too Congressman Turner."

"Well, thank, you Matthew, you are a very impressive young man," said Turner. "You will go far in this life."

McClure continued, "Matthew, we want to take you into our confidence and share some information that I believe you will find of interest as a member of the Senator Jordan protection detail in Detroit."

"We represent some very influential people within the government and business sectors," said Turner, "and they do not believe it is in the best interest of this country for Senator Jordan to become president at this stage in history. Our economy is in shambles, and our image on the national stage is greatly tarnished."

"I couldn't agree with you more, Congressman. I think his campaign has been divisive to the country and his presidency would be a tremendous embarrassment," said Foster.

"Well, we're glad to see that you agree, but I must ask, to what lengths would you go to see that he doesn't get there?" asked McClure.

Somewhat caught off guard by the straightforward question from the Congressman, Foster responded

‚"Well sir, whatever it would take, short of something like an assassination."

"Are you firm in your convictions on this?" asked Turner.

"Absolutely," replied Foster.

McClure continued, "Well then, I must state this directly. We know of people who would remove the threat of his presidency and at the same time catapult your career to the top. We have an informant who is in contact with a radical who wants to assassinate Senator Jordan. However, we could only condone an attempt that leads to no more than Senator Jordan being slightly injured. We do not wish him serious harm. You see, we have it on very reliable information that Senator Jordan's wife is so concerned for his safety that he will withdraw from the race if a serious threat to his life occurred."

"Yes sir, as a member of his protection detail, I can confirm that concern on her part myself," replied Foster.

"Well, excellent. It is always good to corroborate these facts from different sources," said Turner.

"What we propose is that we guide his plans in the manner we wish and do not stop this assailant until the last minute, until the time where you can stop him and become the hero in front of millions on national television," added Turner.

Foster smiled at the concept and thought; This is my chance to avenge the shame my family has felt since the assassination of President McKinley, while at the same time gaining recognition.

"If things work out right, not only will you become an instant hero, I can assure you that due to your participation and support of the cause, our mutual friends will ensure that you will have a very prominent political career ahead of you," declared McClure.

"Count me all in, gentlemen!" said Foster in an excited voice.

"That's great, Matthew. Now let's get down to the specific details of the plan," said Turner. "We want to limit the assailant to a light caliber handgun to assure that Senator Jordan is not seriously harmed. We are also aware of the Rostrum's protection capabilities against a handgun, so our people will need to gain access to the panels in order to replace the normal panels with ones of lesser protective quality. That way the bullets will penetrate the Rostrum with only enough energy and velocity to cause a flesh wound to whoever is behind it, and Smithson Integrated Engineering will take the blame for a defective product."

McClure piped in, saying, "What we need from you is to provide us with the details regarding security alarm coverage in the Jordan campaign headquarters, a couple of pictures of your campaign identification card, and enough seals to replace the tamper-indicating seals on the Rostrum."

Foster replied, "The only alarm coverage is a magnetic switch on each of the doors and windows. I can get you the seals with no problem, because even though they are serialized and tracked, the database is not very secure. In fact, I had to cover a mistake I made once when I lost a seal by modifying the database. A cyber tech friend told me to try logging into the database as 'admin' and use a blank password. Worked like a charm," Foster said. "It seems that this is a default configuration on the database software. Most people change it when they initially install it because the rules for accreditation require them to complete a checklist. However, whenever they reload the software, the blank admin password gets reactivated. I know most of the IT guys that support the system, and I was not surprised when I found that that little trick worked." Foster added, "If you have a camera, we can take those pictures now."

After an assistant took pictures of Foster's campaign identification card, they concluded their discussions with McClure, saying, "Matthew, we need to make sure that you are close to the podium so you can be in a position to shoot the assailant. How do you propose that we do that?"

"Not a problem. As one of the junior agents, I will be on the auditorium floor just forward and to the side of the Rostrum. If the assailant comes down along the cleared aisle in front and crosses the line before he shoots, I will have a clear shot without putting others in the line of fire," replied Foster.

"Excellent! The assailant thinks he has insider support, so we'll set it up so that he takes the path you suggest to the shooting position. We wouldn't want to jeopardize the safety of anyone else," said Turner. Having concluded their business Foster shook the Congressmen's hands and departed the office, thinking of how proud his family will be when he stops the would-be assassin.

Chapter VII
The Escape

It had been almost a month since Thompson had heard anything from Candy. Since his last meeting with her, he had identified Kenneth Günter Collins as a person of interest to be monitored, began researching leads concerning the KGC, and gathered new information on the street about the Copperheads. Thompson was sitting at his desk looking over his field notes, while Danovich was seated at his desk talking on the phone in the background. As he hung up the phone, he looked towards Thompson and asked, "Hey Stan, how are you coming on that KGC thing? Have you seen Candy lately?"

"No, the last time I talked to Candy was about a month ago. Ya know, she was saying something about new members of the Copperheads being fresh out of

Jordan and Yemen. I guess I wasn't paying much atten-tion to what she was saying. I guess I was watching her small silver cross hanging by its chain just above her cleavage. It was very distracting," Thompson admitted.

Danovich gave a big smile and said, "Yeah, I think these are more like dates to you than field interviews buddy."

"Well, I should have paid more attention to what she was saying."

"Oh yeah, why?" asked Danovich.

"Other sources are now corroborating what she was saying: that the Copperheads leadership was making it a priority to recruit these skilled military types over the last year. Candy had mentioned earlier that all the new recruits recently initiated into the ranks of the local gang were young ex-military types. Now I've got other sources indicating that the gang has seen an extraordinary rate of growth. Candy said that some of these new guys included Army Rangers, Special Forces, and Navy SEAL veterans with recent combat experience."

Danovich frowned at the thought. "Those are some tough and well-trained guys. Imagine the chaos a gang filled with guys with that kind of skill and experience could create."

"Yeah, I know, that's exactly my point. They could be real trouble," asserted Thompson.

"If I were you, I'd follow up with Candy again and see what's been going on during the last several weeks."

"I'm already on it. I'll be meeting with her tomorrow afternoon at the playground near the elementary school," said Thompson.

"Well, let me know if something else comes up."

Thompson turned back to his desk and agreed, "Don't worry, I will."

Thompson arranged to meet Candy at a playground near a local elementary school in the early afternoon the next day. As he pulled into the outer school parking lot, Thompson saw that Candy had arrived before him, and she was sitting on one of the playground swings, waiting. Getting out of his vehicle, he closed the door, looked around for anyone that might be watching, and then walked over to where Candy was sitting.

"Hey Thompson!" she said as he approached. "What's up?"

"Well, that's what I wanted to ask you," Thompson responded as he leaned against one of the support posts of the swing. "Are any new guys joining the gang lately?" he asked.

Candy replied, "Yeah, five more in just the last week, all of them just back from combat assignments in either Yemen or Jordan."

This concerned Thompson, and it showed on his face.

"Is that odd?" asked Candy.

With a grimace, Thompson said, "Yes, it is odd and disconcerting, because these guys give the gang an advantage over local law enforcement, especially if they're armed."

Candy replied, "Well, I don't know much about weapons, but they have been going down to the quarry shooting quite a lot."

"Was that at the old Kendal Mine quarry down near the river?" Thompson asked.

"Yes, the owner has given them permission to shoot down there," said Candy.

"Do you know who the owner is?" asked Thompson.

"No, but I think they're somehow connected to Smithson Integrated Engineering. I heard one of the guys mention them in conversation with a couple of the gang lieutenants," Candy answered.

As they talked, Candy's brother Ben pulled into the Sunoco gas station across the road in his old pickup truck, got out of the cab, and began to fill his gas tank. With the nozzle stuck in the gas tank and the pump running, Ben leaned up against the truck with his forearms against the side of the truck bed and began to look around killing time. Though it was some distance away, Ben recognized Candy sitting on the swing, and he could see that she was talking to a guy he didn't recognize. When his gas tank was full, he returned the nozzle to the pump and went inside the store to pay the cashier. Noticing that Candy and the guy were still there when he came out, curiously Ben sat in his truck, lit up a cigarette, and watched the two while they talked.

"Have you heard any more about KGC?" inquired Thompson as he continued his discussion with Candy.

"A couple of days ago I overheard Jake say something to Ben about freedom coming soon for KGC," Candy answered.

"Listen, Thompson," Candy added in a quiet, slightly shaken voice. "I'm a little concerned about us being found out by the gang. If they ever even thought, I was talking to a fed I'd wind up in pieces in a dumpster."

In a reassuring voice Thompson said, "If you have any indication that someone knows, you call me. I will come get you and keep you safe." Noticing that Candy was wearing her hair differently, Thompson said, "I like your hair that way. It highlights your eyes."

"Thanks," she said as she twisted a strand of her long, brown hair around her left index finger. "Thompson," she said in a curious voice, "do you think a person can begin their life over and forget about all the bad things they've done in the past? I mean really start over?"

"Well, sure," replied Thompson. "There are all sorts of reasons to do that. Look at me, I got divorced and had to start over."

"No," she responded. "I mean change who you are, what you believe in, and what your vision of love can be?"

Getting into unfamiliar territory, Thompson stumbled for the right words. "Well, I guess so ...I mean sure you can. Listen, of course you can! You just have to know in your heart what that change should be and then do it, no matter what the consequences. If you really, really want it, it can happen."

"You really think so?" she asked.

"Yeah, I know so. If and when we are done with all of this and you're ready to make a change, I'm there for you," he replied.

"Thanks Stan. That means a lot to me." Looking down at her watch, she stood up quickly from the swing and said, "Shit, I'm going to be late to meet Jake. Gotta go. I'll call you if something else comes up. See you later." Candy quickly left the playground, returned to her car, and drove off with a slight squeal of her tires on the pavement.

Thompson waved goodbye as she sped off and headed back to his office to call the corrections officer at Big Sandy. On his drive back, he fantasized about being Candy's knight in shining armor; he would gladly be her protector if things went badly. Her expression of vulnerability about being found out by the gang and the idea of changing her life was the closest thing to an emotional connection with him that he had ever gotten from her. If being her security blanket was the best he could do for now, he could accept that because it was real, not just something he imagined to be true.

Across the road, Ben had watched as Candy and Thompson said their goodbyes and kept an eye on Thompson as he returned to his car. Though from their body language he thought they would, he was glad to see that they did not kiss or hug to indicate they were romantically involved, because that would really piss off Jake if he found out. But what he noticed next was probably even worse. As Thompson opened the car door to get in, Ben noticed that the vehicle had U.S. government plates on it, so he decided to covertly follow Thompson to his next destination. Driving through the city streets, Ben maintained his distance behind Thompson's car so that he wouldn't know he was being followed. As Thompson pulled into the underground parking garage of the Federal Building, Ben pulled his truck over into a metered parking space across from the building.

Agitated by what he had just seen, Ben struck the steering wheel hard with his right fist and said out loud, "Damn it, Candy, you've really screwed up this time, girl." He then put the transmission into drive and sped off down the street.

Back in the office, Thompson placed a call and was holding on the phone with the Big Sandy Penitentiary. Danovich walked over to his desk and looked at Thompson a couple of times because he was not saying anything on the phone.

"Hey, Thompson, what are you doing?" asked Danovich.

Thompson replied, "I'm on hold with the Big Sandy Penitentiary, waiting to be forwarded to my contact on the floor in the prison unit where Collins is."

When Officer Johnson came to the phone, he said, "Hey Agent Thompson, I was going to give you a call."

"Why?" asked Thompson. "Is something up with Collins?"

"Well, last week Collins admitted to a murder that occurred over seven years ago," said Officer Johnson.

"Why would he do that?" asked Thompson.

"Everyone thinks he's finally reformed and trying to set things straight. He even waived a jury trial and is going straight to sentencing as part of a plea deal," stated Officer Johnson.

Perplexed, Thompson said, "I don't understand. It doesn't fit with the information I received earlier today."

"Well, believe it, or not he's going to be sentenced tomorrow at the Federal Courthouse in Huntington, West Virginia," said Officer Johnson.

"What?" yelled Thompson. "You're going to transport him to Huntington tomorrow? That's a big mistake. Let me talk to your warden right away!"

"Okay, hold on. It'll take a minute to get you transferred up to him," replied Officer Johnson.

Thompson placed his hand over the phone's microphone, turned to Danovich and said, "Can you believe this? They were going to take Collins out of the security of the prison walls to appear in court almost sixty miles away!"

At his request, Thompson was transferred to the warden's office immediately.

"Agent Thompson, this is Warden O'Conner. How can I help you?" asked the warden.

In an excited voice, Thompson explained, "Warden, you can't let Kenneth Collins appear in Huntington tomorrow. I have information that leads me to believe he's a flight risk. He must stay within the prison walls. If not, something is going to happen and he will escape!"

"Alright, alright! I'll postpone the sentencing, but your information better be solid," replied the warden.

"Thank you, sir, you won't be sorry. I'll get back to you in the next couple of days with some more information," said Thompson.

Warden O'Conner ended the call by saying, "If anything changes, you better let me know pronto."

The warden hung up the phone and immediately called District Attorney Vince Davidson in Huntington, West Virginia to postpone the sentencing hearing. Answering the phone in the outer office, the secretary said, "District Attorney Davidson's office, how may I help you?"

On the other end of the line, Warden O'Conner answered in an excited voice, "Rita, this is John O'Conner. I need to talk to Vince right away."

"Yes sir, Warden, I'll let him know you're on the phone," replied the secretary. She placed the phone on hold, got up and walked into DA Davidson's office and said, "Excuse me Mr. Davidson, but Warden O'Conner from Big Sandy is on line one and wants to talk to you. He says it's urgent."

"Thanks, Rita, transfer him in," replied DA Davidson.

The secretary stepped back to her desk, picked up the phone handset and punched a couple of numbers on the phone console. Immediately the phone on the DA's desk buzzed. Answering the phone, DA Davidson said, "Warden O'Conner, what can I do for you?"

"Vince, I got this call from an FBI Agent in Little Rock that says he has information that Kenneth Günter Collins is a risk of escape tomorrow. He wants me to stop his transfer to the courthouse up there tomorrow for sentencing," claimed the warden.

DA Davidson paused for a second and then said in a very firm tone, "John, this is a very big case, one that gives us a check in the win column without a fight. We haven't had many wins lately, John. I can't tell you how much that means right now. The media is already setting up outside the courthouse and broadcasting on an hourly basis. We are not going to delay this sentencing hearing. You do whatever you need to do to make sure nothing bad happens and you get him here on time before the judge! You hear me?"

"Well yes, I hear you Vince, but let it be known for the record that I am doing this under protest. This better be worth the potential risk," replied the Warden.

"It's worth whatever risk there is! We are really hurting for some good publicity in the media. Right now, the people believe there is no real justice in our criminal justice system, and we have to show some progress," responded DA Davidson.

"It won't look very good if he escapes on route to or at the courthouse," the Warden stated in an irritated tone.

Pausing for a second to keep his composure, DA Davidson responded by saying, "John, it is your job to make sure nothing happens. You get him here bright and early in the morning, cleaned up and ready for his picture to be plastered on every newspaper front page and six o'clock news cast for two hundred miles." With that said, the DA slammed the phone down onto its cradle, ending the conversation. Immediately, the DA closed the door to his office, pulled his cell phone out of his pocket and hit a speed dial number programmed into it.

On the other end of his call he heard, "Congressman McClure's private line, this is Jane, how may I help you?"

"Jane, this is Vince Davidson. Is the Congressman available?"

"Congressman Turner is with him right now. Is it important enough for me to interrupt?" she inquired.

"Yes. It's good that Congressman Turner is there to hear this as well," replied DA Davidson.

On the congressman's phone intercom Jane announced, "Congressman McClure, Vince Davidson is on your personal line and would like to talk to you and Congressman Turner immediately."

Hitting the speaker button on the phone console, Congressman McClure said, "Hello Vince! What's all the fuss about?"

"Congressman, as you know we are planning to get Kenneth Collins to the courthouse for sentencing on the plea deal we concocted to facilitate his rescue tomorrow," answered DA Davidson.

"Yes, yes, Congressman Turner and I are fully aware of its importance to the cause," replied McClure.

"Well, I just hung up with the warden at Big Sandy, and he said he was contacted by an FBI agent out of Little Rock who picked up some intelligence information about our operation to get Kenneth Collins out of custody."

"Is our plan in jeopardy?" asked Congressman Turner.

DA Davidson replied, "No sir, I told him that he needed to do whatever he needed to do to get him to the courthouse. I don't know what measures he's going to implement to improve the security of the convoy."

"I'll inform Brother Whittaker of the developments so that our men can be prepared for whatever they do to counter the threat. I will also make a phone call or two to see if I can get this FBI agent pulled off track as well. Thanks for the heads-up, Vince. Make sure things go well at the courthouse tomorrow," responded Congressman McClure.

"Yes sir," replied DA Davidson. "We'll take care of things on our end."

Back at Big Sandy, the warden became concerned after he had hung up with DA Davidson and began to second-guess the relatively unknown and unconfirmed source of this newfound information. During his conversation, the DA had been rather defensive about the subject, and he didn't want to further agitate such a powerful man with wealthy connections and a promising future in the political field ahead. With his hand on the phone, he thought for a moment, then picked up the handset and called the SAC at the Little Rock FBI field office to confirm the intelligence information that Thompson had provided.

The phone rang in the FBI's Little Rock Office, and the warden was connected to the SAC. "Special Agent Brenner, this is Warden O'Conner at the Big Sandy Federal Penitentiary in Inez, Kentucky," began the warden. "I was talking to Agent Thompson of your office, and he says he has information that would indicate that an inmate in our custody is planning an escape tomorrow. I just wanted to touch base with you to confirm the threat."

SAC Brenner replied, "Oh he did, did he! He hasn't communicated this threat information to his section leader, and he did not bring it to my attention before he went outside this department by contacting you. Frankly, Warden, Agent Thompson is not one of my best agents, and I would question the veracity of his source of information. I will speak to him about this; I wouldn't change anything at this point. Thanks for the heads-up. I'll call you later." Upon hanging up the phone, SAC Brenner realized he was late for another meeting, grabbed his suit coat, and dashed out of the office.

Warden O'Conner hung up the handset, picked it up quickly again and punched a number. The prison operator answered, "Yes Warden, how can I help you?"

"Sally, get the transportation security team in here for a meeting, please."

"Yes sir, they'll be right in," she replied.

A few minutes later, three prison supervisors joined the Warden in his office so he could brief them on the transportation details for the next day. "Gentlemen, whether it's legitimate or not, this information about

Collins being an escape risk has me a little concerned, so we're going to beef up the security detail for tomorrow's transfer." He directed them to beef up their security detachment for the fifty-nine-mile route and to be prepared for anything. "In addition to the normal driver and security officer on the inmate transport bus, I want an escort car with two officers in front, the Lenco Bearcat armored truck with a driver and five tactical officers in back, and I will ride in the helicopter to provide overwatch and command and control for the convoy. In addition to your handguns, everyone will be armed with an assault rifle, with 120 rounds of ammunition each. Everyone will wear their tactical body armor during the entire move. We'll depart first thing in the morning. I want all the inmates scheduled for court loaded on the bus and ready to roll out at 0700 hours," instructed the Warden.

The next morning, things went according to plan; the convoy was loaded and ready to hit the road at seven o'clock. Warden O'Conner gathered his men in a circle, gave the escort detail their final briefing and said, "Men, we want to keep a keen eye out for anything that looks suspicious. If you see anything that doesn't look right, don't hesitate to get on the radio and let everyone know about it. If there really is anyone out there trying to break Collins out, we want to see them first, jump on them quickly, kick their pansy asses and make it home before Momma calls us for dinner. To confirm our radio call signs, I will be Eagle One, the lead vehicle will be Echo One, the bus will be Echo Two, and the Bearcat will be Echo Three. Any questions? Okay, let's move 'em out."

With a loud unison clap like a football team breaking out of a huddle, the escort detail broke from the circle, did one last check of their equipment, and loaded into their vehicles. Keeping a fifty- yard separation between each of the three vehicles, the convoy proceeded along the planned route. In their individual vehicles, members of the escort detail were on edge and exhibited a heightened level of awareness concerning everything along the planned route. Every horn honk and vehicle with more than one occupant that went by caused the men to tense up and scan the roadside out their windows. About midway along the convoy route, the Warden spotted a road crew ahead of the convoy, picked up the radio microphone and transmitted to his units below, "Eagle One to all convoy units. Pull over on the shoulder and come to a full stop. There's a road crew about a half mile ahead blocking one lane of northbound traffic. I want to check it out before we get to it. Echo One, proceed ahead of us and check the crew out; Echo Three, deploy a two-man team to the east and west sides of the road about ten yards into the woods to secure our flanks; and Echo Two, hold what you've got until we determine what the situation is."

One of the officers in the Bearcat opened the top hatch and took up a covering position with his rifle, while the back door opened and two officers hit the ground running to take up positions to the east of the road, followed by two other officers who proceeded to the west in similar rapid fashion. As the lead escort vehicle began to drive forward, the Warden did a visual scan of the wood line to either side of the bus. A few minutes later the silence was broken by the speaker on the radio: "Eagle One, this is Echo One."

"Echo One, go ahead," the Warden responded.

"Nothing unusual to report here, sir. They're legitimate and will hold the rest of the traffic until we can get through," reported Echo One.

"Okay, hold your position until we fall in behind you and then proceed. Break. Echo Three, load up and let's roll," ordered the Warden.

Once the four officers were back inside and buttoned up in the Bearcat, the driver of Echo Three flashed his headlights at the bus, and then the two vehicles proceeded onward to link back up with Echo One at the location of the road crew. Proceeding along the route with similar intensity and tension, the convoy finally reached Huntington without incident.

As the convoy drove up to the Federal Courthouse in Huntington, the scene was something of a circus atmosphere. Numerous media broadcast vehicles were set up outside in front of the old courthouse to cover the event. Pro-civil rights protestors lined the sidewalk holding signs and chanting, while neo-Nazis gathered across the street and began to cheer as the convoy came into sight. Quickly, the convoy proceeded past the crowd and pulled into a fenced portal that served as the main vehicle entry point to the Federal complex. Once inside the portal, the gates were closed behind the convoy and the vehicles proceeded to the side doors of the building. Ten additional officers in riot gear swiftly formed a lined corridor between the prisoner transport bus door and the entrance to the courthouse. The escort detail unloaded the bus, rushed the prisoners into the courthouse and secured them in the holding cells in the building's basement.

Having landed in the rear of the complex, Warden O'Conner walked up to the escort detail that had gathered in the hallway. "Well guys, according to the court docket, we have a long wait ahead of us," lamented the warden. "Collins won't appear until later this afternoon. We'll stand by as an emergency response force to augment court security elements. From the look of the crowd out there, things could go bad real quick. Stay ready."

Later in the day, Collins was removed from the holding cell and was escorted by more than ten court security officers. As he entered the side door of the court-room, the camera flashes from the horde of press corps members were just short of blinding. Making his way in leg and belly chains to the defendant's table, he quickly sat beside his court-appointed attorney. As the door leading to the judges' chambers began to open, the bailiff forcefully announced, "All rise, the Honorable Patricia W. Burns presiding." Respectfully, everyone in the courtroom, even Collins, stood as the white female judge in her early fifties took her position behind the bench. Though Collins was racist, he was very respectful of recognized authority.

Judge Burns struck the gavel and said, "Be seated." Everyone took their seats as she thumbed through the case folder presented to her by the bailiff. Looking to Collins' attorney, Judge Burns asked, "As I understand it, the prosecution and the defense have reached a plea deal that is acceptable to both sides. Is that correct, counselor?"

Standing up to answer, Collins' attorney stated, "That is correct, your honor. We are ready to enter a plea."

"Mr. Collins, to the charge of second-degree murder of Curtis Peoples, how do you plead?" asked the judge.

Standing beside his attorney, Collins replied, "Guilty, your honor."

"And as I also understand, under the conditions of the plea deal, you have come to an agreement upon the terms of incarceration and are prepared to proceed to formal sentencing. Is that correct?" asked the judge.

Collins' attorney responded, "Yes, that is correct, your honor. We are ready for you to impose the agreed-upon sentence at this time."

"Okay. Then we will proceed. Mr. Collins, for your part in the murder of Curtis Jackson Peoples, I hereby sentence you to fifteen years' incarceration at the Big Sandy Federal Penitentiary, to be served consecutively with your current term of incarceration. Bailiff, remove Mr. Collins from my court and return him to the holding cell pending transportation back to Big Sandy," pronounced the judge. Collins then turned and walked back out of the courtroom through the door he had entered.

After the day's court session was concluded, Collins and the other inmates were loaded back on the bus. The convoy was ready to return to Big Sandy at 4:30 in the afternoon. After the stress of the drive up, waiting for something to happen that never did and the long wait at the courthouse, the officers on the prison escort detail were tired and were not as vigilant as they were on the ride up. On their way back, the tactical officers in the rear of the Bearcat were dozing off, and the rest of the officers were looking forward to getting home for a good dinner with their families. After all, Collins had been sentenced to another fifteen years in prison. If there was a planned escape, everyone expected it to be attempted before he entered his plea and was sentenced.

As he drove along with the convoy, the bus driver said to the security officer on board, "I'll be glad to get these guys back in the lockup and get home. My wife has a roast cooking for dinner."

"Yeah, the sooner we get these guys back home, the better I'll feel too," remarked the security officer.

With almost a laugh, the bus driver replied, "Oh, hell. They're not going to try and get Collins out now. He already pled guilty and was sentenced. If they were going to break him out, they would have done it on the ride up or at the courthouse."

"Yeah, I guess you're right," the security officer said in a relieved tone.

"Sure, I'm right. Just sit back and relax," assured the bus driver.

Along Highway 23 just south of Luisa, Kentucky, a pickup truck driven by a woman with a tarp draped over the bed of the truck pulled in unnoticed behind the Bearcat, keeping a distance of approximately fifty yards back from the end of the convoy. Seemingly unthreatening to the convoy, the warden did not pay any additional attention to this vehicle as it followed along behind the convoy. As the convoy entered a roadway cut through a wooded hillside that rose above the convoy on either side, a massive explosion from a roadside bomb erupted in a shattering crack that ripped through the side of the lead escort vehicle, nearly cutting it in half. The bus driver quickly slammed on the brakes, causing the wheels to lock up in a short screech of the tires and brought the bus to a halt near the burning hulk of the lead vehicle. Afraid to proceed further for fear of another improvised explosive device, the bus driver leaned over the steering wheel, scanning the outside to assess the situation, too frozen in fear to react. After all, these were tactics employed in Yemen against American forces, and the corrections officers in the convoy had no experience in reacting to such attacks. Immediately, each of the white inmates on the bus dropped flat on the floor for cover, with the two closest to Collins piled on top of him, shielding him with their bodies. Two loud and almost simultaneous gunshots from outside the bus broke the deafening silence that seemed to linger forever after the escort vehicle was thrown violently into the air by the blast. With deadly precision, two snipers located on the edge of the wood line scored head shots on the driver and security officer in the front of the bus, coating the inside of the bus's cab with a slick red film containing chunks of scalp and skull fragments and leaving an ever so slight crimson mist hanging in the air. In the rear of the convoy, the Bearcat had come to a skidding halt in immediate response to the horrific scene that was rapidly unfolding in front of them. The tactical team leader yelled, "What the shit was that?"

At that very moment, the tarp on the bed of the pickup truck following the convoy was thrown off and two figures in camouflaged battle uniforms stood up in the truck bed shouldering Russian made RPG launchers. Looking out one of the back portholes, one of the officers recognized the threat and yelled, "RPGs at six o'clock! Get the fuck out … now!" As the tactical officers in Echo Three grabbed their weapons and fumbled with the doors of the Bearcat to exit, detonation of the expellant charges of both RPGs created a tremendous back blast behind the truck, accentuated by a large puff of gray smoke that swirled in the calm breeze. Immediately after the secondary rocket motors ignited to propel the warheads toward the Bearcat's rear doors, the armor-penetrating shaped charges in the nose cones pierced the rear armored panels of the Bearcat, sending two jets of flame and molten metal into the armored compartment, searing flesh and creating an incredible overpressure in the confined space of the armored truck. As the top hatch of the Bearcat opened, a dazed and bloodied tactical officer tried to exit through the hatch. Immediately he was hit with rifle fire from the wood line, and his limp body fell back into the Bearcat. The sound of a long whistle blast was heard, at which time smoke grenades were deployed within the ambush zone to conceal all actions on the ground from observation by the unarmed helicopter above. While support team members provided covering fire and flank security, assault team members armed with AK-47s rapidly assaulted the Bearcat and dropped grenades in the open hatch of the roof to ensure that all the occupants were dead.

At the edge of the wood line, Todd Fuller, a member of the assault team, steadied one of the Russian SA-7 Grail heat seeking anti-aircraft missile launchers on his shoulder aimed at the helicopter. Noticing Fuller's readiness to engage the helicopter, the ambush leader yelled out to him, "Fuller, don't engage the helicopter! Deceit will serve our needs better than destruction right now."

The assault team leader gave two long blasts on his whistle, and immediately the southern support team left from its security positions and began to board the inmate bus. One team member assumed a kneeling position at the bus's front wheel, covering any threat from the road in front of the bus. A second team member assumed a cover position ten feet to the rear of the bus door, and a third knelt about ten yards away from the bus directly in front of the door, systematically scanning the bus windows for threats. Two other men used a wrecking bar to quickly open the bus door. As soon as they breached the exterior, the two cover men entered the bus with their AKs aimed toward the back of the bus in preparation to engage potential threats that remained. Immediately behind them, the two breachers then stepped onto the bus, grabbed the legs of the dead officers, and pulled the bodies of the driver and security officer onto the roadway. One of the breachers swiftly cut the high-security padlock off the prisoner compartment cage door, and both breachers entered and began to cut the restraints off the white inmates while the cover men provided overwatch.

In a commanding voice, one of the cover men yelled out clear instructions to the inmates. "White inmates to the back of the bus, black and Hispanic inmates to the front. Move, do it now!" Everyone reacted as instructed by the AK-wielding assault team member.

Two other men entered the bus with duffle bags stuffed full of street clothes for the white inmates to change into. Making maximum use of the cramped space, one of the cover men maintained security while the other climbed into the driver's seat, put the bus into gear, and began to drive it around the crumpled hulk of the burning escort vehicle, continuing south on Highway 23. About 100 yards down the road, the bus made a left-hand turn onto a dirt side road through a heavily wooded area, where additional smoke grenades had been deployed to fill in the gaps of the tree cover so that the helicopter could not see what was happening underneath.

Warden O'Conner looked at the pilot and said, "I can't see them, can you?" The pilot shook his head as he tried to peer through the smoke and trees to see what was happening on the ground. Losing contact with the bus for less than two minutes, from his perch on the helicopter the warden again spotted the bus as it emerged from the smoke traveling slowly on the dirt road towards a paved secondary road. "There it is! Continue to follow it," directed the warden. He watched as bus then made the turn onto the hard-top road and drove east towards the West Virginia state line. When the warden observed this movement at the edge of the trees and smoke, he instructed the helicopter pilot to follow the bus along the road east towards the town of Luisa. By this time, the warden had notified dispatch of the assault and was relaying the progress and every movement of the bus in its attempt to elude the helicopter's pursuit.

Warden O'Conner looked ahead of the bus along its projected route and transmitted over his radio, "Eagle One to all responding law enforcement units! The prison bus is now traveling east on County Road 7 and is approximately five miles east of Highway 23. State and county units, set up a roadblock just west of Luisa. Let's get them stopped before they get into West Virginia."

From the point of the attack, the ambush leader watched as the helicopter flew out of sight. He held his radio to his face and transmitted to the others, "Decoy and helicopter are clear. Back the bus back onto the highway and let's go." He gave three long blasts on his whistle and the remaining ambush members retreated to the wood line, where they had stashed a couple of SUVs for their getaway. The real prison bus backed out from under the cover of the trees, where it had entered the dirt road earlier, back onto Highway 23. Once back on the hardtop-road, the bus proceeded south a few hundred feet, turned right onto a paved county road, and continued driving to the west.

Prior to the ambush, the assault support team had pre-staged a similar painted bus under the trees, ready for use in a masterful sleight-of-hand switch. The actual bus containing all the inmates had pulled in close behind the second bus under the combined concealment of smoke and tree coverage. Then, like a choreographed group of Las Vegas magicians, under the concealment of the smoke the support team members quickly removed the black and Hispanic inmates from the real prison bus and loaded them onto the second bus, which was parked immediately ahead of the actual prison bus. Having transferred the black and Hispanic inmates, they finished removing the prison shackles from the white inmates, and who began to change into street clothes as they were handed out. This operation was executed with such rehearsed precision and timing that the helicopter crew was unaware that there were two buses beneath them, so they bit hard on the diversion and drew all responding units away from Collins' location with them.

Within three miles of Highway 23, the real prison bus pulled into a dirt drive leading to a farmhouse and a large red barn whose doors were already standing wide open. Collins' bus and the vehicles carrying the ambush force drove into the barn, and the doors were quickly closed behind them. Exiting the bus, Collins greeted the ambush leader with a hug and asked, "After you got those niggers and spics switched over to the other bus, how did you keep them from stopping once they were clear of you?"

With a big shit-eating grin, the ambush leader replied, "I told them that we had booby trapped the bus with explosives and asked them if they had ever seen the movie *Speed* with Keanu Reeves. The guy we picked as the driver said he had, so I told him he was now playing the part of Sandra Bullock and once he got going, he better not stop!"

Collins asked, "You didn't waste good Russian Semtex explosives on those worthless assholes, didja?"

With his shit-eating grin turned into a great big smile, the ambush leader responded, "Nope, but after seeing the patrol car in front of them blown ten feet in the air earlier, they didn't seem to question the authenticity of my threat."

"I'm sure by now those guys are jumping out of the windows at about forty miles an hour all along the route. That will keep those cops busy for a while," laughed Collins.

"Let's give the guys their new credentials, load everything into the other vehicles, and let's get out of here before this area becomes saturated with cops," said the ambush leader.

Collins responded by hollering out in a commanding voice, "Let's do it! Load up, guys. Get those barn doors open and let's roll."

As the barn doors opened, a television news helicopter flying east from Lexington on its way to cover the ambush site happened to notice activity near the barn and spotted the rear of the prison bus inside the barn.

"Hey, what's that over there?" asked the news reporter on the helicopter.

"I don't know; let's get a closer look," replied the pilot.

When the ambush leader saw the helicopter, he yelled, "Fuller, destruction would be the appropriate choice NOW!"

Fuller shouldered the SA-7 Grail, locked it on the target, and fired the missile. Seeing the smoke of the rocket trail rapidly approaching, the pilot tried to take evasive action, but it was too late. With deadly accuracy, the heat-seeking warhead found its intended target, sending the helicopter to the ground in a smoking, rotating mass that erupted in flames when it hit the tree line. Collins and his men with fresh street clothes and

false identification credentials, loaded into several vehicles and quickly left the area along different routes
towards the west. Collins and his men were headed west
to Lexington to take U.S. Interstate 75 north to Cincinnati, his intended destination.

Chapter VIII
Damage Control

Sitting in his office in Little Rock, Agent Thompson overheard a couple of other agents in the office talking about a developing story on the news about a terrorist attack on a prison convoy over in Kentucky between the cities of Huntington and Inez. One of the agents yelled to Thompson, "Hey, Stan, you ought to come see this. This looks pretty bad!"

Thompson sprang to his feet to see the television coverage now on all the national TV news sources. He couldn't believe what he was seeing. The other agent said, "Didn't you say the prison transfer from Big Sandy was going to be postponed?"

"The warden said he would cancel the sentencing hearing. What the hell just happened?" replied Thompson.

Just then, SAC Brenner stormed into the work area with Thompson's supervising agent and said, "Thompson, in my office now!" They proceeded to the office, where Brenner slammed the office door shut. "Why didn't you inform us about your lead on this Collins escape threat?" Brenner demanded.

"You would have just blown me off, apparently just like the warden at Big Sandy did!" yelled Thompson. Thompson thought for a second and then asked, "How do you know I had a lead on Collins anyway?"

SAC Brenner's face lost all expression; he looked down and said, "Because the warden didn't blow you off; he called me yesterday afternoon to ask about you and your credibility."

"Yeah, and you probably told him I was a fuckup, didn't you. Well, who's the fuckup now Brenner?" Thompson said in a loud, angry voice.

"You should have kept us better informed Thompson; some of this blame still lies on you as well. We have to help clean this up," said Brenner in response. "Get over to Inez as quickly as you can, to see if you can help the local FBI Field Office in Louisville, Kentucky make sense of this attack. You'll link up with one of their agents in Lexington and then take a Bureau helicopter over to the ambush site." Brenner looked over towards Jackie Kerr, who had joined them in the office, and added, "Jackie will have the admin staff set up your air travel, and she'll make the final arrangements with the Louisville office."

Somewhat shaken, Thompson left SAC Brenner's office, returned to his own office, and then sat at his desk to collect his thoughts. He sat and wondered if there was something else he could have done to prevent this tragedy. Finding himself short on answers, he decided he had better get going. Still in a state of shock, Thompson went to the garage, got in his car, drove to the airport, and hopped the first flight to Lexington he could get. The flight seemed to take forever, but when it finally landed at the Lexington airport, he was met by an agent from Louisville as he exited the boarding ramp.

"Agent Thompson?" asked a slender man in his thirties.

"Yes," responded Thompson as he reached out his hand.

Shaking Thompson's hand, the man said, "I'm Agent Jim McCartney. Glad to meet you. I hope you got something to eat on the plane because we have a helicopter cranking and ready to take us to the ambush site."

"Not really, but I haven't had much of an appetite since I heard what happened to the prison convoy," admitted Thompson. "Let me make a quick head call and I'll be ready to go."

"Alright, the restroom is just down the concourse here. We've got some bottles of water and sodas in a cooler on the helo in case you're thirsty," offered Agent McCartney.

"Thanks," replied Thompson. "I could use something to wet my whistle after I take care of business here."

Once they exited the door of the airport concourse onto the tarmac, airport security drove them over to the flight line, where they boarded the Bureau helicopter and took off for the ambush site. On route to the crime scene, McCartney told Thompson, "Not long ago we were informed that the Channel 11 news helicopter went missing shortly after the ambush. They were flying from Lexington when they heard the radio traffic about the attack and diverted to cover the story. About twenty minutes after the ambush, they lost radio contact."

"I wonder if somehow Collins was able to commandeer the helo, or maybe the pilot was in on it from the start," responded Thompson.

"That's a possibility, but we've got ground units checking the area to see if they can spot a crash site just in case they had mechanical problems," said McCartney as they approached the location of the ambush.

As the helicopter circled the ambush site before landing, Thompson surveyed the devastation inflicted upon the two escort vehicles and the personnel who were in them. Nearly cut into two pieces, the patrol vehicle lay on its side halfway on the road and halfway on the shoulder. Sitting in the middle of the road about seventy yards from the patrol vehicle, the armored vehicle gave the appearance that the driver had simply parked it and walked away. Only the thick, sticky red pools of blood, which had formed under the chassis after it dripping from the holes in the Bearcat's floor, betrayed the otherwise normal scene.

Agent McCartney leaned over to Thompson and shouted over the engine noise, "There were no survivors other than the warden and the pilot who were in the Bureau of Prison's helicopter overhead when the attack kicked off. They fell victim to the diversion with the duplicate bus and unknowingly cleared Collins' escape path to the west. Eventually the diversionary bus was stopped, but law enforcement agents were fully occupied in trying to round up all the inmates running loose who were scattered across the countryside with various injuries from jumping out of the moving bus. We haven't yet figured out why they just didn't stop along the way."

The helicopter landed on the roadway to allow Thompson and Agent McCartney to examine the scene on the ground. They walked over to a panel truck, where a forensic explosives technician from the Bureau of Al-

cohol Tobacco Firearms and Explosives (ATF) was recording his test results and findings on his laptop computer.

Thompson asked, "What can you tell so far?"

Pointing to the right side of the road across from the
wreckage of the patrol vehicle, the ATF tech explained,
"Based on the available evidence and the eyewitness
accounts from the warden and pilot, I've determined
the massive explosion that initiated the ambush and
annihilated the lead escort vehicle originated over
there in an orange, water-filled road barrier positioned
on the shoulder of the road. It could have been positioned there for weeks, and sometime before the day of
the transport someone had drained the water from the
barrier, placed an elongated high explosive charge of
approximately fifty pounds inside, added ball bearings
and heavy lag screws to the roadside face of the charge
and then refilled it with water. The non-compressing
hydraulic pressure created by the water hammered the
vehicle like an anvil, while high-velocity projectiles of
ball bearings and lag screws ripped through the soft

metal skin of the patrol vehicle, obliterating the occupants at the very start."

Looking under what was left of the hood of the lead escort vehicle, Thompson could see large lag screws deeply embedded in the engine block. The ATF tech continued explaining, "This was no amateur gadget. Whoever built this improvised explosive device knew exactly what they were doing. Trace analysis by our portable Beringer explosive detection system on the sample swipes we collected identified the explosives used to construct the device as Semtex, a Russian-made military high explosive. Though it is similar to our C4 plastic explosives, this is not something commonly found in the US."

Agents McCartney and Thompson then walked over to the Bearcat, looked inside one of the side doors, and saw that the interior was scorched, covered with blood, and riddled with shrapnel. Looking back toward the rear doors they could see two relatively small holes burned through the armor plate that allowed two beams of sunlight to shine through and project circular light spots on the floor. After searching the ground near the rear of the Bearcat, Thompson found a twisted stabilizing fin. "Well, based on the small entry holes burned through the armor doors and this rocket fin, it's almost certain that the weapon used against the armored vehicle was a Russian RPG," surmised Thompson.

"Two shots," Agent McCartney said as he examined the rear doors of the Bearcat. "They didn't leave anything to chance, did they?"

"No, they wanted to make sure the team inside was incapacitated so they didn't pose a threat," replied Thompson.

Another agent came running up to Agents McCartney and Thompson and said, "They found where the TV 11 news helicopter went down not far from here. If you guys arc done here, we'll hop on the helo and go check it out."

Though it was hard to find a place to set the helicopter down in the heavily wooded area, they managed to land not far from the site of the TV 11 helicopter wreckage. McCartney, Thompson, and the other FBI agents walked up to the crash site from where their helicopter set down. Stretched in a forty yard radius around the downed helicopter fuselage, yellow crime scene tape marked a perimeter to control access in order to protect potential evidence. At a point in the perimeter, a sheriff's deputy manned an access point established by a gap in the tape. Thompson and McCartney showed their badges and entered the perimeter after the deputy logged their entry into a form on his clipboard.

Not surprisingly, both the pilot and reporter were dead, their charred bodies still positioned in the cockpit of the helicopter. "Before now, no one knew what had happened to the TV 11 bird; it had just dropped off radio communications with no explanation," McCartney told Thompson.

The engine and transmission area on the helicopter's fuselage showed telltale marks and damage of an anti- aircraft surface to air missile. Thompson examined the marks and said, "Looks like it was hit by a heat seeking missile that tracked and targeted the engine exhaust. After it was hit here in the engine and transmission area, it would have pretty much fallen out of the sky."

Thompson looked around the outside of the crime scene perimeter and said to the other agents, "If this was a shoulder-fired missile, the launch location shouldn't be very far away." Pointing to a dirt road that he could see through the trees some distance away, Thompson asked one of the local officers, "Where does that dirt drive across the road lead to?"

A sheriff's deputy from the area, who was assisting the federal officers, said, "That road goes over to a small farm owned by Jeb Smith and his wife. They're real nice folks; they wouldn't be mixed up in anything like this voluntarily, that's for sure."

"Let's check out the farm then," said Thompson. "We'd better approach this carefully. They should already be gone by now, but as the prison convoy found out, you never know when all hell's gonna to break loose."

McCartney looked at the other FBI agent and instructed, "Form up an entry team and let's go check out the farm." The on-scene agents and supporting local law enforcement officers quickly formed a makeshift tactical team and then moved in a tactical formation through the woods to the edge of the farm. Using available cover and concealment, the state and county officers set up containment around the perimeter of the farm's structures to prevent the escape of anyone who may be hiding there. McCartney and Thompson viewed the scene from the edge of the woods and provided command and control of the actions. On the front porch of the old two-story farmhouse, the entry team of agents stacked close to each other in a line and prepared to make a tactical entry to clear the house. Thompson gave the go-ahead and with a quick nod of the team leader's head, the front team member kicked the door in, and the team quickly entered the structure and began a slow, methodical clearing of each room before entering the next. Thompson lost sight of them once they entered the house. After what seemed an eternity, the team leader broke the silence of the radio and reported, "We found Smith and his wife. They're dead in their upstairs bedroom, each with single gunshot wounds to their foreheads."

McCartney responded, "Okay, make your way to the barn and clear it."

"Roger that, exiting now," replied the entry team leader.

The entry team then moved to the barn and once again stacked for entry. While the scout covered the door with his M-4, the team's breacher moved to the door with a Hooligan Tool pry bar in hand. Placing the tool underneath the lock's hasp he forcefully removed the lock and opened the door, and the team entered the barn to clear it. A few seconds later, a single arm extended out the barn door with its hand in a thumbs-up position. Once the entry team leader gave that all-clear signal, he called for Thompson and the other agents to enter. Inside they found the abandoned prison bus, orange prison jumpsuits scattered everywhere, and the spent launcher tube from the Grail anti-aircraft missile.

Impressed with the efficiency of the operation, Agent McCartney stated, "These guys had it planned out, alright; this wasn't some pick-up game of amateurs. They did their reconnaissance in advance, selected their base of operation, set up their ambush location, and executed a flawless plan with military precision."

Thompson nodded in agreement and added, "These guys had a lot of Russian-made weapons, ammunition, and equipment items. We need someone in the ATF to work that angle to see where they came from."

"I'll get someone on that," replied McCartney.

McCartney looked around the barn at the other agents and turned back towards Thompson saying, "These guys will process the crime scene, and we'll head back to Louisville, where we'll focus our resources on trying to figure out where Collins may be headed from here. When you get back to Little Rock, call me directly if you find anything."

"Will do. Now let's head back to the helicopter and get on it," Thompson said before he started walking for the barn door.

Immediately, the local agents began to secure the crime scene in preparation for the technicians who would begin to process the scene for available evidence once they were completed with the ambush site.

Returning to the field office in Louisville later that evening, Thompson provided all of his information to the other agents ...except who his informant was. He was not going to expose Candy and subject her to any risk with these guys; after all, Candy was his and no one else's.

"These guys used Russian-made weapons and equipment, so while the ATF is focusing on determining the source of the hardware, we should concentrate on the operators themselves," said Thompson. "They had to train and rehearse somewhere; you guys should check the areas around here that you know to see if anyone's been doing some heavy-duty shooting. I will check on the quarry back in Little Rock to see if I can determine what types of weapons the Copperheads were shooting back there and whether there's some connection with Smithson Integrated Engineering in this mess."

Back in Little Rock, Thompson was at the county clerk's office early the next morning to go through property records to determine who the owner of the Kendal Mine quarry was. As he stepped inside the main door, Thompson paused and looked around the room. As he scanned the area, he saw many dusty shelves filled with record books and several library- type desks with computer workstations. Behind the main counter he observed an old man looking through some papers on the counter. The elderly Record Clerk's reading glasses were perched on the end of his nose with a cord attached to the end of the earpieces to keep them around his neck when he wasn't using them. Thompson walked directly over to the old man and stopped with his hands on the counter in front of the old man. Before Thompson could ask for assistance, the Records Clerk pulled his glasses off his nose, let them hang by the cord and asked, "How can I help you, young man?"

Pulling his FBI badge and credentials out from the inside pocket of his sport coat, he showed them to the Records Clerk and introduced himself, "Special Agent Thompson with the FBI." Thompson closed his leather credential holder and placed it back into his coat pocket. "I'm looking for some information concerning the old Kendal Mine quarry outside of town here."

While scratching his head and looking up in the air, the Records Clerk responded, "Well, I don't know much about it right off the top of my head, but I can help get you set up over there with one of the computers and you can go to town on searching the property database."

Looking over at one of the workstations and then looking back at the old man, Thompson gratefully replied, "That would be most helpful, sir."

The Records Clerk then walked Thompson over to one of the desks and showed him how to access the county databases. "This menu will get you pretty much anywhere you want to go. You can look things up by owner, parcel number or property street address."

Thompson nodded, took a seat in front of the computer screen, said "Thank you," looked back down and began to type on the computer keyboard.

As he searched the electronic files that had just recently been converted from old microfiche property records, he found the listing for the quarry. Talking out loud to himself, he said "Here it is, hmmmm, just as I thought." He again read through the property description to make sure he had the right piece of property and then went straight to the section that dealt with ownership. "Wait just one minute, what is this?" he exclaimed. Immediately he looked up from the computer, attracted the attention of the Records Clerk and motioned for him to come back over. "Come over here please, and take a look at this."

As the Records Clerk approached and leaned over the computer monitor, Thompson pointed to a name on the screen. Seeing what Thompson was pointing at, the old man put his glasses on his nose, he said the name out loud as he was reading, "Kensington Global Corporation."

Thompson asked, "Are you familiar with the company that holds the lien for this piece of property?"

Turning from the screen to look at Thompson, the old man replied, "No, that's not a finance company that I can recall ever seeing before, but that's not unusual. There are thousands of them just in this state."

"Could you please check your state database to see if it is an Arkansas company?" Thompson asked.

Already taking a step towards the main counter, the Records Clerk said, "Why sure I can." Stepping behind the counter, he entered a query in the state database he had access to on his computer. "Nothing in the state database but hold on just a second." He then moved from behind the counter and to another console on the table next to the one Thompson was using and began to type on the keyboard.

"And there you go! Now, back in the old days I couldn't have done this, but this here Internet has just about taken all the work out of it. It used to be, we had to get authorization to use the long-distance phone line, then make a bunch of out-of-state calls, then wait for a couple of weeks and then..." Thompson interrupted the old man before he could finish his sentence.

"I don't mean to be rude, but I'm in a bit of a hurry. Can you just tell me what you found, without the history lesson?" pleaded Thompson.

"Well, certainly I can, I know you FBI agents are just so busy chasing all those Islamic terrorists and such that you don't have much time to hear what we used to..."

"Please..." Thompson interrupted again, "..just tell me what you found."

"Well, this company here isn't an Arkansas Corporation or Limited Liability Company or such, but the Google search I did shows it as being a California corporation located in San Francisco. Look here you can read the company website by yourself, 'cause I know you FBI fellers are educated and up to date with these newfangled search engines and..."

"Thanks very much, I can take it from here." said Thompson with a rather short attitude.

As the records clerk walked back behind the counter, Thompson read through the company's various webpages, and over the next hour checked several other websites and databases as well. After reading a line on one website, Thompson quickly grabbed for his cell phone to call Agent McCartney back in Louisville to pass on this information. When he answered the phone, Thompson said, "Agent McCartney, this is Stan Thompson back in Little Rock. I reviewed the county and state records regarding the quarry up here where the Copperheads gang had been shooting."

"Okay, so what did you find out?" asked Agent McCartney.

"Well, I confirmed that the property is owned by Smithson Integrated Engineering, but in looking at the lien holder, it was financed by, get this, the Kensington Global Corporation," replied Thompson.

In response Agent McCartney asked, "So what's unusual about that? Am I supposed to know who this company is?"

"Well call me paranoid if you will, but their initials are KGC, and every time in the last few weeks where I've come across those initials something bad is found underneath when we kick the rock over," said Thompson.

"So, you think there is a connection between Kenneth Günter Collins, the Kensington Global Corporation and the fabled KGC of the 19th century?" questioned McCartney.

"I don't think we should count it out at this point. Besides, in addition to owning several properties across the country where a group could do such things as, let's say shoot big guns without raising any interest from the local population, they are also big in the international import-export shipping business. I think we need to check out their shipping and receiving facility in the San Francisco Bay area. If they are connected to Collins, this could be where the weapons used to make his escape came into the country," Thompson explained. "Here's the real clincher; the Chairman of the Board for Kensington Global is an old-money mogul by the name of Franklin Whittaker in Cincinnati, who also just happens to sit on the Board of Directors for Smithson Integrated Engineering," added Thompson.

"That does put an interesting spin on things," replied Agent McCartney, "but there isn't anything that directly ties him or Kensington Global to Kenneth Collins." Agent McCartney continued the conversation, saying, "I'll get the San Francisco Field Office and ATF to check out Kensington Global's Bay Area port facilities tomorrow."

"Alright then, I'll check out the quarry tomorrow to see if I can determine what types of weapons were shot by the gang there and if I can recover any evidence that could potentially tie them to the prison break," responded Thompson.

Just before hanging up, Agent McCartney said, "Hey Thompson, watch your back out there. Let me know what you find out."

"Will do," replied Thompson and then closed his cell phone to end the call.

Thompson opened up his cell phone again and called the general manager of the Smithson office and fabrication facility there in Little Rock. Answering the phone, the manager said, "Smithson Integrated Engineering, Jerry Jackson, manager. How can I help you?"

"Mr. Jackson, this is Special Agent Thompson of the Little Rock FBI Field Office. We're looking into an interstate automobile theft ring, and we had an anonymous tip that someone may be disposing of vehicles in the quarry lake at the Kendal Mine. I was told that Smithson owns the property. Is that correct?" Thompson inquired.

"Our company has owned it for many years, but we hardly have any use for it except for recreational activities. It certainly came in handy with this Rostrum project since we used the property to conduct blast and ballistic testing of the panels for the Secret Service.

Now, if somebody is dumping stuff up there in the lake, I definitely want to know about it, cause I don't want anyone messing up my prime fishing spot," replied Mr. Jackson.

"I don't think there is any real basis for this automobile dumping claim, but I would like to get permission to drive out there and take a look for myself, if that's okay," asked Thompson.

Mr. Jackson responded in a helpful voice, "Well sure, that would be just fine. Would you like me to go with you, or can you find your way out there okay by yourself?"

"No sir, I don't want to waste your time for something that will probably not pan out. If it's alright with you, I'll just go out by myself," said Thompson.

"Well actually, I'm snowed under here at the plant getting the last of those Rostrums out the door to the Secret Service. Why don't you just come on by when you're ready and get the key to the lock on the main gate to the quarry?" responded Mr. Jackson.

"Mr. Jackson, I really appreciate your help. I'll be right over to pick up the key and directions and then I'll head out there and look around. I'll have the key back to you in the morning, if that's okay," Thompson asked.

"Sure, that will be just fine. We'll see you in a few minutes," replied Mr. Jackson.

As soon as he hung up the phone with Agent Thompson, Mr. Jackson picked up the phone handset and dialed another number. After a couple of rings, a voice answered on the other end. "Yeah, Jake here."

Quickly, in an excited voice Mr. Jackson said, "Jake, I just got off the phone with a federal agent who said he's checking out reports of stolen cars being dumped out at the quarry. Son, have you and your boys been stealing cars again? I would've thought that your last stay in prison would have cured you of that."

"Daddy, Daddy, slow down. No, no, we haven't been doing nothing like that," Jake replied in a reassuring tone.

"Well, you better not be. At least you better not be messing that quarry up," said Mr. Jackson.

"Daddy, I know that's your favorite fishing hole, and I wouldn't mess that up. Hell, I won't even let the other guys piss in that water, much less drop an oily old car in there," Jake stated in a convincing voice.

"Well, okay. That agent is coming by in a few minutes to pick up the key and go nose around out there anyhow," informed Mr. Jackson.

Jake ended the call with, "Okay Daddy, I'll talk to you tonight. Bye."

Quickly ending his call, Jake immediately dialed the phone number for the quarry overwatch position. The person currently on duty at the position answered the phone and said, "Ben here."

"Ben, this is Jake. There's a federal agent coming out there to look around. He'll probably get there before we can get there, so keep an eye on him. If he gets close to the explosives cache, take him out if you have to. We'll deal with getting rid of the body when I get there," instructed Jake.

Ben replied, "Will do, Brother. See you in a few" and hung up the field phone.

Jake hung up the phone and then briefed a couple of his guys about the situation, "We gotta get out to the quarry. Some FBI agent is going out there to nose around." They grabbed their coats and headed out to his truck where Candy was sitting impatiently waiting for him. Jake opened the driver's door, climbed in, and stuck the key into the ignition. "Sorry, Baby, we've got to go out to the quarry real quick like. Breakfast will just have to wait a little while longer."

Candy rolled her eyes and crossed her arms in a huff. Jake shook his head, annoyed with her reaction as he started the engine, put it into gear, and screeched the tires as he began to drive the truck down the road.

On the edge of town Thompson, stopped by the aging Smithson factory to pick up the key. As he exited out of the old office door, he looked down at the large key ring he was holding in his hand. In addition to the handful of keys on a four-inch diameter brass ring made from a brazing rod was an eighteen-inch piece of broom handle. Thompson thought to himself, "I guess they don't want to lose these." He opened the driver's door to his car and tossed the key ring onto the passenger seat, where it skipped off the upholstery, bounced off the passenger door armrest and fell between the seat and door sill. Thompson took off his sports coat, sat behind the wheel, started the car up and began the thirty-mile drive out to the quarry. Shadows from the many tall trees that passed rapidly broke the steady stream of sunlight that showed through the windshield along the way. The drive was very peaceful on the two-lane county road until a group of three motorcycle riders pulled up behind him and followed his car for a few minutes. He wondered if they were members of the Copperheads gang that Candy's boyfriend was a member of ...the guys he was checking out. When the procession came to a long straightaway, the motorcycle riders passed by him with their loud exhausts roaring like the sound of rocket engines straining against gravity and continued to pull away from him along the roadway. As it turned out, he could tell from their jackets as they passed by that they were just wanna-be bikers. Probably some lawyers, doctors, or dentists cutting out from their busy work schedule, just out for a morning ride in the country on a sunny morning. Still, he began to wonder whether it was a good idea to go to the quarry alone and without telling anyone else where he was going. As an afterthought, he grabbed his phone to call the office to send another agent out as backup. Unable to get a wireless signal out there, he decided to continue out to the site alone. He didn't even try his mobile radio in his FBI government pool vehicle because he knew he was out of range this far out from the city. Realizing he had just passed the turnoff onto the gravel road that led to the quarry, Thompson slammed on the brakes and skidded to a stop about fifty yards beyond the unmarked intersection. He would have kept on going if he hadn't noticed the bullet- hole riddled, rusty signs overgrown by poison ivy vines just off the road to the left. Putting the transmission into reverse, he backed the car up in the middle of the road where he could read the sign: "Kendal Mining Operations – Quarry #1 Truck Access." Quickly he changed to the forward gear, gave it some gas, and made the turn down the gravel road leading to the quarry.

Arriving at the front gate to the quarry about two hundred yards off the paved road, Thompson saw or heard nothing to indicate that anyone was in the area. As far as he knew, he would be completely by himself out there. Looking around from the seat of his car, he could see that the gate to the quarry was an old rusted and mangled two-piece chain-link fence secured with a single padlock and chain that swung inward to the open position. It looked as if, over the years, the gate had been swiped quite often by the dump trucks that used to enter and exit this old quarry regularly when it did a steady volume of business. Now it lay dormant; after the housing bubble burst, there wasn't much road construction in the Little Rock area to keep it operational anymore. Exiting his vehicle, he unlocked and opened the gate, drove through, and then closed and secured the gate behind him before continuing on down the drive another half mile to the quarry itself. As he approached the quarry, he noted that this could be a very treacherous place in the dark as the sheer rock face just a few feet on the left edge of the road dropped off thirty to forty feet to the clear, greenish water of the lake below. Arriving at the end of the main drive, Thompson turned his vehicle around and parked in the direction of the gate just in case he had to make a quick exit.

As he got out of the vehicle, the small hairs on the back of his neck stood on end. Scanning the area quickly, Thompson felt as though someone was watching him, but he couldn't spot anything out of the ordinary. He was totally unaware that high up on an overlooking ledge across the lake, one of Jake's men, camouflaged with a Ghillie suit, was watching him through the scope of his Dragunov. As he peered through the rifle scope, Ben recognized Thompson as the guy he saw Candy talking to several days ago at the playground and followed to the Federal Building. Ben flipped the safety off on the rifle and placed his finger lightly on the trigger. Keeping a good sight picture through the scope on Thompson at all times as he moved around his car, Ben made sure that Thompson was alone, and also that he was ready to take Thompson out with a single, well-placed shot if need be.

Thompson walked over to a makeshift firearms range, where shooting lines had been carefully measured off and marked at twenty- five, fifty, one hundred and two yards from a target line in front of a long earthen berm used as a bullet backstop. Looking across the lake, he could make out a shooting bench that he figured must provide a shooter a steady platform for a four-hundred-yard shot. As he walked downrange, he looked on the ground along each of the shooting lines; it was clear that past shooters had performed a very effective "police call" to pick up all expended brass cartridges. This would be odd for most of the lazy weekend recreational shooters who routinely left their brass where it lay on the ground. Thompson knew that if the group had shot a lot of ammo, they had to have missed a piece of brass or two here and there ...and he was correct. As he kicked the sand and gravel along the shooting lines, he looked closely for any glint of the shiny gold color from a single piece of brass as it was exposed to the bright rays of the sun above. He was right; there, in amongst the sand and gravel at different spots, he found five spent casings with military markings on their bases. Examining the brass cases, he identified four of them as 7.62 x 39 mm, the same size cartridge used in Russian type AK-47 rifles. The other, which he found at the two-hundred-yard mark, was a 7.62 x 54 mm, which Thompson identified as the unique round used for a Russian Dragunov or similar former Soviet-era sniper rifle.

Thompson stepped back to his car, placed the spent cartridges in his trunk, and grabbed a small shovel and sifter. Moving downrange to the impact berm, he selected a couple of spots where frequent bullet impact was evident, removed a shovel or two of the dirt and sand on top, and tossed it aside. He then dug another shovelful of dirt and sand, dumped it into the sifter, and began to shake the sifter back and forth. Steadily the level of the dirt and sand worked its way down, until all that was left in the screen of the sifter was a handful of expended bullets and pebbles. Picking up a representative sample of these expended bullets from the batch, he examined it carefully, noting its solid copper jacket with rifling marks clearly present and its hollow base filled with lead.

The size and construction of the ammunitions components were consistent with a 7.62 mm military full-metal jacket cartridges, which were relatively cheap to manufacture in great quantities. Within the last ten years, ammunition like this for the AK-47 or SKS rifles produced in Russia, China or Pakistan had been abundantly available at inexpensive prices at almost any gun store, gun show or on the Internet. What was different were the casings for the Dragunov; they weren't as common as the casings for the AK-47.

Hearing vehicle motors approaching, Thompson quickly moved back to his vehicle, secured his evidence in the trunk, and closed it before any vehicles came into view. Just then, a red rusty pickup truck with the silhouettes of a driver and passenger, as well as two men on motorcycles, came around the last curve and headed straight for Thompson, who was now seated in his car with his door open and his feet on the ground. Thompson wanted to be sure he could exit his vehicle and draw his Glock 22 quickly if he had to. Now he was really second-guessing himself about coming out alone and not telling anyone except Agent McCartney in Louisville what he was planning to do. His hands began to get clammy, and his heart began to pound as though it was going to leap out of his throat if he opened his mouth to speak.

As the truck was pulling up to the side of his car, he noticed that the passenger was Candy and that she looked scared. Thompson thought to himself, "The driver must be Candy's dirtbag boyfriend. I sure wish our first meeting was on better terms than I have right now, when he has the upper hand."

From his perch across the lake, Ben continued to watch the scene through his rifle scope as the pickup truck came to a short, sliding stop on the gravel adjacent to Thompson's car, with the truck's door directly across from his open door about twenty yards away. Candy's boyfriend Jake, wearing a faded and well-worn blue jeans jacket, rolled down his window, let his left arm hang limp out the open window, looked Thompson's car up and down, and said, "From your license plates and vehicle I'd say you was a government man. Now am I right or am I right?"

Thompson responded to the question, saying, "You sure are right, buddy. I'm with the Environmental Protection Agency, and we had a report of some form of chemical contamination in the lake water that could be affecting the water downstream from here. My office sent me up here to take a look for myself to see if there was any basis for concern. From what I've seen, the water looks to be as clear and clean as a swimming pool, and since everything else here looks in order, I was just about to head back to the office to let them know there is no cause for concern."

With a big smile, Jake said, "Well, that's great to hear, 'cause me and my bitch here like to get naked and go swimming in that water in the summer. Matter of fact, if it was just a little warmer, I'd have her strip down and jump in right now just to give us something to get our hearts pumping.

"Is your heart pumping already, Mr. Government man?" Jake asked in a sarcastic tone.

Embarrassed by the comment, Candy turned her head and looked out the other truck window so Thompson couldn't see her face. Thompson felt bad for her having to put up with such crap from this lowlife piece of shit, and if he thought he could get away with it, he would pull out his service pistol and quickly put two rounds into the boyfriend's chest and one to the head.

But keeping in character with his cover story, Thompson replied, "That might be pretty exciting, but I have lots of paperwork back at the office, and they're waiting for me to report in, so I'd better head on out."

Jake said, "Go ahead and leave if you have to, but come on back anytime you want. I'll get this little gal here to put on a show for us all that you won't soon forget. Oh, by the way, as you go outta here, don't worry about closing the gate behind you. We'll make sure it's closed; after all, we don't want any riffraff coming in here unannounced, do we?"

With his heart still pounding like a jackhammer, Thompson politely said goodbye, closed the car door and drove off with his fingers clenched tightly around the steering wheel while the dust swirled in his car's wake behind him. Not only was he hopped up on adrenaline from his intense encounter with the Copperheads, he was also concerned for Candy's well- being. He was pissed that he had to leave Candy there with those assholes; but he did, and that's what bothered him the most. He sped out through the open gate to the quarry, turned onto the county road, and headed back to town.

Chapter IX
The Preparation

After the brutal ambush on the prison convoy, Collins and his Copperheads quickly made their way up Interstate 75 to Cincinnati and to the expansive mansion and racehorse training complex belonging to Franklin Whittaker. Just days before the planned national speech by Senator Jordan, Collins and Whittaker were working on the final preparations for implementation of their ambitious plan. Both men had spent most of the day on the phone coordinating logistical arrangements and ensuring that preparations and deployment of the troops were going according to plan.

Whittaker and Collins were about to conduct a final mission planning and coordination briefing via a webcast conference that connected them to their leaders in the twenty U.S. cities they had chosen for their operation. The webcast was being hosted from a spartan command post with concrete walls, hidden well within the mansion. In the center of the room was a large center table with several computer workstations and stacked with files and papers. A large LED screen on one wall showed a live picture of the section of the room where a podium was standing on display. Whittaker and Collins stood by the table looking over several documents, maps and photos while discussing their plan. "Brother Collins," Whittaker began, "the primary race has come to a crescendo, and we are only days away from the nationally televised speech that will lock in Senator Jordan as the Democratic Party's candidate for the presidency. Are we ready to execute our plan?"

Responding very respectfully to his superior, Collins said, "We are. We've been on the phone all morning double-checking our logistical preparations. This video conference we're about to conduct will be the final briefing to ensure that our commanders at each of the key cities fully understand their responsibilities."

"Yes, the timing of several interrelated events is crucial to the success of the mission; once it begins, everything will have to happen fast," Whittaker elaborated. "There will be no time to give additional instructions or directives. Everyone must know their jobs and how they affect the subsequent actions."

"That's correct, sir. Speed and coordination are the keys to success of this plan. By the time the government can react to one event, the next event must already be underway if we're to keep the federal authorities off balance until it is too late," said Collins.

As during the dinner conference months earlier, the electronic security technicians were actively monitoring for transmissions from eavesdropping devices that would alert authorities to the details of the plan. A technician was making the final connections over a secured network line and finishing a roll call to ensure that everyone was on the line. He then turned to Whittaker and Collins and said, "Gentlemen, the connection is secured, and all twenty sites are on line and ready to begin."

Whittaker began the conference, saying, "Gentlemen, in just days we will initiate a monumental offensive action that will change the course of history. Never have the conditions been so favorable and the key chess pieces in their optimal strategic positions on the board of play. You have prepared well; your training has been excellent, as was demonstrated in our operation to extricate Brother Collins from federal incarceration. Our victory on the field of battle that day was complete. The federal force was annihilated with not so much as a scratch to any of our soldiers. Now we make our final preparations. I will now turn over the floor to Brother Collins to lay out our final battle plans." Whittaker stepped out of the camera's view to allow Collins to take center stage.

Turning to his elder, Collins began by saying, "Thank you, Brother Whittaker. These plans could not have reached this stage of implementation without your support and leadership to us all." Turning to the camera, Collins continued, "Gentlemen, each of you is responsible for executing actions in your tactical theater of operations. In just a few days, Senator Jordan is scheduled to give a nationwide address that many believe will ensure his nomination to the Democrat's presidential ticket. This is something that we cannot and must not allow. The events that will follow his first words will overextend the federal government's ability to cope with internal conflict. Everything is in place to facilitate the planned attack on the Senator; then it will be your turn to execute your assignments."

Turning to a video clip of the Black Lives Matter protests following the killing of George Floyd, Collins said, "Here you see what the killing of one insignificant black man can do. Imagine if this event were to occur in every major city, with these people being manipulated into a violent frenzy. After the attack on the good Senator, the ignorant blacks in the inner city will pour into the streets in an unorganized manner; with a little help, we will ensure that they get organized and directed where we want them."

Pulling up a sample email on the screen, Collins explained, "Over the last year, our computer technicians have hacked into the computer networks of numerous prominent black ministers in each of your areas and are prepared to send this email from the ministers to the black congregations. As you can see, it instructs them to grab everyone they can and go to a specific location in their neighborhood for, and I quote, 'a peaceful candlelight vigil in remembrance of Senator Jordan.' Once the crowds start to gather, a few of your men will covertly set off store alarms and firebomb several of the local businesses with Molotov cocktails. This will bring in police riot response forces, who will assume that the gathering crowd committed these offenses. The police units will therefore create riot lines, and possibly deploy and use less-than-lethal-force weapons against the crowd. These actions will escalate the tensions between the police and the crowds. At that point, two or three of your men, posing as police snipers, will assume clearly observable positions on building rooftops where the news cameras can see them. Each one will select two or three targets among the rioting crowd and then blow their brains onto close bystanders."

A voice from the conference call asked, "Brother Collins, are we to target the leaders in the crowd, as is the normal practice to quell a violent mob?"

"No," Collins responded, "we want their leaders to remain safe so that they can incite the crowd further. If you can pick out the most agitated leaders in the crowd,

I would target a young child or woman in close proximity to them and take that target out with a head shot. This will inflame the situation beyond the control of local law enforcement, causing the President to call out the National Guard and implement the national Continuity of Operations Plan, or COOP as they call it." Collins added, "This is the completion of Phase I agitation."

Another voice from the conference call asked, "It's at this time we withdraw our men and prepare for Phase II, correct?"

Collins replied, "Exactly. We'll let the situation develop overnight and wait for the National Guard forces to be deployed. We believe that before the Jordan speech, the President will be in the White House to watch the national coverage from his residence. Within just a few hours of the attack on Jordan, the major riots around the country will be in full swing. Once the President calls for implementing the COOP, he will go to the south lawn of the White House to board his helicopter and move to a more secure facility. His protective detail will consider it a domestic threat scenario and will avoid moving him by motorcade because, from what they know, the streets in the District will pose the greatest threat." Referring to his Washington, DC commander, Collins asked, "Brother James, will you now present the actions of your team?"

James answers, "Thank you, sir. As Brother Collins described, we will anticipate the President's departure by use of his helicopter assets. We will have a forward observer located at Andrews Air Force Base waiting for Marine One to take off on route to the White House. We will also have five mobile three-man teams in pickup trucks; a driver, security man, and anti-aircraft gunner in the back of each pickup armed with SA-7 Grail missiles like we used to take out that news helicopter after the ambush. These teams will be in positions where they can engage the President's helicopter from multiple locations when it takes off from the White House lawn."

"Doesn't the President's air transport detail use three helicopters in a shell game approach when he moves from the White House?" asked a voice from the video conference participants.

"Yes," answered Brother James.

"Then how are you going to accurately determine your target?" another participant questioned.

"Our reach in the government is long, including the Executive Branch. We have a supporter on the President's staff who will be there in a position to know the load plan a few minutes in advance. He will text me in a coded format to designate which chopper to target," responded Brother James. "Thanks for that question. Are there any others, gentlemen?" asked Brother James, who paused for a moment to field any other inquiries. After a brief moment of silence, he turned to Collins and said," Looks like there are no other questions, sir. I'll turn it back over to you."

Once again assuming control of the conference, Collins said, "Thanks, Brother James. It sounds like your specialized detail is ready to go; I've already seen firsthand how effective our men can be with one of those Grails." Collins continued the briefing, saying, "At that point, the country will be sufficiently destabilized and preoccupied with the internal crisis for our Russian brothers to mobilize their forces, cross the borders and retake Georgia and Azerbaijan with massive force. Our Chinese brothers will cross the Taiwan Straits, attack Taiwan, and liberate it from the illegitimate capitalistic regime in power. The Russian and Chinese central governments will assume that their generals are taking the initiative on their behalf, so it is unlikely they will interfere, and the U.S. government will be powerless to act. Without the U.S., the United Nations will be incapable of responding as well."

"During Phase II of our agitation plan," added Collins, "the National Guard will assume control of riot response in all the major cities. However, they will be ill prepared and equipped to deal with the situation. This time, our special operatives will assume shooting positions to the rear of the crowd, where they will engage the National Guard troops with accurate small-arms fire, only this time your aim will be to take out the officers and senior noncommissioned officers. Without effective command and control, the National Guard troops, believing that the crowd fired on them, will likely return fire into the crowd, further inflaming the situation, and the troops will eventually abandon their positions. Soon the will and ability of the National Guard to counter the uprising will degrade to the point of being totally ineffective.

"Middle- and upper- class white citizens, sitting in their homes in the suburbs, will watch these scenarios play out on their big- screen televisions. We will instigate events to make them think that these events are beginning to spill over into their own neighborhoods, and they will see that a headless federal government is too paralyzed to act on both the international and national levels. They'll watch Russia and China forcefully take back that which is rightfully theirs and also see what they believe is their own country spiraling into chaos. They will lose confidence in their government's ability to keep them safe and to maintain the standard of living they're accustomed to. That is when we bring in our main body of Copperhead militia forces who know nothing of the agitation tactics we were using in the inner cities. Our Copperhead militia will ruthlessly put down the perceived rebellion with force, thereby bringing safety and security back into the citizens' lives. By restoring calm to this threatening situation, they will support our cause, and we will be able to step in to replace the individual state governments with our modern feudal system of government," Collins concluded.

To end the conference, Collins asked, "Are there any questions about your individual parts in implementing this plan?" With no other questions, Collins said, "Thank you, gentlemen. You may continue with your final preparations."

Turning to Collins, Whittaker said, "The plan is good, our people are dedicated, and our preparations are almost complete."

Collins' cell phone rang. He answered it, saying, "Yeah Jake, what can I do for you?" Pausing for a minute to listen, he responded, "Okay, well, he's sniffing around too much now, so take care of it. Okay, bye."

He turned to Whittaker and explained, "One of our guys in Little Rock says there was an FBI agent looking around down at the quarry today."

"Did he find anything?" Whittaker asked.

Collins answered, "The agent picked up some brass and dug up some spent bullets from the range before our other guys could get down to him."

"Does he pose a threat?" asked Whittaker.

"Not anymore. I told them to remove him from the equation," Collins replied.

"Let me know if this agent becomes a problem. We don't need any interference this late in the game," demanded Whittaker.

"Yes sir," responded Collins. "I'll keep you informed of any unusual developments."

Chapter X
The Evidence

When Thompson got back to the office from his visit to the quarry, he sat down at his desk and began to bag the bullet evidence he had collected and fill out the chain of custody forms. As he was finishing up his end of the required paperwork, one of the Bureau's evidence technicians came by his desk. "Thompson, the boss said you had some important evidence that we need to put a rush on."

Thompson looked up and said, "Yeah, I was just finishing up the chain of custody forms. Here you go." As he handed him the bagged and tagged evidence, Thompson continued, "This is the most important case we have right now. Important enough for Brenner to have you come here to get it, instead of me coming down to your hole in an office in the basement."

"Must be the Collins case, huh?" the technician asked. The evidence technician looked the bags over, read through the chain of custody forms, and then signed them. Tearing off one of the copies of each form, he handed them over to Thompson. In turn, Thompson opened a desk drawer full of files and put them in one of his hanging folders marked with a tab labeled KGC.

"We need to cross-reference these bullets with those that were collected at the ambush site and the farmhouse where the elderly couple was killed in Kentucky. Call me as soon as you have something," Thompson instructed.

"Sure thing. We're on it." The technician stuck all the evidence bags into a box and headed straight for the lab downstairs.

Getting on the phone, Thompson called Agent McCartney to give him an update and find out what the San Francisco Office had discovered. When the agent answered the phone, Thompson said, "McCartney, it's Thompson. I just got back from the quarry, where I recovered some Russian rifle brass and bullets. I instructed the lab to expedite processing so we can compare them to the bullets you guys recovered at the ambush site crime scenes."

"Great! The labs have been given instructions from the top that anything associated with the Collins case has top priority," replied Agent McCartney. "Did you see anyone out there?"

Thompson said, "Yeah, while I was there three of the Copperheads drove up and began to check me out."

"Did they know you were an agent?" inquired Agent McCartney.

Thompson replied, "No, I told them I was with the EPA checking out a report of contamination in the water out there at the quarry. But what do you have for me?"

McCartney reported, "I got word back from the San Francisco Office that the ATF ran the trap lines of their informants on the shipping docks and came up with a real potential. One of the informants was working late one night around Kensington Global's warehouse unloading cargo containers that just came in from China and cleared customs. A forklift operator screwed up and ran into the side of a cargo container, making a big gash in its side wall. Later on, this informant peeked into the container through the hole and saw wooden weapons crates with Russian markings."

"Can this guy distinguish Russian Cyrillic print from Greek?" asked Thompson doubtfully.

"Not only can he distinguish it, he can read it; he's a Russian immigrant from the Balkans. And get this: the print on the crates said they contained AK-47s," responded Agent McCartney.

Thompson asked, "Did he actually see any rifles?"

"He didn't see them open the crates that night, but he said when he went back the next day he saw a couple of Aryan gang types cleaning the packing grease out of a couple of AKs in the shipping office," replied Agent McCartney.

"How many cargo containers were there?" asked Thompson.

"He said there were about thirty or so, and twenty of them were being transported to several major cities in the U.S. He also said he didn't know where the rest of them were being sent, but the first one went to your neck of the woods," Agent McCartney said.

Thompson asked, "Here? When did this occur, and why didn't this guy report this activity to his ATF handlers when he first saw the weapons?"

"Seeing that they were Russian weapons he thought the Russian mob was involved and was somewhat intimidated. Remember, this guy was from Russia and saw firsthand what the Russian mob could do, so he was more afraid of them than he was of the ATF. This all happened about six months ago," replied Agent McCartney.

"Based upon the information from my CI, the timing would correspond to approximately the same as when the gang began to shoot down at the quarry here," Thompson surmised. Thompson knew that one shipping container would hold more than enough weapons to outfit the gang in Little Rock. "So where did all the other cargo containers go?" he asked McCartney.

"No clue; the guy didn't know any more," replied McCartney.

Hearing a beep on his phone, Thompson said, "Gotta go, I've got another call on the line. Let me know if you hear anything else." Pressing the blinking button on the phone, he answered, saying, "Agent Thompson here. How can I help you?"

It was Candy on the line, and she sounded pretty upset. "Thompson, good, I was worried that you wouldn't make it back to the office. Are you okay?"

Thompson replied, "I'm fine. How are you? I didn't want to leave you there with those guys, but I had no choice."

"I'm fine too," Candy replied. "They had a guy watching you through a sniper scope the entire time you were there, so they didn't buy your bullshit EPA story. They could've killed you right then and there."

"Well, they didn't, did they?" Thompson asked rhetorically. "What did your boyfriend do after I left?" asked Thompson.

"When we got in close enough to get cell coverage again, he immediately got on the phone and reported about your snooping around at the quarry," she replied.

Thompson asked, "Could you tell who he was talking to?"

"When the guy on the other end answered, he called him Collins," Candy answered.

In an excited voice Thompson said, "Collins! That's a real break! Did you hear anything to indicate where he was?"

"No, I didn't hear much more than that. Collins gave him some instructions, but I couldn't hear what he was saying," Candy replied.

"I sure hope your boyfriend used his own cell phone," Thompson mused.

"Yeah, he used his phone. Why?" responded Candy.

Thompson explained, "Give me his number and I'll get our guys to see if they can pull up the number Collins used. The can try to locate where his cell signal's coming from."

Thompson quickly took down the number, told Candy to be careful, and ended the phone conversation. Immediately he dialed Agent McCartney. "Thompson here. I've got a cell phone number that was in contact with Collins earlier today. I need you to pull some strings and get the tech guys to make maximum use of that Patriot Act so we can determine Collins' number and locate where the call originated from."

Agent McCartney replied, "Hell yeah, give me the number and timeframe and I'll put a boot in their ass to get something for us. By the way, your evidence guy in Little Rock emailed pictures of the rifling marks on the bullets you found to the central lab processing the ambush evidence. They did a quick comparison based on the pictures and the preliminary determination is that two of the twenty bullets you collected at the quarry matched bullets taken from the ambush crime scene. Now they still need to get the bullets into the lab to confirm their findings with a side-by-side comparison, but that does tie the Little Rock gang with the ambush operation."

"That's good to hear! We can work on that to identify the guys involved in the ambush, but something bigger is going on here. There were at least nineteen other cargo containers sent to other cities, and it's obvious that Collins is not here in Little Rock." Thompson considered for a moment. "So, what else is going on with this that we're just not picking up on?"

Agent McCartney said, "I'll have the San Francisco office conduct a search of the Kensington Global warehouse for weapons. I'll also get a nationwide alert out to our other field offices to give them a heads-up, so they can be looking into related events in their areas."

"That's a good idea. Call me back if anything else pops up," replied Thompson.

Thompson hung up the phone, swiveled around in his chair and turned to Danovich as he walked into the work area. "Well, the threads of this case are beginning to come together into a larger piece of string that I can just about grab hold of now. I know I'm getting close. Soon I'll be able to pull that string to unravel this mess and get to the bottom of it."

"Sounds like your day is coming to a productive close," remarked Danovich, "but you need to get home and get some sleep. You look like shit."

"Yeah, I'm just flat tired; I haven't slept well since I viewed the ambush scene," said Thompson.

In a confused tone, Danovich asked, "You've seen plenty of dead bodies before and they've never affected you this way. Why now?"

Looking off into space right in front of him, Thompson said in an unemotional voice, "It wasn't the blood and the dead bodies of the correction officers that bothers me. What bothers me is the level of violence and speed of action in the ambush. It caught all those officers off guard and totally unprepared; they had no chance at all. They were out-positioned, out-gunned and out of luck. To think that that morning the officers woke up, kissed their wives and kids goodbye just like any other day, but because they were assigned to guard a hate-filled criminal like Collins, someone else had already decided that they weren't coming home, except in a body bag. That's what bothers me!"

"It's the futility of it," Danovich lamented in agreement.

"Yeah, and that's why I have to bring those responsible to justice," responded Thompson.

"Well, you're not going to get it done if you're worn down to the point you can't think straight. You better get home, clean up and hit the rack for a while."

In a fatigued tone, Thompson said, "You're right. I'm headed for home now. See you later." He picked up some files, stuffed them into his soft-sided attaché case and walked towards the exit of the bullpen while Danovich watched.

As Thompson was about to go out the door, SAC Brenner passed Danovich on the way back to his office. "Where's Thompson going?" he asked.

"Home. He needs some rest. He's worn out," explained Danovich.

Brenner saw the door close behind Thompson, turned his gaze on Danovich, and said, "I should probably assign someone else to that case. Someone who will follow through!"

Danovich shook his head in disagreement. "I wouldn't do that just now, Chief. This case has changed Thompson somehow. He is definitely not the same; he has a purpose, and come hell or high water he is going to track these guys down."

"Well, I hope you're right, 'cause this thing could turn ugly fast." Brenner turned and continued to walk back to his office, where he entered the door and closed it behind him.

When Thompson got home, he fumbled with his keys as he unlocked the door to his drab, one- room efficiency apartment, entered the kitchen area, turned as he closed the door and made sure it was locked. He turned back around from the door, scanned the interior and his old furnishings. They were old and didn't match, even as to decade, but they were his ...about the only things he could call his own these days. He set his attaché case and coat on an old table that looked like it was used on the set of Leave It to Beaver. Making a bee-line directly to the kitchen cabinet over the stove, he opened the door, grabbed his half- full bottle of Jack, and set it down on the countertop. Thompson reached down into the sink, picked up a dirty glass, wiped it out and poured himself a large drink from the bottle. He screwed the bottle cap back on, walked to the TV, picked up the remote, turned it on and sat down in his old recliner. As he flipped through the channels, he drank down his Jack in three large gulps. He finally stopped channel surfing on the all- night news channel and fell asleep before he got to the first commercial.

At five minutes after midnight Thompson's cell phone rang, waking him from a restless, Jack- induced sleep. He quickly glanced at the clock on the wall above the sink. Noting the time he answered the call, "Thompson here. This better be good."

It was Candy. "Thompson, I've got some important information for you that can't wait. Meet me at the playground near the school at 1:30 a.m. and bring my money with you." Before Thompson could ask any questions, Candy hung up the phone without even say- ing goodbye. Thompson asked out loud to himself, "Bring her money?"

Thompson immediately called her back, but she didn't answer her cell phone. Instead, he got her voice mail: "Hello, it's Candy. I must be partying right now so can't answer your call. You know the drill just wait for the beep."

Thompson hung up and looked at the clock again. It was now 12:20 a.m. With a thirty- minute drive to the playground, he didn't have much time to prepare for the meeting. Grabbing a few things, he went out the door, jumped in his car, and headed out. On the way to the playground, he wondered what Candy had for him, why she was so matter of fact, and what was this about bringing her money?

Thompson got there early and was already on the playground when Candy's car rolled up to the parking lot. It was very quiet, except for a dog barking off the distance. As he started walking over to where her car was parked, Candy opened the door and stepped out of the passenger side of her car. Catching Thompson off guard, Candy's boyfriend Jake stepped out of the driver's door, and another Copperhead stepped out of the rear passenger door, each carrying an AK-47. As Candy ran over to Thompson, he could see a long cut on her right cheek that hadn't quite stopped bleeding yet.

Crying as she approached, she told him, "I'm sorry, Thompson, but they overheard my last call to you about the quarry and they made me call you here. I tried to warn you when I said to bring my money."

Thompson responded," It's okay, it's okay."

Both men approached with their rifles pointed at Thompson from their hips, while he held his hands up at his sides in a sign of submission. Jake said with a big smile as he raised his rifle to his shoulder and took aim, "Well, well, well, Mr. Government Man; you've been pokin' around where you shouldn't have been this time. Looks like you're off the case now."

As soon as the butt of his rifle found its place on his shoulder, a single shot rang out across the playground, and multiple muzzle flashes erupted from the barrel of Jake's AK-47. Jake's body fell limp to the ground with a single shot from an FBI sniper's bullet to the head, and an FBI tactical team emerged from the shadows, yelling instructions to the other gang member. Danovich was leading the team and shouted, "Drop the weapon, drop the weapon! Get down, get down or I'll put a bullet in your head too!"

The Copperhead dropped his rifle and put his hands in the air. Candy reached out for Thompson and clasped her arms around his neck as the weight of her body began to hang heavier and heavier on his shoulders.

Looking down at her face, Thompson could see that she was turning pale, and her hands were cool to the touch on the back of his neck. Thompson could feel that his right hand, which was positioned on Candy's back to hold her up, was wet, and he could feel drops dripping from his fingertips onto the ground behind her. As he eased her to the ground, he could see that she had been struck in the back by one of the bullets fired from Jake's AK-47. It had passed through her body and exited below her sternum. "Someone call an ambulance!" he yelled. "Candy, stay with me! We'll have help here in just a minute, hold on!"

"I tried to warn you," she said weakly.

"You did," he replied. "How do you think I knew to have the tactical team provide cover for us?"

Sitting down, he cradled her head on his lap; he always wanted to hold her, but not like this. Looking into his eyes, she said in a soft, calm, unsteady voice, "Thompson .... it's okay ... it's okay. You need to warn them." Stopping in an attempt to catch an elusive breath she continued, "I heard them say something about one Marine and Jordan." With her right hand still behind his neck, she pulled their heads together and gently kissed his lips. Then she lay her head down, smiled, and closed her eyes for the last time.

Chapter XI
The Attempt

Back in Detroit, Rostrum #71 had arrived at the Jordan campaign headquarters a couple of months ago and had been used for several local speeches already. When not in use, it was securely stored in the campaign headquarters storage building along with portable stages, chairs, signs, banners, and other campaign-related equipment.

Not coincidentally, at the same time as Thompson was scheduled to meet Candy at the playground in Little Rock, the KGC initiated its plan to remove Senator Jordan from the race for President of the United States. Collins had felt that Thompson was getting close to stumbling on something that could interfere with the KGC's intricate schedule of events that had taken many years to develop to this critical stage. Collins had instructed Jake to remove Thompson from the equation at a time that would cause the FBI's team of investigators to focus on the murder of one of their own in Little

Rock and distract their attention away from Detroit and Senator Jordan.

Simultaneous to the meet between Thompson and Candy, a team of KGC operatives was positioned outside Jordan campaign headquarters, preparing to breach the security envelope and execute their actions to switch the panels on Rostrum #71. Dressed in dark-colored street clothes, they quietly exited a black van parked in the alley near the Jordan headquarters. Two of the men moved to either end of the alley and positioned themselves so they could observe the approach of anyone that could threaten the secrecy of their mission. Three other men opened the rear doors of the van and began to unload their heavy cargo onto a handcart. When the last item was loaded on the cart, the third operative quickly proceeded to a panel of electrical junction boxes bolted on the wall and scanned them with a small flashlight with red LED bulbs to protect his night vision. Once he found the one he was looking for, he cut the padlock off and slipped a thin, L-shaped tool into the gap on the edge of the box's cover. Carefully he fished around for the small pressure switch that would close the electrical circuit if the cover were opened, causing the alarm to activate. Because he had performed this operation many times, he found the switch with ease and held it down with the tool as he opened the cover. Without having to look, he reached down to where he had already torn several pieces of duct tape and lightly attached them to his leather jacket, removed a single piece and secured the switch in the down position with it. On the terminal block of the alarm panel, the operative clamped a wire with an alligator clip on each end to two contact points. This action bypassed the electrical circuit, thereby disabling the entire alarm system. He checked with his lookouts to ensure that the coast was clear and then moved to the rear door of the Jordan campaign headquarters' storage building.

With the building's alarm system disabled, the operative used an electric lock-pick tool to unlock the door, and the team entered the facility quickly, quietly, and undetected. They swiftly moved down the corridor, pulling their handcart to the room where Rostrum #71 was being stored and beginning their work to remove and replace the ballistic panels.

Switching out the armor panels in Rostrum #71 took only a few minutes, because the replacement panels had been carefully prefabricated at Smithson's factory and the operatives had practiced the operation until they could do it with their eyes closed. Once all of the panel wells were closed up again, the operatives peeled off the old Secret Service seals along the edge of the seams of Rostrum #71. They then replaced the seals with the ones they had received from Agent Foster so that no one would be able to tell that the panels had been tampered with. Eager to report back to their leaders that the mission had gone flawlessly, they exited the building, removed the alarm bypass, and replaced the lock on the junction box. They loaded their hand cart and the old panels in the van and drove off ...unnoticed and, as far as they knew, completely undetected. However, in their haste to complete the mission and exit before a rent-a-cop security guard was scheduled to return on a routine patrol, one of the operatives failed to secure the corner of one seal completely to the surface of Rostrum #71.

After Candy died in his arms, Thompson stayed with her body until the coroner was prepared to take her away. It was predawn when the attendants placed her in the body bag and loaded her unceremoniously in the back of the coroner's van. As they cranked the van's engine, Thompson stood in the middle of the parking lot and watched as the coroner's vehicle pulled away and disappeared down the street into the first rays of dawn. SAC Brenner walked up to Thompson and said, "I'm sorry, Stan, but we need to debrief you. Why don't you run home, get a shower and meet me at the office in a couple of hours. We'll try to make sense of all this mess." Thompson said nothing; he just nodded, got in his car, and drove off.

At 8:00 a.m. Thompson, Brenner and other agents sat in the field office to go over the current status of the case. Brenner walked into the meeting from his office with a stack of files and began the meeting. "Okay, let's get started. A lot has transpired in the last several hours. Ballistic evidence has already connected the assault rifles used at the playground with the weapons used in the ambush of the prison convoy. We have a single suspect from the playground, but he's already lawyered up and isn't talking. Agent Thompson, I believe you have some new information."

Thompson stood up and walked to the front of the room to address the group and bring them up to speed on the recent developments in the last few hours. "Agent McCartney called me about an hour ago and told me that the San Francisco office raided Kensington Global's warehouse last night. They found a couple of cargo containers of new Russian weapons, including AK-47s, Dragunov sniper rifles, RPGs and RPK machine guns. They also found an empty crate for SA-7 Grail shoulder-fired heat seeking anti-aircraft missiles. We know that one was already used to down the news helicopter after the prison break, but there could be others out there somewhere. In addition, there were several documents found in the warehouse to indicate that there are armed Aryan gang militias preparing to do something ... what, we don't know ... around the country, so they're putting out a national intelligence alert to all FBI field offices and other law enforcement agencies. Based on the information I got this morning from Candy ... excuse me, my CI ... we think that they plan to take out Senator Jamal Jordan."

SAC Brenner interjected, "Senator Jordan's campaign has been picking up a lot of steam. Jordan took the lead in the last primary and is starting to widen the margin in the polls. If things continue to progress as the national media outlets project, his opponent, Senator Crawford, will have to bow out of the race for sake of solidarity within the Democratic Party. Tonight, Senator Jordan will be making a special televised speech in Detroit, so Stan, I want you to go up there this afternoon to coordinate with his Secret Service protection detail."

"Yes, sir," replied Thompson. "There's one other thing we haven't quite figured out. My CI said something about one Marine. I think she could have meant Marine One, the President's helicopter, It could somehow be involved in whatever they're planning."

Alarmed at the implication, SAC Brenner responded quickly, "Well, before we go get the White House's panties in a wad based on a sketchy comment from a questionable CI way off in Little Rock, Arkansas, we need to have something tangible from another source to link to this potential concern. You better grab some things and head to the airport soon to catch your plane to Detroit."

"Yes, sir, I'll get out of here, pack a bag and get to the airport. I'll call you after I've hooked up with Senator Jordan's protection detail and see what future travel plans they have for him," replied Thompson. He grabbed his notebook computer case, some papers, and left the building.

Later that morning in Detroit, all the preparations for the speech were well underway by 9:00 a.m.; everyone was scrambling around transferring equipment to the large auditorium in the center of town. A forklift was brought into the storage building to load Rostrum #71 onto the back of a truck, where it would be secured for the short trip. Outside the closed loading doors, two Detroit police officers watched as the doors rolled up to reveal Rostrum #71 sitting on the forks of the lift. One of the workers opened the back of the truck, and the officers watched as the driver of the forklift carefully eased the load into the cargo compartment and then backed out, leaving Rostrum #71 sitting in the middle. Workers used straps to secure the podium in place and the roll-up door of the truck's cargo compartment was pulled down, locked, and then sealed.

The police officers jumped into their sedan, and the truck pulled away from the loading dock and pulled out onto the main street with the police following close behind. Upon arriving at the venue for the speech, the truck was unloaded and Rostrum #71 was moved to the stage, front and center. As a campaign worker was wiping it down to remove the dust that had settled on it while in storage, he noticed that the corner of one of the tamper-indicating seals on Rostrum #71 was not completely stuck to the surface. He had cleaned Rostrum #71 each of the times it was used before and had never noticed it in this condition. The campaign worker reached into his pocket and pulled out a spreadsheet printout that contained the serial numbers of the seals assigned to safeguard each of the Rostrums. He scanned down the page and then read the number on the suspected seal and confirmed that it was listed on the authorized list. Still, he felt he should bring it to the attention of one of the agents on the Secret Service detail. From his position kneeling on the floor, he noticed the legs of a man in a suit pass close by him. "Hey, come look at this seal. It doesn't look quite right. I checked the serial number against the database printout, and it's correct, but see right there? The corner isn't completely stuck down; I've never seen it that way before."

Kneeling down to take a look at what the worker was talking about, Agent Matthew Foster studied the corner of the seal closely, then pressed the corner down with his finger and said, "No problem. We did a recent inspection of the panels, and we must have missed that corner. See, now it's good as new." Agent Foster stood back up and walked away.

Accepting Foster's explanation, the worker continued with his activities to prepare the stage for the evening's events. After connecting the power, the worker performed a sound check with the internal infrared communications link. Everything was just about ready for the speech; banners were hung in strategic spots to ensure that wherever the TV cameras were pointed, there would be a campaign banner directly in view.

Network camera crews were double-checking cable connections and panning the room with their cameras to check camera angles and lighting, and to send test signals to the production trailers located behind the building.

Agent Foster stepped into a private office, closed the door, and sat in front of a desk. Once he was seated and sure he was alone, he pulled out his cell phone, punched in a number and hit the call button. After a couple of rings, a voice answered the phone. "Agent Foster, has the Rostrum arrived?"

"Yes, it arrived earlier today. It is in position and ready," Agent Foster replied.

"Did you receive the pictures of the suspect?"

"Yes, I did," answered Agent Foster.

"Are there any changes to the security plan?"

"No changes. Things are going to be in place as planned. All attendees coming in the front doors, including staff, will be scanned just like TSA does at the airports," Agent Foster explained. "Your guy will have to come in the back doors, where most of the staff will enter unchecked. The doors are automated with a badge reader. The badge he has will not work because it's not encoded, but he can tailgate in behind someone who is able to open the door. All they will do is make sure he has a staff badge and check his picture to see if his face matches. Then they'll let him in. They do it all the time."

The voice acknowledged the process. "He's already been instructed to enter this way. Once inside, he'll wait until the last minutes before the speech to approach the stage. He'll come down the center aisle and stop just short of the barrier in front. He will make his move as soon as Senator Jordan begins his speech. He believes you will help by clearing his exit. Are you sure you'll be able to recognize him?"

Agent Foster replied in a matter-of-fact tone, "There's no doubt in my mind. I've looked at his picture so much, I've been seeing him in my sleep."

"Good, then everything is set to make you a national hero and enable you to reclaim your family name," remarked the voice.

With a grin and visions of press conferences, Agent Foster replied, "Things are moving along here. We're not far from show time."

"Well, I will say my congratulations early. You're doing a great service for your country," added the voice.

"Thank you for the opportunity to do so," responded Agent Foster.

"I'll you soon after it's over; talk to you then. Bye."

Agent Foster ended the call, placed his phone inside his coat and exited the office to check on the progress of final preparations. People had already begun to process through the security gauntlet at the front doors and began to take their seats in the auditorium. By 6:30 p.m., the crowd had packed the auditorium. Everyone felt the excitement of the event and knew this would be a moment that would be recorded in the history books. Scheduled to begin at 7:00 p.m., the speech would be televised on all major news channels and would last twenty minutes. Immediately after Jordan's speech, there would be ten minutes of reporter commentary and then Senator Crawford would provide a similar speech from her hometown. Things were abuzz backstage as the last few minutes ticked by.

Senator Jordan was going over his notes one last time, and his wife had begun to pace as she became more apprehensive about the whole evening. She saw Agent Foster, walked over to him, and said, "I don't feel good about this, Agent Foster. Something just doesn't feel right about his speech!"

Empathetically, Agent Foster consoled her, "Mrs. Jordan, please don't worry. The other agents of the protection detail and I will take good care of him. I'll be in front just to his right, and I won't let anything happen to him." Mrs. Jordan appeared to be comforted by Agent Foster's comment because she knew in her heart that he would do everything he could to keep her husband out of harm's way.

In the background a telephone could be heard ringing, and the stage manager went over and answered it. After listening for a moment, the stage manager could be heard saying, "Yes, I see one of the Secret Service agents right now. Wait just a minute; I'll put you on hold." As he placed the phone handset on the cradle, the stage manager looked over at Agent Foster and waved him over. "Hey Agent Foster, I have an FBI agent on hold for you on line three."

Agent Foster acknowledged the call and proceeded to the phone. Picking up the handset and pushing the line three button, he said, "Agent Foster. How can I be of assistance?"

On the other end of the line a voice answered, "Yes, Agent Foster, this is Agent Stan Thompson with the Little Rock office of the FBI. I just landed at the Detroit airport, and I'm headed to your location."

"Well, we're kind of busy here right now getting ready for the big speech. Is there something I can do for you?" asked Foster.

Thompson responded, "I've just recently come across some information that indicates there's a plot to kill Senator Jordan."

Concerned that this might disrupt current plans to allow him to stop an unsuccessful assassination attempt, Agent Foster replied, "Yes, we've heard something along these lines already, and I can tell you that everything is in place here to ensure nothing happens tonight. When you get here, we can discuss this threat in more detail."

Thompson was caught a little off guard that Agent Foster had already heard something about the potential threat. "Okay, I'm glad you guys are prepared for the worst. I'll be there in a few minutes."

Anxiously, Agent Foster replied, "Alright, we'll see you when you get here. Gotta go."

For his part, Thompson was somewhat relieved that he had contacted someone in Senator Jordan's protection detail. Thompson hung up and headed for his waiting rental car. After his conversation with Thompson, Agent Foster looked around to make sure no one was close enough to hear and punched in a speed dial number on his cell phone. On the second ring, the voice he had been talking to earlier in the day answered by asking, "Agent Foster, aren't you getting ready for the speech?"

"Yes, things are a go here, but I just got off the phone with an FBI agent from Little Rock by the name of Thompson who knows there is a threat to Senator

Jordan. He's on his way here. I'm afraid he'll mess things up here."

"When did he call, and where was he calling from?" asked the voice impatiently.

"I just hung up with him a minute ago, and he said he was calling from the airport," Agent Foster explained.

In a less impatient tone, the voice continued, "Don't worry. By the time he can get there, things will be finished, and you'll be the hero. Keep with the plan, Agent Foster!"

Relieved, Agent Foster responded, "You're right, I shouldn't have bothered you. I'll call you after it's all over here."

In a pleasant tone, the voice added, "I look forward to your call. Break a leg."

Agent Foster ended the call, put his cell phone away and headed over to join the other agents of the protection detail.

As Thompson drove in his rental car on his way to the auditorium, his cell phone rang. Pulling it out, he answered, "Agent Thompson."

Brenner was on the other end of the call. "Thompson, Brenner. Have you gotten to Jordan yet?"

Thompson replied, "Not yet, but I talked with his protection detail. They said they had already heard about the threat."

"No one here has talked to them. How did they know about it? Who did you talk to?" Brenner asked.

"I talked with an Agent Foster. He indicated that they were ready for anything," explained Thompson.

"Well, maybe they heard about another threat. It could be that there's something else going on out there that we're not aware of. You would have thought information-sharing would have gotten better since 9/11. Anyway, give me a call once you establish face-to-face contact with them and brief them on what Candy told us," advised Brenner.

"Will do. Talk to you later," Thompson said before he ended the call and continued to drive towards the auditorium.

Ten minutes before the speech, everyone on the Secret Service protection detail had taken their assigned positions near the stage. As he stood alone in the isolation aisle in front of the stage, Agent Foster scanned the audience, looking for the person he was seeing at night in his sleep ...the shooter. He began to get a little nervous; was he the only one who knew what was going to happen and who the shooter was? But he finally spotted the shooter in the back of the auditorium. "He looks just like the picture," Foster thought. "It must have been a very recent picture. How did they do that without him knowing?" As the shooter made his way to the front, Foster thought, "If he only knew what was about to happen to him ... he's royally screwed; they're double crossing him in real style. He thinks he's going to make history, but in reality, I'm going to make *him* history!"

Reaching the last point before crossing the barrier tape marking the front edge of the isolation isle, the shooter stopped and crossed his arms. Looking at the shooter's fake identification badge, Foster said to himself, "That is a real good forgery! Even I would let him in if he presented it to me for access. No wonder he was able to get in with no problem."

At 7:00 p.m. on the dot, Jordan had reached the podium and, after the applause subsided, began his speech. Agent Foster and everyone else quickly recognized that Senator Jordan's first words out of his mouth were not coming out over the loudspeakers. Simultaneous, the shooter nervously and urgently reached inside his jacket, removed a small silver object, and began his arm movement in the direction of Senator Jordan. Reaching for his Sig 229 semi-automatic pistol holstered on his waist band near his right kidney, Foster felt like everything was moving in slow motion. Everything was so clear and sharp; he could make out every detail of the shooter. Foster had already identified the point of aim on the shooter's body that would assure an incapacitating and fatal shot. In this moment of clarity, as he drew his pistol from his holster, he identified the object in the shooter's hand. It wasn't a gun at all! It was a ...television remote control! The shooter fully extended his arm and pointed at the front of Rostrum #71.

Foster watched as the shooter's thumb began to press one of the remote's buttons. In a blinding and numbing flash of bright, white-hot light, Rostrum #71 exploded with such force that anything or anyone within fifty feet was almost vaporized by the massive positive blast wave that expanded outward, pushing with it secondary fragmentation of every conceivable kind. Within a matter of split seconds, the negative blast wave then collapsed inwardly on its point of origin to fill the void created by the rapid cooling of the hot expanding gases generated by the explosion.

No one in the entire auditorium was left standing. Hundreds of torn and bleeding bodies lay about the blood covered concrete floor. Even people who were lucky enough to have not made it inside before the speech lay bleeding in the parking lots and sidewalks outside, victims of flying glass from the auditorium windows. Jordan was positioned at the focal point to the rear of this massive charge at the time of detonation; there wasn't much of him left to find, at least nothing recognizable. Because they were so close, Agent Foster and the shooter were the first to be hit by the fragmentation and blast wave, and they too were gone. A cloud of the choking, dense black smoke that military explosives produced hung in the air like the fog over Lake St.

Clair to the northeast of the city. An eerie calm fell on the scene for a brief moment before the initial shock of the event began to subside. As if on cue, the screams and groans of the dying and injured began to rise in a crescendo of terror. The devastation of the site was complete and total.

Driving up in his rental car, Thompson was in a direct line of observation of the auditorium only a block away when the blast occurred. Slamming on his brakes, he had come to a skidding stop as the debris began to fall in front of the auditorium. Exiting his vehicle, he moved along the street to the front door of the auditorium itself. Looking into a glassless front window, he scanned the interior of the auditorium and briefly surveyed the devastation, looking for anyone who could tell him what had happened. No one alive there really knew what happened or was capable of telling someone else what had occurred.

Remembering that the national news channels were supposed to cover the speech, Thompson ran around the side of the smoldering and shattered building to the adjacent parking lot, where he found one of the TV production trailers. He ran up the stairs and entered the production trailer. Though not physically affected by the blast itself, the production crews were in a dazed state of disbelief, trying to comprehend what they had just witnessed through their monitors and heard and felt with their own bodies. Thompson found the production manager, pulled him to the control board of the trailers, and said, "Agent Thompson, FBI. I have to see what happened just before the blast. Reset the digital recording to ten minutes before the blast."

Still a little shaken, the production manager said, "Yeah...yeah..I can do that...let's see...what angle do you want to see first?"

"Let's take the widest angle we can and then narrow down if something catches our eye. Do you know who everyone is on the screen?" Thompson asked.

"No," replied the production manager as he turned his attention to a nicely dressed woman standing against the wall who could not grasp what had just happened. "But Lesley over there is one of Jordan's public affairs staff. She'll be able to point everyone out for you. Lesley, are you alright, dear?"

Still visibly shaken, Lesley walked over to the control board and yelled, "No! What the hell just happened here?"

Thompson touched her shoulder and responded, "With your help, that's what I hope to find out. I'm Agent Thompson with the FBI. We're going to replay the coverage; I need you to tell me who's who. Can you do that for me?" he asked in a reassuring tone.

"If it will help you get the bastards that did this, tell me what you need," she said.

Thompson said, "Okay let's start rolling."

"I'll put the widest shot here on the center monitor and synchronize all the other camera angles," explained the production manager.

Looking at the video, Thompson could see three of the protection detail agents taking their positions on the stage and in front of the podium. He asked the Jordan staff member to tell him the names of the three Secret Service agents and point them out. "Can you tell me the names of these Secret Service agents?"

They paused the screen, and the young PR woman pointed to each of the agents. "That's Miller to the left and Burns to the right on the stage, and that's Foster down in front."

"Foster..," Thompson said out loud. "He's the guy I talked to from the airport."

As they advanced the recording, Thompson spotted a guy walking up the center aisle to a position in front of the barrier tape and stop. "Back that up a few seconds," he asked.

The production manager backed it up and began to play that section again. "Okay, there you go. Do you see something?" he asked.

Thompson told the others, "Maybe. See how Agent Foster is focused on this guy as he walks up front, turning his head as he moves; it's as if no one else existed. What is it about this guy that Foster doesn't like?"

Turning to the PR woman, he asked, "Do you know who this guy is?"

She replied, "Oh yes, that's Jeremy. He's a new campaign worker. I don't think Agent Foster had ever met him before."

"Why is he walking up to the front and standing there in the center aisle, anyway?" asked Thompson.

"We were having problems with the public address system in the Rostrum before the speech, so as a safety precaution, George Harper, the sound engineer, gave Jeremy the remote control for the system and instructed him to go stand there in case the system failed to work when Senator Jordan spoke. If the systems didn't work right off the bat, he was supposed to use the remote to reset it," the young lady replied.

As they continued the recording, they watched as Senator Jordan began to talk, and the public address system wasn't working. They saw Jeremy reach into his pocket and pull out the remote. Thompson said, "Stop! Play that back, right there. See how Agent Foster appears to be going for his gun? He thinks Jeremy is a threat. Zoom in on Agent Foster's face."

As the picture closed in on Foster, Thompson asked, "See how, as he is reaching for his gun, the expression on his face goes from conviction to confusion?"

"Yes," the production manager said. "He goes from knowing exactly what to do to not understanding what to do next …like he's been fooled about something."

"Exactly. It looks to me as if both Agent Foster and Jeremy were used. Keep it in slow motion," Thompson instructed.

As they continued to play the recording, they saw that as soon as Jeremy pointed the remote control at the Rostrum, the explosion occurred. The production manager was able to rewind the recording and pause it to catch the initial red glow of the blast expanding from the front of the Rostrum.

"My God," cried Thompson, "the Rostrum was the bomb! There can be no mistake; the center of the blast came from the podium itself. I want to know the last person who even touched that Rostrum."

"Well, I think that would be the guy that cleaned it when it was set up, and I just saw him outside," said the young woman.

"Get him in here right now!" demanded Thompson.

Pulling the worker inside, Thompson asked him, "When you cleaned that podium, did you notice anything odd?"

"Sure did," the worker replied. "I noticed that one of the corners of a seal on the panels wasn't stuck down all the way. I brought it to the attention of one of the Secret Service agents, and he told me that they had just inspected the interior panels and that it was okay."

"Which one of the Secret Service agents did you point the seal out to?" asked Thompson.

Looking at the video from before the blast occurred, the worker pointed to Agent Foster and said, "It was that one right there. He said it wasn't something to be concerned about, so I believed him."

"So, Agent Foster was the one that told you the seal was okay, the one that I warned before the speech and did nothing, and the only agent that reacted to Jeremy when he came up front. It would appear that Agent Foster was a willing insider who was, in the end, double-crossed himself," surmised Thompson.

Answering his ringing cell phone, Thompson said, "Thompson here."

"Thompson, it's McCartney. Are you okay?" asked Agent McCartney.

"Yeah, I'm okay, but it's really a mess up here. They took out Senator Jordan and about a hundred and fifty of his supporters, including other prominent political leaders," Thompson replied in a fatigued voice.

Wanting some additional information about the situation, Agent McCartney asked Thompson, "What type of explosive device does it look like it was and where was it placed?"

"You're not gonna to believe this shit, but somehow, they got to the Rostrum before the speech and replaced the ballistic panels with high explosives and ball bearings, creating a huge Claymore mine. It devastated this place like nothing I have ever seen before. My guess is that one of the Secret Service agents provided the access, but obviously didn't know what they were replacing the panels with since he was at ground zero when it went off," explained Thompson.

"This is what Candy was trying to tell you about Jordan before she died. Now if we only knew how Marine One was involved," said Agent McCartney.

"Yeah, that still bothers me; we aren't thinking of something," sighed Thompson.

In an excited voice, Agent McCartney said, "Hey, Thompson, I was just handed a message that they've zeroed in on Collins' cell phone signal. Get this, he's in Cincinnati at the residence and horse stable complex of one Franklin Whittaker."

"Interesting! That completes the circle. Smithson Integrated Engineering made the Rostrum; the Rostrum was made into a Claymore mine; Kensington Global Corporation smuggled in the weapons and explosives for Collins' escape and Jordan's assassination; we find out Whittaker is the Chairman of the Board for Kensington and on the Board of Directors for Smithson; and now, when we finally triangulate Collins' cell phone signal, it's pinpointed on Whittaker's property," explained Thompson.

"Let's go get him then," said Thompson. "While I turn over this information to the investigating agents here, you get arrest warrants issued for Collins and Whittaker. I'll contact the Cincinnati field office to call out their tactical team, activate the closest Marine

Corps reserve company, and begin planning for an assault on Whittaker's compound. I'll have SAC Brenner contact the Attorney General to request that the President enact the Insurrection Act so that we can use the Marines in direct action in support of the assault. If we encounter what I think we might, we're going to need their skills and capabilities. I would have the FBI Hostage Rescue Team join us, but somehow, I think they'll be needed in DC for the next few days. Rendezvous with me at the Cincinnati airport at 4:30 a.m.; they'll have a hanger for use as a planning and staging area."

"I'm on it. See you in Cincinnati," replied Agent McCartney.

Chapter XII
The Fall

Once Thompson had passed on the information he had gathered at the scene to the on-site investigating agents, he headed to the Detroit airport to hop a plane to Cincinnati. As he drove his rental car, he listened to a local radio station's report of public gatherings across the country in all major U.S. cities. In Detroit, the initially peaceful gatherings were quickly turning into riots, and with every mile he drove the level of violence continued to escalate. Thompson pulled out his phone and called in to the office. It rang until Thompson heard the answer, "Brenner here."

"Hey, chief, it's Thompson."

Brenner asked, "Thompson, what's your status?"

"I've turned everything over to the local field office, and they're working the scene. I'm on my way to the airport to catch a flight to Cincinnati," he reported.

"Have you been keeping up with developments across the country? The major cities are a powder keg ready to go off. People are rioting in the streets," said Brenner in an uncharacteristically nervous voice.

Hearing the concern in his tone, Thompson replied, "Yeah, I've been hearing it on the car radio. What started out as peaceful demonstrations have been growing into all-out riots and sounds like it's getting worse. Downtown Detroit is ablaze in several areas."

"Thompson, it's that way in about two dozen major cities," Brenner replied.

As he pulled into the airport rental car return lane, Thompson brought the car to a stop and continued his discussion. "This looks bad, boss," he said as he got out of the car and started to look around at the signs giving him directions to the terminal. He shut the car door and handed the keys to the rental car attendant. "I'm at the airport, so I'd better get to the ticket counter."

Brenner closed by saying, "Okay, check in every now and then to let me know your progress."

"Will do," said Thompson as he ended the call. He spotted the door he needed and headed there, leaving the rental car attendant holding out his receipt.

"Sir, your receipt!" hollered the attendant, but Thompson didn't hear him and rushed inside.

Inside the airport terminal, Thompson ran up to the ticket counter ahead of other scared and frustrated people in line and got the attention of the ticket agent. "I'm Agent Thompson, FBI. I've got to get to Cincinnati. What do you have available?"

"I'm sorry, sir, but due to the riots the airport has just been closed. All inbound flights have been diverted to other cities, although from the sound of it on the news, similar situations and conditions are developing in the other cities as well. If you want to get to Cincinnati anytime soon, you'll probably want to drive; it will take you about four and a half hours down I-75," the ticket agent explained while holding the phone in one hand with the other covering the microphone.

Thompson headed back out the door toward the rental car return area. As he rushed up to the booth, the rental car attendant was standing there, still holding his keys and receipt. "I need that car back," Thompson quickly instructed.

"I kinda figured you would, based on the looks of things," the attendant replied as he turned back to a television monitor, where live news coverage of the riots was being shown. Thompson paused long enough to catch up on recent developments by watching as the news anchor sent the coverage out to a field reporter in downtown Detroit.

The young woman on the screen began her report. "This is Marla Cohen reporting from Third Street and Seldon Avenue. What initially began as a peaceful protest against the assassination of Senator Jordan first became an unruly crowd and has now become a potentially violent mob. Just blocks from here, storefronts and businesses are ablaze, and the fire department cannot respond due to the danger posed by these crowds. As you can see behind me now, the police have established a riot control line to stop the advance of this unrest, and it appears to be successfully holding the growing stream of demonstrators at bay. They seem to be achieving results and calming the situation. One thing we have just seen is the deployment of police riflemen on a couple of the rooftops overlooking the crowd. As you can see, these police riflemen are only positioned in case things were to really get out of hand ...oh my God! Did that officer just shoot into the crowd below?... There's another shot. Turn the camera over there ... I just heard more shots ... Look there ... in the front of the crowd ... There are women and young teenagers on the ground bleeding. People are screaming. The officers on the riot lines seem to be as much in shock as the people in the crowd. Jim, it's getting very dangerous here and we need to move to another location, so I'll send it back to you until we can get to a safer place."

Quickly the coverage returned to the studio anchor, "Thanks Marla, be safe out there. Don't take any risks." Turning his attention to the audience, he continued, "Well, as you can see, things are beginning to deteriorate downtown, so it is advised that you stay home."

Thompson grabbed his things and the keys to the rental, rushed over to the car and got back in. He opened up the map in the car to determine the most direct route to Cincinnati. Tonight was no night to be on any inner-city side street. His fingers followed a route on the map that took him through Toledo and Dayton, Ohio south on Interstate 75 to Cincinnati. Thompson set the map down, started the car, entered his destination into the GPS, and drove out of the airport onto I-275 on his way to I-75 south. In contrast to the dark night sky, Thompson could see that parts of the city were in flames. He passed several cars that were overturned and on fire. As he drove, he scanned the satellite car radio for news channels so that he could keep up with developments across the country. The way it looked, things were going to get ugly real fast.

Only thirty minutes into his drive, Thompson caught one news radio person already talking about the problems in New Orleans. "Just minutes ago, a very large mob near the Superdome overran the police lines and has beaten several police officers to death. Police units all over the city have had to withdraw with their injured to their parish and district headquarters just for self-preservation. Folks, I hate to say it, but by the time it is all over with, the wrath Hurricane Katrina unleashed in 2005 may look like nothing compared to what the people of this town are doing to New Orleans," reported the news man in a somber voice.

As he turned to different channels, he heard of similar happenings in Memphis, Houston, and St. Louis. Cities in the Eastern Time Zone were probably luckier than those in the Pacific Time Zone; at least the approach of early morning hours might take some of the momentum out of the violence in the east, whereas the west had three more hours for it to get a rolling head of steam before there would be any sign of daylight. At 3:10 a.m. EST, he got a call on his cell phone from SAC Brenner. "Thompson, where are you now?"

"I'm a few miles north of Dayton on I-75, trying to get to Cincinnati by 0430 hours," replied Thompson.

"Well, get there in time, but be safe; you're a key element in this operation. We're still waiting for the approval to use the Marines in the assault on the Whittaker estate. We really need them, because the long-range forward looking infrared radar on a Marine

Longbow helicopter shows the presence of several fortified fighting positions covering key avenues of approach, and lots of heat signatures from what we think are Copperhead ground troops moving around down there. Oh, by the way, the President has just implemented the COOP, and he'll be relocating from the White House to a more secure location. Marine One is set to pick him up in the next hour or so," continued SAC Brenner.

In an excited voice, Thompson responds, "Marine One...that's it..that's the missing link. You have to get on the horn and tell the White House not to use Marine One to transport the President."

"Thompson! The District is a great big riot zone right now. He can't be traveling by ground!" exclaimed SAC Brenner.

"You have to do it. There may be other SA-7 Grails out there that we don't know about," explained Thompson.

"I don't know ...let me think about it. Anyway, the Marines and our Cincinnati and Louisville field office tactical teams are finishing final plans for the Whittaker estate assault in case the President approves implementation of the Insurrection Act. The Marines are putting containment units in place as we speak; at least that doesn't violate the Posse Comitatus Act. I'll see you in Cincinnati," closed SAC Brenner.

At 4:15 a.m. in D.C., Brother James called Collins on his cell phone as Marine One flew over his position near the Washington Monument to land on the south lawn of the White House. "Brother Collins, Brother James. Turkey has come home to roost. I say again, the turkey has come home to roost."

Collins replied, "Happy hunting, gentlemen. Let me know when you bag one."

"Roger, out," responded James. As he began a status check on his five mobile anti-aircraft units, he monitored the status of Marine One. With the police busy with the riots, each of his anti-aircraft units was able to move into position around the White House undetected. A couple of the units were able to gain access to rooftop positions within a quarter mile of the south lawn. Brother James' mobile phone notified him of an incoming text message with the sound of a sonar ringtone. He quickly pulled it out and read the encrypted message he had been waiting for, to designate the intended target. On the screen of his phone he read the text, "I think the movie I was trying to remember the other night was Rio Bravo." In reply, Brother James typed back, "That is a great classic western. I think I'll rent it tonight. Thanks." Putting his phone back in his pocket, Brother James reached for a hand-held radio and began to conduct a status check of his units. "All units be advised to target Bravo, I say again target Bravo. Unit One, do you copy?"

After only a second or two of silence, the unit replied, "This is Unit One, I copy Bravo. We have eyes on the target and are ready."

"Unit Two here; copy Bravo. We're up and operational."

"Unit Three ready; copy Bravo."

"Unit Four ready; copy Bravo."

"Unit Five ready; copy Bravo."

Brother James acknowledged their report and gave a preparatory command. "Roger that. All units are ready. Stand by."

The first helicopter had already landed, paused, and taken off, and the second was sitting on the White House lawn waiting to load its passengers. A few minutes later as the second helicopter, the actual Marine One transport, began to gain altitude, James gave the order, "All units engage. I say again, all units engage."

With that order, the skyline of the District was illuminated by multiple rocket launch back-blasts and golden streaks of light that all converged towards a single central target. In a desperate but futile attempt, Marine One ejected flares intended to draw the heat-seeking missile's aim, and then took what limited evasive action it could at such a low altitude and air speed. With staggered timing, one by one the missiles impacted the lumbering helicopter until the third struck the fuel tank, causing the explosive fuel to erupt into a bright, glowing fireball above the Old Executive Office Building just hundreds of feet west of the White House.

In a fiery hunk of burning metal, Marine One tumbled awkwardly to the ground with a thunderous crash.

Seeing the burning wreckage on the ground, James called Collins back and reported the kill. "Start the dressing, the turkey is cooked."

Collins replied in a cheerful voice, "Good job, Brother James. Now you and your men should support the local militia in their ground operations. Collins out."

At 4:40 a.m., Thompson pulled up to an outlying structure off the runway at the Cincinnati/Northern Kentucky Airport, quickly exited his rental car, and entered a hangar that had been transformed into a busy Tactical Operations Center, generally called the TOC. As he approached a large table full of maps and reconnaissance photos, he spotted Agent McCartney, SAC Brenner, and several others huddled around a television monitor tuned to a local news station. Live shots of D.C. firefighters hosing down the smoldering hunk of twisted metal that used to be Marine One were being displayed as they watched in horror.

Thompson saw those scenes on the monitor and in a heated voice yelled, "You see Brenner, I told you to call the White House! Now the President is dead when one call from you could have avoided this."

"Calm down, Thompson. I did make the call. Thanks to you, the President didn't get on the helicopter at the last minute; he's safe and remains at the White House," said SAC Brenner. "Because of that, he just gave us the approval to use the Marines on the Whittaker estate assault. After Marine One was shot down, he called me personally and said to go get those sons of bitches for the crew of Marine One."

"Well, we'd better get on with it then." replied Thompson. "What's the plan?"

Agent McCartney walked with Thompson to the planning table and introduced him to the Marine company commander. "Agent Thompson, this is Captain Nowak, the commanding officer of Lima Company, 3rd Battalion, 25th Marines, 4th Marine Division out of Columbus, Ohio. They brought 153 men, most with recent combat experience in the Middle East."

Shaking the Captain's hand, Thompson said, "Glad to have you guys with us. If I'm right, we're in for a real battle. McCartney, how about briefing me on the operations plan."

"Alright," said Agent McCartney, "The Captain has already deployed units in containment positions near the estate. Marine units will be used to engage all exterior opposing forces so that the FBI tactical teams can be inserted by helicopter on the roof to enter and clear the mansion."

Thompson added, "Captain, make sure that those ground troops are kept busy in case they have any more of those SA-7 Grails; we don't want them to take out the FBI teams before they get on the roof."

"Not a problem sir," said the captain. "Those positions that we can't kill right off the bat, we'll put enough suppressive fire on so that they won't even lift their heads to get a breath of fresh air."

Agent McCartney continued with his mission summary. "Since the fighting positions shown on the reconnaissance photos cover both of the drives to the main house of the estate, Marine assault elements will move by foot using stealth from the south to secure the outer buildings first. The weapons platoon has covertly taken up supporting positions on the high ground to the west to provide overwatch and covering fire for the assault elements. Unfortunately, we cannot open fire on their positions until the suspects on the grounds have demonstrated hostile intent. Once the assault elements have secured these outer buildings and taken their final position of cover and concealment, on order they will begin to move towards the perimeter. If they should receive fire, the weapons platoon will initiate a heavy volume of fire upon the enemy positions, and the assault elements will use fire and maneuver to breach their perimeter. Once they've established a foothold, they'll then systematically eliminate all defensive positions around the mansion. At the point when the Marines have breached the perimeter, three FBI teams will approach by helicopter, fast rope-down onto the roof and enter the door on the south wall, which opens to a stairwell. Team Three will insert first, enter, secure the upper level of the stairwell, and then proceed to clear the third floor. Team Two will insert next, moving right behind Team Three to enter, search, and clear the second floor. Team One will insert last, immediately behind Team Two, and move to clear the first floor. Thompson ,you'll follow along behind Team One. Our goal is to take Whittaker and Collins alive. Each of the teams has been rehearsing, and they're making final preparations."

"Sounds like a well thought- out plan. When will we be ready to go?" asked Thompson.

"All the Marine units are in position, and our teams are ready to load on the helicopters. Grab an MP5 and body armor, and let's get to the helos," replied Agent McCartney.

In the predawn darkness, three Blackhawk helicopters sat on the flight line with their rotors turning as three lines of ten tactically clad FBI agents trotted to their assigned helicopter and loaded. Just before loading on the Blackhawk, Thompson looked back at SAC Brenner as he stood near the hangar. They shared a gaze and Thompson nodded, turned, and climbed into his seat on the chopper. Once Thompson was seated, the group of choppers simultaneously increased power and one by one, they lifted off the ground, turned towards the west and flew off in trail formation, one following the other. The Blackhawks flew by nap-of-the-earth towards their final staging area on a high school football field just two miles south of the Whittaker estate. As he sat on the helicopter in flight, Thompson saw the fires from the downtown riots glowing on the still-dark horizon. Setting down on the football, field the pilots kept the helicopter blades turning and waited for the command to insert their occupants into the fight.

Just before first light, the Marine assault teams had successfully cleared the outer buildings without incident and were in their final positions of cover and concealment. Now was the time that all hell was about to break loose. Reporting to command, the pilot of the lead chopper radioed to the tactical commander, "Charlie One, Air One."

"Go for Charlie One," responded Captain Nowak.

"All air assault units are in final staging positions," reported Air One.

"Roger that, Air One, stand by. Break. Charlie One to all units: Execute. Proceed to Phase Line Alpha. I say again, proceed to Phase Line Alpha," instructed Nowak.

On the command to execute the assault, the ground units began to use bounding maneuvers to cover the ground between them and the KGC defensive perimeter. The Marine weapons platoon could observe the KGC defensive perimeter of the Whittaker Estate. Camouflaged soldiers with AK-47s manning sandbagged entrenchments could be seen from the Marine overwatch positions using their night vision scopes. Some of the KGC soldiers were seated in their fighting positions drinking coffee, completely unaware of the approaching forces they would soon battle. Marine ground assault units took covering positions on the edge of the wood line. Ahead of them, across approximately fifty yards of open ground, lay a barn and stables. A squad of Marines, using the shadows to mask their movement, left their concealment at the wood line and moved to the two doors of the building. There they paused, and with perfect timing, they entered both doors simultaneously in two fire teams. After a moment, an arm was extended out the door with a thumbs-up sign. Seeing this, the overwatch team still at the wood's edge got up from their cover positions, quickly moved to the barn, entered, and joined up with the other Marines.

Successful clearing of the barn and stables completed the first phase of the operation to ensure that no hostile threats from these structures could jeopardize the Marine units' advance towards the KGC defensive lines. Achievement of this milestone was reported to the tactical command. "Charlie One, this is Golf One. We have reached Phase Line Alpha, I repeat Phase Line Alpha."

"Roger that. Proceed to Phase Line Bravo," instructed Captain Nowak.

Golf One acknowledged, "Roger, moving."

Knowing that contact with hostile forces was imminent, the weapons platoon leader passed an arm signal down the line to get ready to engage. Seeing this signal, the Marines took aim with their assigned weapons and the machine gunners quietly pulled the charging handles on their M-240 belt-fed machine guns to the rear and returned them to their forward locked and loaded position. Members of the ground assault used bounding overwatch movement techniques to approach the KGC defensive lines. Half the squads would set down in covering positions, while the others moved forward with only the predawn darkness to conceal their movement. Once the maneuver element had moved approximately thirty yards, they would then lie down and in a good fighting position and signal to the overwatch element to get up and move ahead of them as they covered the advance. Only a few yards out from the defensive perimeter, one of the KGC soldiers caught sight of the Marine advance and yelled out, "Inbound movement on the perimeter at sector three!" He then opened fire with his AK-47.

Immediately upon compromise of the Marines' position, the hillside to the west of their position lit up with multiple muzzle flashes, and the KGC positions began to take a heavy volume of incoming fire from the Marine weapons platoon on the hill. Red tracers from their M-240 machine guns lit up the finely manicured lawn surrounding the big house, while 40-mm grenades from their M-203s created brilliant flashes of light when they impacted on and around the KGC fortifications. Some of the KGC troops were hit as they tried to get back to the cover of their fighting positions. Those who were in their positions were pinned down by the incoming bullets, to the point that they couldn't place effective fire on the Marine assault elements.

Quickly, the Marines were able to overtake the KGC positions as the weapons platoon shifted its fire off of the primary defenses and placed it on positions that threatened the ground assault's flanks. Overtaking the first group of KGC defensive positions, the Marines reported their progress and then split to assault other defensive positions on each flank. "Charlie One, Golf One. Reached Phase Line Bravo, I say again Phase Line Bravo. Sir, we have broken through their perimeter and we are systematically clearing the fighting positions. We have secured the corridor for helo insertion."

"Roger that, Lieutenant, keep the pressure on. Break. Air One, this is Charlie One. The ground corridor has been secured. You are a go for insertion," instructed Captain Nowak.

Immediately the lead pilot responded, "Charlie One, Air One. That's a roger. We're pulling pitch and on route."

All three helicopters increased power, and one by one they lifted off with about forty-five seconds of delay between them to afford them sufficient spacing for individual hovering insertions at the target location. Flying at treetop level, the three Blackhawks made their approach to the roof of the mansion. Riding on the last bird, Thompson could see the deadly light show on the ground as they flew over the ground battle that raged below. The streaking glow of tracers from the machine guns and the flashes of hand-grenade detonations illuminated the battle space in an eerie dance of light, shadows, and smoke. In blacked-out mode, the pilots used night vision equipment to one by one skillfully find their mark and hover just long enough over the house for the fast ropes to be dropped and all the occupants to quickly slide down the ropes and disappear in the shadows of the rooftop below. Thompson was the last to slide down the rope as the Blackhawk banked off to the east side of the building.

As the last bird cleared the roof and gained speed, distance, and altitude to leave the hot zone, a KGC soldier exited a side door of the mansion, shouldered an SA-7 Grail, and took aim at the helicopter as it began to bank. The missile was launched in a streak of light that found its mark in the exhaust port of the right engine of the Blackhawk. Losing power quickly, the pilot was able to safely auto-rotate the big bird down into a horse pasture approximately five hundred yards from the house. As quickly as he appeared, the Grail gunner was immediately struck with machine gun fire from a Marine assault element, causing him to fall to the ground in a heap.

Up on the roof, Team Three breached the roof door and quickly entered a large, square-shaped stairwell that extended down to the ground floor. Hallways for each of the three floors extended from the stairwell, where each of the FBI tactical teams began clearing their assigned areas. Team Three moved down one flight of the stairwell and then moved down the third-floor corridor, clearing each room as quickly and effectively as possible. With precision timing, Team Two passed the third floor as the last member of Team Three exited the stairwell and entered the third-floor corridor. Team Two moved down the stairwell, entered the second floor and began their clearing operations. As a member of the last team to enter, Thompson followed his team as they entered the stairwell and moved quickly down to the first-floor landing. Shots and muffled yelling could be heard on both floors above as Team One, followed by Thompson, entered the first floor. From a door down the long main hallway, several bursts of un-aimed automatic fire were directed towards Thompson's team as they entered from the stairwell. Focused on the threat, the team returned fire, neutralized the gunman and continued to clear the hallway.

As the tactical team systematically cleared the main hall, including the rooms and side corridors along the way, Thompson followed at a distance of approximately fifty feet behind the main team, acting as an additional rear guard for team movement. Thompson would briefly look into rooms the team had cleared as he followed their progress. Ahead of him, he could see that the team had encountered a T-shaped intersection at the end of the corridor. In a well-coordinated movement, the team negotiated the intersection, requiring the team to break up into two separate maneuver elements to clear the remaining sections of the first floor. Still a distance away from the T intersection, out of the corner of his eye Thompson briefly caught what he thought was the movement of a shadow down a side corridor that the team had already cleared. Looking back down the hall in an attempt to signal the tactical team before it moved on, Thompson saw that both of the two team elements had already separated and moved down the two opposing corridors out of direct line of sight. Seeing that the team was gone, and not really positive of what it was that he saw, Thompson then redirected his attention and muzzle of his MP-5 back down the side corridor, determined to confirm or disprove what he thought he saw for himself.

He moved smoothly and quietly down the corridor with his MP-5 at the low-ready position, his heart beginning to pound rapidly like a bass drum at a rock concert. As he was trained at the academy, he moved with his weapon off safely and his trigger finger extended along the lower receiver of the MP-5 just outside the trigger guard. In an instant, he was ready to quickly raise the muzzle towards his intended target, place his finger on the trigger, identify the threat, and squeeze off a well- placed series of shots: two to the body and one to the head. As he moved to the edge of a door jamb, he could see just inside the room where he thought he'd seen the movement of the shadow just moments ago. Only partially opened, the door opened inwardly and away from him, with the hinges on the door jamb located opposite his position in the hall. Through the small crack between the door jamb and the door near the hinges, a shadow again passed in front of him, but much deeper into the room. When he peered intently through the crack along the left wall of the room, he could see a desk with a lamp on it and a man behind the desk looking through the main middle drawer and gathering papers. In one quick, fluid motion, Thompson partially crossed the threshold of the door, pushed the door completely against the left wall and assumed a standing barricade position with his weapon aimed at the suspect. "Freeze! FBI!" Thompson yelled at the suspect.

Caught off guard, the man immediately dropped the papers onto the desk, stood up straight and raised his arms to shoulder level so that Thompson could see that his hands were empty. As the light settled on the man's face when he stood erect, Thompson immediately recognized the face as the one on the numerous photos from the case file. "Collins!" Thompson yelled. "Keep your hands where I can see them." Thompson gave Collins a cursory visual search from where he stood and could see the strap of a weapons sling, showing that Collins had a rifle slung to his right side, just barely tucked away around behind him.

"Who are you?" Collins asked.

"Special Agent Thompson of the FBI. You move, and it will be the last thing you'll do," he responded.

With a smile, Collins said, "I thought Jake had gotten rid of you back in Little Rock. Well, that just goes to show that you just can't get good, dependable help these days, can ya?"

Thompson knew he had to get some help from the team to take such a dangerous criminal into custody, so he decided to use his radio to call for assistance. As he removed his left hand from the fore stock of his MP-5 to reach for his radio, Collins dropped to one knee behind the desk and brought his AK-47 pistol to bear on Thompson's position with a burst of automatic fire. Thompson pivoted back into the hallway just in time to keep from being hit with a fatal round. Two of Collins' shots passed through the wooden door, with one of the bullets grazing Thompson's right side just above his hip and through the limited protection of the soft side panels on his body armor. It felt as if someone had taken a glowing red branding iron to his slide. Thompson stuck the muzzle of his MP-5 in the doorway and returned fire with a short burst of his own, but Collins had already moved from his shooting position behind the desk to a door leading into a smaller adjacent room.

Thompson yelled out, "Collins, give it up! There's no place to go."

"There's always a place to go ...it just may not be where you meant to end up," shouted Collins over the undetermined sound of wood sliding against wood.

Covering the door with the muzzle of his weapon, Thompson moved to the left side of the door, paused, and pulled a flash-bang from his pocket. Holding down the grenade-type spoon with his left hand, he pulled the pin with his right, kicked the door open and tossed it into the room. Almost instantly it erupted into a brilliant flash of white light and thunderous blast, immediately after which Thompson made a buttonhook movement into the room and quickly scanned the room for a target. Collins was gone! "How could that be?" Thompson said to himself. There were no other doors or windows to this room; how could he have just disappeared? Frantically knocking and pushing on all surfaces that could be a hidden panel, he desperately looked for Collins' escape route, to no avail. Confused and bleeding slightly, Thompson exited the room back into the passage. By now the gunfire inside the entire house had stopped and he could hear the teams yelling "clear" with every successive room they entered and secured.

Grabbing his radio, he transmitted, "Thompson to all units. I just lost Collins in a room on the first floor with no visible exits. This old mansion must be full of hidden passages. Captain Nowak, notify all containment units to be watchful for hidden exits outside the main house."

Captain Nowak responded on the radio, "Wilco."

Thompson continued on the radio and asked, "Team One, any sign of Whittaker?"

Team One's leader responded, "Negative."

"Team Two?" asked Thompson.

"That's a negative," Team Two responded.

"Team Three?" asked Thompson again.

"That's a negative here too," replied Team Three.

"Well, keep looking. Whittaker and Collins have to be here somewhere," Thompson concluded.

As Thompson was giving these instructions over the radio, Collins was exiting a secretive tunnel opening two hundred and fifty yards to the east of the mansion near the bank of the river, well outside the Marines' established containment ring. When he emerged from the tunnel, he scanned the area while the muzzle of his AK-47 pistol followed the direction of his eyes. Assuring himself that the area was clear of federal forces, Collins stealthily moved down a trail to the river's edge, where he located an equipment cache point. After removing a camouflaged tarp off the top of a one-man kayak, Collins pushed the watercraft into the meandering waters of the Ohio River tributary, got in with his AK-47 slung and began to paddle downstream unchallenged. In the FBI's haste to assemble an assault team, their tactical plan counted on the exterior containment ring to prevent the escape of suspects and did not factor in potential waterborne exfiltration routes. In the pale light of the early morning hours, Collins slipped away under cover of the dense fog rising off the river's placid surface.

Frustrated that he had missed the opportunity to catch Collins and that even a second search by the FBI teams could not determine where Whittaker was, Thompson walked into the great hall of the mansion.

Off this great hall was a large, stately library, where he envisioned Whittaker sitting in one of the overstuffed leather chairs in a smoking jacket, sipping a glass of brandy and laughing out loud about how he had completely outwitted Thompson. Just the thought of this imagined scene angered Thompson to the point that he yanked a book off the shelf, threw it across the room and watched as it slid across the plush wool carpeting. Walking over to the book he picked it up, set it on a small table, and realized that his fingers were wet with a deep-red fluid. Rubbing it between his index finger and thumb, he could see that it was fresh blood. Taking a closer look at the floor, he could now see the blood trail that the book slid across; he hadn't noticed it earlier because it blended in so well with the red oriental pattern of the carpet. As he examined the blood trail, he saw where it had originated in the great hall and entered the library. Carefully, Thompson tracked the blood trail through the library until it ended at the base of a section of the built-in bookcase in the wall.

Seeing that there was no corresponding arch pattern on the carpet to indicate that it opened outward,

Thompson deduced that this particular section of the bookcase must swing inward from the library into a hidden room behind the wall. Searching for the latch release mechanism, Thompson started to examine all the books on the shelf until he spotted a blood stain on the last one on the right end of the third shelf. Unable to remove it, he tilted the top of the book forward until he heard a metallic click sound behind the bookcase. As he pushed on the bookcase, the section opened inward into a dark corridor. Making sure that the flashlight on his MP5 was working, he entered the opening and saw that the blood trail continued on the floor along the narrow passageway. Forty feet ahead, Thompson observed that the passage made a right-hand turn and that the corner was illuminated from a source down the other passage.

Thompson approached the corner slowly and quietly and then began to edge around the corner little by little, looking over the sights of his weapon. Hearing movement in the next room, he moved closer and saw the body of a KGC soldier lying at the end of the blood trail. After he made a rapid entry into the room,

Thompson caught Franklin Whittaker off guard as he was stuffing documents into an attaché case.

"Whittaker, get your hands up!" demanded Thompson as he aimed his MP5 at Whittaker so that the red dot of the tactical laser clearly marked its intended target: the center mass of his chest.

"No need to point that weapon at me officer, I will not resist whatsoever. I have plenty of lawyers for that," remarked Whittaker. "After all, I am the victim here. These men took over my estate and have been holding me hostage for the last several days."

"You can try, but you're not going to sell that bull-shit line to me," replied Thompson.

"I don't have to make you believe me, just all the judges, politicians and prominent people of this community with whom I have established long standing relationships," laughed Whittaker. "While you and I both know that I am only guilty of trying to correct the errant path that this country is moving down, no one outside this room will ever hear me say it. Who are you anyway, officer?" Whittaker asked.

"Agent Thompson of the FBI," he replied.

"Ah yes, you're the bright agent from the Little Rock office. Sorry for that little unfortunate event at the playground, but Mr. Collins felt you were becoming too much of a threat that could derail our plans for Senator Jordan. You have done very well in piecing together bits of the puzzle so far, but you still don't understand the broader objectives. You're smart, I'll give you that; and you know, our cause could use a sharp man like you. I could make you a wealthy man. What do you say to switching teams?" asked Whittaker.

Without hesitation, Thompson said, "No, I'm going to make sure that you and your group of hate mongers pay for what you have done to this country over the last several months. You're going to stand before the wives and children of the men killed in the prison convoy and be held accountable."

In a stern voice, Whittaker repeated his offer, saying, "Think about it hard, Agent Thompson. The weakened federal government you currently represent will never be able to convict me of anything more than the feeble crime of harboring an escaped convict while under duress. What do you say? I will not make the offer again."

Pondering the uncertainty of being able to make the charges stick and get a solid conviction, Thompson asked Whittaker, "Are you sure that no one outside this room will hear what we agree to here?"

"Absolutely no one will hear anything. These old walls are soundproof, the turns in the corridor reduce sound transmission down the hallways, and active countermeasures are in place to prevent electronic eavesdropping. No, what we say and do down here will remain just between the two of us. After all, we were able to complete our communications from our command center to our commanders and troops across the country without any concern for potential compromise. So, I can assure you that no one besides me will hear you accept my proposal," said Whittaker.

Thompson was resolute in his decision and said, "You're right; no one will hear me accept your offer, not even you. Now I may not be the sharpest agent in the Bureau, and I may not be rich, but I don't think I can stoop to treason against this great country like you have." Pausing for a moment, Thompson looked down and continued to speak his mind. "But you may also be right, in that a dozen U.S. District Attorneys working full-time for ten years will probably not be able to even get you in a courtroom, much less convict you of the treasonous crimes you've committed."

Whittaker smiled and replied, "See there, Agent Thompson? You are a realist after all."

"I am at that, I guess. As far as that unfortunate event on the playground you mentioned, Candy sends her regards." With a quick, fluid motion, Thompson raised his weapon and squeezed the trigger, placing two rapid shots in the center of Whittaker's chest and, before his body could begin to collapse, placing a third round in his forehead.

Thompson watched as Whittaker's body fell limp to the ground, and with a smile he said, "I may have graduated last in the FBI academy, but I was the top shooter of the class." Thompson then walked over to the dead KGC soldier at the entrance to the room and, while still wearing his Nomex gloves, picked up a handgun lying on the floor. He then walked back to where Whittaker's bloody, lifeless body lay on the floor, knelt, and placed the handgun in the corpse's right hand. Even though Whittaker probably wouldn't have made it into a Federal courthouse to face charges, he got what was coming to him after all.

Chapter XIII
The Cleanup

Standing over Whittaker's body, Thompson grabbed the remote microphone of his radio and transmitted to the other FBI team members: "This is Thompson. I've got Whittaker down in their command center just off the library behind the bookcase. I left the bookcase door open so you can find it with no trouble. There appears to be valuable evidence and intelligence information down here. Let's get a team down here to work this material to see what else these guys are up to and stop it."

Agent McCartney responded, "Roger that, we'll be there in just a minute. What's the status of Whittaker?"

"Be advised, Whittaker took hostile action when I entered, so I had to take him under fire. He's dead," said Thompson.

In a sarcastic tone, McCartney replied to this revelation. "Couldn't have happened to a more deserving guy. Looks like swift justice found him for the damage he has caused today."

"Yeah, you might say that!" responded Thompson.

"I did just say that," McCartney smugly replied. "We found the hidden passage, and it looks like we're coming up on your position."

Within a couple of minutes, other FBI team members had found their way into the secretive command center and linked back up with Thompson. McCartney and a team of other agents entered the command post and started to look around at the layout to determine what to focus on next. McCartney walked over to Thompson as he stood over Whittaker's body, knelt down and took a quick look over the body. He stood up, still looking at the body, placed his hand on Thompson's shoulder and said, "Hey, nice shot group. Two to the body and one to the head! I want you on my entry team next time."

"Hopefully, there won't be a next time," Thompson replied.

Thompson looked up from the body, scanned the room and saw a couple of computers at workstations on the main conference table. "I bet those computers on those desks over there hold very valuable data. Let's get Special Agent Armstrong and his team of computer techs down here to crack the administrator passwords on these computers so we can take a look inside their electronic files," Thompson ordered.

McCartney quickly responded, "I'm on it." He grabbed his radio and transmitted, "Brenner, this is McCartney."

"Go for Brenner," he responded.

"Can you get Armstrong and his crew down here to start going through these computers to see what they can find?" McCartney inquired.

"Sure thing. They'll be on their way. I'll escort them down there," Brenner replied.

McCartney ended the radio traffic. "Roger that. McCartney out." McCartney walked over to the main table and began to examine the documents for action-able information.

A few minutes later, Brenner, Armstrong and the computer techs walked into the command center and started to work on the computers. Brenner left the computer experts to do their thing, then walked over and knelt over Whittaker's body in a way that blocked the others' view so that none of the law enforcement staff could see what he was doing. A moment later, Brenner stood up and walked over to where McCartney was sorting through the hard-copy documents. Agent McCartney found the operational plans that Whittaker and Collins had prepared and began to read their details and implement instructions. "Hey, Thompson!" he shouted. "You know the police snipers that we heard about that were shooting demonstrators in the streets?"

"Yeah," replied Thompson. "Those guys have done much more harm than good and are the reason the President has had to call out the National Guard to attempt to regain control. They should be rolling into the cities around the country in the next several hours."

"Well get this," said Agent McCartney. "It wasn't the local cops who did it after all. It was a bunch of Collins' men dressed in police uniforms who did it. From their plans, they've intentionally been agitating the crowds and making the cops believe that the demonstrators were responsible for the fires and violence in the streets. They anticipated the government's reaction to certain stimuli, which they generated and controlled."

Reading further in the plan, Agent McCartney became very concerned and told Thompson, "You mentioned that the National Guard is being deployed. Well, based on that anticipated deployment, Collins is about to implement another phase of their plan. Their snipers have been instructed to take out the officers on the National Guard riot lines, expecting that the leaderless troops will think they're under fire from the demonstrators and that they will return fire into the crowd. Thompson, they're deliberately trying to provoke the National Guard into shooting the demonstrators."

Startled at the thought, Thompson looked up from his papers in astonishment and replied, "If they're successful, then the political stability of the entire country will degrade into anarchy."

"They've planned for that too," said McCartney. "Now I know where all those Russian weapons went. The Copperheads have established a large militia in each of the big cities. They'll deploy them in the aftermath of the National Guard debacle and put down the uprising with brutal force. Their goal is to decimate the non-white populations and to firmly establish the whites as the undisputed ruling body of their new political order."

Now feeling a real sense of urgency in the situation, and knowing that time was of the essence, Thompson implored the others, "We can't let that happen. Let's see if we can identify the field commanders and key personnel so we can cut the head off this snake."

They immediately started sorting through the files and papers. After about an hour of sorting, McCartney looked up from the desk and said, "Looks like they were not only well funded, but well organized; they have detailed hard-copy files on each of their lower-level field members." He looked over at Brenner, who was now assisting the computer techs, and asked, "How are those computer techs coming on getting into the computer systems over there?"

Brenner replied, "Armstrong and his team broke the administrator-level passwords a while ago and are doing some quick keyword searches on some of the files to speed up the process. They also ran into a few files that are encrypted with off-the-shelf encryption software, so they're focused on breaking the encryption code."

SAC Brenner's cell phone rang and he answered. "Brenner here. Yes sir, we're going through the files, now trying to get a lead on the elements deployed in the field. Yes sir, we just came across something. Collins' men are going to deploy as snipers behind the crowds of demonstrators to engage the National Guard officers. We need to warn them not to fall for their trickery and end up firing into the crowds. They need to seek out the snipers before they start firing!"

Pausing to listen for a few minutes, Brenner said to the person on the other end of the call, "That's not good ... They must think that we're powerless as a nation to respond ... It sounds like they were just waiting for something like this to happen ... Yes sir, we will focus on the task at hand here and we'll keep you informed of our progress. Out here, sir."

Getting off the phone, SAC Brenner turned to Thompson and said, "That was the Director himself. Things are not only messed up here in the states; there are other threats on the international stage now. Before Marine One was shot down, the Russians were conducting training exercises near the border of Georgia and Azerbaijan. As soon as the news reports of civil unrest on our streets got out and speculation that the President was dead after Marine One was downed, they began to mass their armored divisions on the border. To top it off, the Chinese have redirected their navy into the Taiwan Straits at key choke points and are setting up a blockade to the south, totally isolating Taiwan by sea. There have already been some Silkworm missile exchanges with the much smaller Taiwanese naval forces; they are fighting back but are severely outgunned by the Chinese fleet. Intelligence imagery from our satellites tells us that landing craft already partially loaded in Chinese naval bases are being readied to set sail within hours. Our Pacific fleet is headed for the island as we speak, but they have a long way to go. A smaller carrier group in the Indian Ocean is not far from being able to put planes in the air to reach the southern tip of Taiwan."

In a concerned tone, Thompson replied, "There has to be a connection here. Collins' troops were equipped with Russian weapons that were smuggled in by way of Chinese freighters. And just before all of this broke out here, there just happened to be fully combat-ready Russian armor divisions near the Georgian and Azerbaijan border conducting scheduled military exercises, and the Chinese already had landing craft partially loaded for deployment in an amphibious assault. There's no way all of this is a coincidence; those computers hold the key to unraveling this connection."

After he walked over to the area where the FBI computer technicians had set up shop, Thompson began to discuss the status of their scans. "How's it going?" Thompson asked one of the computer techs.

"Since we've cracked the password accounts, we've gained total access to their systems, but they've been using sophisticated encryption software to secure some of their data files. We've been pounding on the encryption keys for some time now," responded the computer tech. "In fact, even while we work here, some of these files are remotely being subjected to a brute force attack using some of Los Alamos National Laboratory's most powerful supercomputers. Brute force attacks are not very hard to use, but they can take some serious time, depending on the sophistication of the password or encryption key. Essentially, they create every combination on the keyboard, including special characters, and combine them in every conceivable combination and password length. That, my friend, is a metric butt-ton of possible combinations."

Thompson replied, "Well, there's a lot at stake riding on you guys giving us access to the information in those files. If you don't do it soon, in the future you won't be seeing any more product labels saying made in Taiwan."

Overhearing this discussion, Special Agent Armstrong, the onsite FBI cyber team lead, suddenly had an idea. "You know," he said, "sometimes you just need to take a few steps back to see if there are other approaches that could work. So, let's dumb this down a little." Speaking to the computer tech, he asked, "Can you see the file extensions of the encrypted files?"

"Yep, they're Microsoft Word documents. Why?" the tech responded.

"Thompson, why don't you think up some words that you would expect to be in these encrypted files? That will help us zero in on the areas of interest," Armstrong said.

While Thompson contemplated, Armstrong explained his thinking. "You see, every time Microsoft Word opens a file, it creates a temporary – and unencrypted- version of itself and stores it in the hard drive," he said. "That's how the program knows enough about your file to recover it, in the event of a computer glitch. If everything closes out normally, Word doesn't need the temporary file anymore, so it discards it. But all that really happens is that the reference to the file is removed, so the program can no longer access it through the file system. The file is still on the hard drive; we just need a way to get to it."

The tech screamed, "Of course, temp file recovery - why didn't I think of it?! There is a software tool that allows us to easily browse, or keyword- search deleted files on a hard drive. Of course, it won't help us see the encrypted files, but we can certainly see their unencrypted cousins, as long as they haven't been overwritten by other files or by a forensic clean- up tool."

Thompson said, "Okay, try KGB, Collins, Russia, China, and Jordan. Make 'em case sensitive if you can. Let's start with Russia."

"No problem o," said the tech as he typed in the keywords. Almost immediately, keyword hits started to pop up on the monitor.

At Thompson's request, the computer tech expanded the text surrounding the keyword, Russia. "Would you look at that?" the computer tech said after opening a file listed under the search results. "Here's a list of the KGC Russian contacts and operatives. It looks like these Russian generals were tired of waiting for democracy to bring them wealth. They were going to break away from the Russian military, take over Georgia and Azerbaijan and set up their own separate feudal network, with each participating general having his own kingdom."

Looking over the data in the file, Thompson remarked, "I'd bet Moscow would be interested in all of this information. How about searching for China?"

Conducting a similar keyword search for China, the computer tech came up with similar information. Seeing this information, SAC Brenner surmised, "Apparently these commanding generals in both countries were using their military troops and equipment for their own personal gain, without the knowledge of their respective central governments. So it isn't just a matter of direct defiance by the two central governments as we thought before."

After evaluating this new information, Thompson turned and said to SAC Brenner, "Sir, as you well know I'm no politician, and I'm not versed in matters of international relations, but I think that the President should let the world know that he is alive and well and that he's in firm control of the U.S. He should also share this information about these rogue generals with the Moscow and Beijing governments and let them deal with these events instead of us escalating the potential threat. "

"You know ...for once, I agree with your political assessment of the situation, Thompson," replied SAC Brenner. "I'll run this information up the chain while you guys focus on finding out how to stop the KGC plans in the cities. We need to know who their field echelon leaders are and how to find them."

"We're on it," replied Thompson.

SAC Brenner left the command center while the computer techs continued to search the files for information on the domestic threat. Locating a high-level file folder holding twenty individual file folders labeled with major U.S. city names, the computer tech opened the Atlanta file subfolder and began to review the files contained within.

"Bingo!" the computer tech said excitedly. "Here's a file containing the background, description, assignment and pictures of each member of the Atlanta KGC militia. Here's another file with the locations and phone numbers of the field headquarters and staging points for their operations."

Looking over the information in these files, Thompson said, "This is everything we need to go after these bastards. I want you to email copies of each city's files to their respective FBI field office so they can round these guys up and end the violence out there. They're going to need help from their reservists and National Guardsmen and since the President has already enacted the Insurrection Act, there are no barriers to using them in a direct- action operation."

Thompson, Agent McCartney, and the other agents continued to process the crime scene and to look for additional information that might be useful in stopping the violence and prosecuting everyone involved with this treasonous operation to the fullest extent of the law.

Thompson pulled out his phone and called Brenner. "Brenner, it's Thompson. We're making good progress and are about to wrap things up here."

"The information you've been passing on has been valuable in the field," said Brenner. "The reports are coming in now that the National Guard troops are taking up positions in the cities as we speak. We've passed along our information to them so they'll be prepared."

Somewhat relieved, Thompson replied, "That's good. For a change it feels like we're getting ahead of the power curve and not playing a game of catch-up with the KGC. We'll pack up things and join you back at the airport in the TOC. McCartney and I should be there in the next hour or so."

"Alright, when you two get back to the TOC, get some rest; we have some cots set up. You guys deserve a break. See you in a bit" Brenner instructed.

After hours of work, they secured the scene and transported all the evidence and intelligence information to the TOC back at the airport. Returning to the TOC, Thompson was dead tired, and once he had turned over the information to a set of fresh agents, he found a portable cot in the makeshift rest area to get some sleep.

At the same time, National Guard troops were deployed in Atlanta, as in other major cities, to confront the growing unrest and keep the violence from escalating and spreading further. Young enlisted men called up from their normal jobs were deployed on the riot control lines and were nervously positioned in front of a hostile crowd that seemed to be growing exponentially with every minute that passed. Several buildings behind the crowds of yelling demonstrators smoldered from the fires set by Collins' covert operatives. As an occasional bottle or rock was hurled at their lines, the officers and sergeants of the National Guard did their best to reassure the troops on the riot lines that everything would be just fine. Without their consistent, calming influence, the troops would have either run in fear or unleashed a tremendously brutal assault against those they thought were the antagonists. The tension on the line was high enough already, and the risk of things getting out of hand was growing with every minor clash with the crowd.

A KGC sniper deployed in an overwatch position over the Atlanta city park where the demonstration was taking place began to survey the field of play for potential leadership targets in the National Guard riot lines.

Through the scope of a Dragunov rifle, the sniper lined up his crosshairs on the chest of an Army officer behind the riot control line who was using a bullhorn in an attempt to calm the agitated crowd. The sniper radioed his commander, "Kilo Base, this is Sniper One. I am in position and have a shot on a primary target."

From his command post several blocks away, Kilo Base responded, "Roger that, Sniper One. Hold until the other sniper units have checked in. Break. Sniper Two, what's your status?"

"This is Sniper Two. I am in position and have a clear shot on my primary target. Standing by for a go code," the second sniper answered.

Continuing, Kilo Base asked, "Sniper Three, what's your status over? Over."

After waiting a few seconds with no response he transmitted, "Sniper Three, this is Kilo Base. What is your status. Over." Still with no answer, he called the others. "Kilo Base to all sniper units. Does anyone have a visual on Sniper Three?"

"Kilo Base, this is Sniper Four. I can see his assigned position but do not have a visual on him ...wait ...I see him taking his position ... Something's wrong. It doesn't look like him. Let me check him out through the scope." In an excited voice, Sniper Four transmitted, "Kilo Base!" and abruptly ended his communication.

Hearing this, Kilo Base directed his units over the radio, "All sniper units you have a go. I repeat, you have a go."

Given the release by Kilo Base to engage his target, Sniper One reacquired his sight picture on the Army officer with the bullhorn, steadied his aim, and began to apply smooth, steady pressure to the trigger. The report from another shot rang out across the alleyway, and Sniper One fell to the rooftop from the impact of a bullet ripping through his chest. An Army Special Forces sniper located on the top floor of another adjacent building reported on his radio net, "KGC sniper down on the roof of the building at corner of Luckie and Peachtree Streets."

After sleeping soundly for a couple of hours, Thompson was awakened by hearing his name called out several times. Opening his eyes, he could see that SAC Brenner had pulled a chair up next to him and was trying to wake him up. "Thompson... Thompson... Wake up, you've been out for hours!" said SAC Brenner. "I need to bring you up to speed on a few things. The President took the information we found and personally called the Russian and Chinese leaders to passed on the information. They were very appreciative and vowed that they'd get their rogue generals under control and bring them to justice. Already, satellite intelligence has confirmed that the military forces have been turned back, and reports from people on the ground indicate that tensions have begun to de- escalate. There have been several eyewitness reports of immediate field executions of some of the officers listed in the KGC files. On the home front, National Guard and Reserve snipers were deployed in counter- sniper operations covering the riots. All that combat experience fighting the Houthis and Hezbollah paid off; they were able to locate and neutralize the KGC snipers before they could cause any further damage."

Thompson sat up and shuffled through all the images Brenner was referring to. He exclaimed, "That's out-fucking-standing! What about the status of the militia forces?"

"The FBI field offices were able to act on the intelligence information we provided. They took down the leaders and rounded up their troops in every city without incident. It turns out that most of the Copperheads' militia troops didn't know what was going on either. Their leaders lied to them and were manipulating them; they thought that they were actually doing good and saving the government instead of overthrowing it," SAC Brenner explained. "One thing strange is that they weren't able to uncover their weapons cache."

"Any word on Collins?" asked Thompson.

"Nope, he's just vanished. None of the roadblocks or searches have come up with anything either," replied SAC Brenner.

"Well, it's a safe bet that we'll hear from him again …just not sure when, where and how," stated Thompson.

"I wouldn't take that bet against you, that's for sure. Why don't you go home and get some real rest. You deserve it," instructed SAC Brenner.

Thompson responded, "Looks like you have it just about wrapped up here. I think I will."

Placing his hand on Thompson's shoulder, SAC Brenner said, "Ya know, I was wrong about you, Stan. You're a damn good agent, and I'm proud to be serving with you." Brenner started to turn away from Thompson and walk off, but then paused and turned back to face Thompson. "Oh yeah, strange thing: Whittaker was left-handed and I found the pistol he threatened you with in his right hand. As a seasoned investigator, what do you make of that?" asked Brenner.

Thompson was speechless and shocked that he'd been found out. Looking at his expression, Brenner added, "I thought so. Don't look so worried. I switched the pistol from his right hand to his left before the crime scene guys showed up."

"Thanks, Chief. I owe you," Thompson replied, sounding embarrassed.

Brenner shook Thompson's hand, looked him straight in the eye and said, "I would have done the same thing if I'd been in that situation. You did the right thing, Stan."

Forcing a grin, Thompson replied, "I hope so!" Thompson then paused for a second and continued, "Hey, Chief, I have a question for you. When the elections get going again, are you going to vote?"

"Yep, I haven't missed a general election since I turned eighteen," responded SAC Brenner. "How about you?"

"Before all this happened, I would have used the election as just an excuse to come in late to work, but not now. Not after we came so close to losing this somewhat imperfect democratic republic that we have. I now understand what a right and responsibility we have. We can let the likes of Whittaker and Collins decide our fate for us, or we can participate and control our own destiny. As for me, I choose the latter. No one is going to decide for me anymore!" Thompson explained.

With a smile on his face, Brenner responded, "That's good to hear, brother. Now gather your stuff and go home before I have you bagging and tagging evidence on this case."

Thompson quickly picked up his gear, climbed into his rental car, and began his drive home to Little Rock. As he drove, he scrutinized every person he passed along the road very closely. After all, Collins was out there somewhere.

About the Author
W.T. Sanders

As a senior-level writer on the topic of protecting the nation's nuclear security assets, W.T. Sanders is uniquely qualified for writing in this genre.

As a former commissioned officer in the U.S. Army and as a U.S. government security contract employee, he rose from a SWAT instructor to a senior executive in some of the largest private security firms within the United States.

He has extensive training and operational experience with various three-lettered federal agencies and is well- versed in military special operations and coun- ter- terrorist/hostage rescue operations. He led inspec- tions of our country's nuclear weapons production fa- cilities that included extensive force- on- force exer- cises to evaluate tactical response to postulated terror- ist threats.

He has written numerous classified and unclassified reports intended for Congressional review, contributed to Congressional testimony, and has written speeches for the U.S. Secretary of Energy and the Administrator of the National Nuclear Security Administration con- cerning the physical protection needs of our nuclear security assets.

In his book *The Rostrum*, Mr. Sanders brings his unique personal experiences to the pages of this intri- guing, politically based crime thriller.

www.ingramcontent.com/pod-product-compliance
Lightning Source LLC
Chambersburg PA
CBHW071924150726
47999CB00001B/91

Ketogenica per la Vita, la Bibbia

Guida Completa alla Perdita di Peso e al Mantenimento del Benessere con la Dieta Chetogenica

Keto Angelica

1. **Introduzione alla Dieta Chetogenica**: Spiegare cos'è la dieta chetogenica, le sue origini e il principio dietro la produzione di chetoni.

2. **La Scienza del Dimagrimento Chetogenico**: Esaminare come il corpo brucia i grassi invece dei carboidrati e perché questo può portare a una perdita di peso più rapida.

3. **Prepararsi al Successo**: Consigli su come preparare la mente e la casa per iniziare la dieta chetogenica.

4. **Pianificazione dei Pasti e Lista della Spesa**: Guida alla creazione di piani alimentari settimanali e liste della spesa ottimizzate per la dieta chetogenica.

5. **Alimenti da Mangiare e da Evitare**: Un capitolo dettagliato sugli alimenti consentiti nella dieta chetogenica e quelli da evitare.

6. **Ricette Chetogeniche Facili e Veloci**: Fornire ricette semplici per colazione, pranzo, cena e snack che si adattano al piano alimentare chetogenico.

7. **Superare la Keto-flu**: Consigli su come gestire e superare i sintomi iniziali di adattamento alla dieta, noti come keto-flu.

8. **Integrazione e Nutrienti Essenziali**: Discussione sull'importanza degli integratori e come assicurarsi di ottenere tutti i nutrienti necessari.

9. **I Benefici per la Salute oltre la Perdita di Peso**: Esplorare altri benefici per la salute associati alla dieta chetogenica, come il miglioramento della funzione cognitiva e la riduzione dell'infiammazione.

10. **Esercizio Fisico e Keto**: Come adattare il regime di esercizio fisico per massimizzare i risultati di perdita di peso sulla dieta chetogenica.

11. **Gestire la Vita Sociale e la Dieta Chetogenica**: Consigli per mantenere la dieta quando si è fuori casa, al ristorante o in eventi sociali.

12. **Chetogenica e Jejum Intermittente**: Integrazione del jejum intermittente con la dieta chetogenica per accelerare la perdita di peso.

13. **Evitare e Superare i Piatos**: Strategie per continuare a perdere peso quando il progresso sembra fermarsi.

14. **Ascoltare il Proprio Corpo**: L'importanza di prestare attenzione ai segnali del corpo e come adattare la dieta chetogenica alle esigenze individuali.

15. **Storie di Successo**: Raccolta di testimonianze e storie di persone che hanno avuto successo con la dieta chetogenica.

16. **Chetogenica a Lungo Termine**: Considerazioni e consigli per chi vuole seguire la dieta chetogenica come stile di vita a lungo termine.

17. **Rischi e Come Evitarli**: Discussione sui potenziali rischi associati alla dieta chetogenica e come minimizzarli.

18. **Chetogenica per Condizioni Specifiche**: Come la dieta chetogenica può essere adattata o è particolarmente utile per condizioni specifiche come il diabete di tipo 2 o l'epilessia.

19. **Superare gli Ostacoli Mentali**: Strategie per affrontare le sfide mentali ed emotive nel percorso di perdita di peso.

20. **Conclusione e Mantenimento**: Concludere con consigli su come mantenere il peso perso e continuare a vivere uno stile di vita sano post-dimagrimento.

1. Cos'è la Dieta Chetogenica?

La dieta chetogenica, comunemente chiamata "keto", è un regime alimentare basato sull'ingestione elevata di grassi, moderata di proteine e molto bassa di carboidrati. Il principio dietro questa dieta è di indurre il corpo in uno stato di chetosi, un processo metabolico naturale.

Durante la chetosi, il corpo diventa incredibilmente efficiente nel bruciare i grassi per produrre energia. In condizioni normali, i carboidrati consumati vengono convertiti in glucosio, che è la principale fonte di carburante per il corpo e il cervello. Tuttavia, quando l'assunzione di carboidrati è drasticamente ridotta, il fegato inizia a convertire i grassi in acidi grassi e corpi chetonici. Questi corpi chetonici servono come fonte alternativa di energia, in particolare per il cervello.

La riduzione dei carboidrati mette il corpo in uno stato metabolico simile a quello del digiuno, ma senza effettivamente dover digiunare. Questo stato di chetosi nutrizionale è il cuore della dieta chetogenica e ciò che la differenzia da altre diete a basso contenuto di carboidrati.

Origini della Dieta Chetogenica

La dieta chetogenica non è un concetto nuovo. Originariamente sviluppata negli anni '20 del XX secolo per trattare l'epilessia nei bambini, la dieta è stata ampiamente studiata e utilizzata per questa condizione quando altri trattamenti farmacologici non hanno avuto successo. Nel corso degli anni, i ricercatori hanno scoperto che gli effetti stabilizzanti dei corpi chetonici sul cervello erano utili non solo per ridurre le convulsioni ma anche per migliorare altre condizioni neurologiche.

Negli ultimi anni, la dieta chetogenica ha guadagnato popolarità anche tra coloro che cercano di perdere peso rapidamente e in modo efficiente. Le persone hanno trovato successo nella dieta chetogenica non solo per la perdita di peso, ma anche come stile di vita per migliorare la loro salute metabolica generale.

Principio dietro la Produzione di Chetoni

Il corpo umano può utilizzare diverse fonti di energia per mantenere le funzioni vitali e le attività quotidiane. I carboidrati sono la fonte di energia più rapida e preferita perché vengono convertiti facilmente in glucosio, che alimenta le cellule. Tuttavia, in assenza di carboidrati sufficienti, come durante un digiuno prolungato o quando si segue una dieta chetogenica, il corpo passa a un'altra fonte di energia: i grassi.

Il fegato inizia a trasformare i grassi in acidi grassi e corpi chetonici, i quali diventano la principale fonte di energia, specialmente per il cervello, che non può utilizzare direttamente gli acidi grassi come energia ma può utilizzare i corpi chetonici. Questo processo non solo supporta le funzioni vitali e fisiche quando i carboidrati sono limitati, ma favorisce anche una perdita di peso sostenuta e può influenzare positivamente varie condizioni metaboliche.

Concludendo, la dieta chetogenica si basa su principi metabolici ben stabiliti e ha radici profonde nella pratica medica. La comprensione di questi principi aiuterà i lettori a capire come e perché la dieta può essere efficace per loro.

La dieta chetogenica si basa su una rigorosa riduzione dell'assunzione di carboidrati, generalmente limitati a meno di 50 grammi al giorno, a volte fino a meno di 20 grammi. Questo drastico cambiamento nella dieta mira a spostare il carburante primario del corpo dai carboidrati ai grassi. Per la maggior parte delle persone, questo cambio non è immediato; il corpo impiega un periodo di adattamento che può durare da alcuni giorni a qualche settimana, durante il quale può sperimentare vari sintomi di adattamento, spesso definiti come "keto flu" o influenza chetogenica.

Questi sintomi includono affaticamento, mal di testa, irritabilità, difficoltà di concentrazione, e voglie di zuccheri, che sono una reazione naturale del corpo all'assenza del solito apporto di glucosio. Durante questo periodo di transizione, i livelli di insulina calano e il corpo inizia a svuotare le sue riserve di glicogeno, che sono forme di conservazione del glucosio, prevalentemente accumulate nel fegato e nei muscoli. Poiché ogni grammo di glicogeno è legato a circa tre o quattro grammi di acqua nel corpo, la rapida perdita di peso iniziale nella dieta chetogenica è spesso attribuita alla perdita di acqua legata al glicogeno.

Con l'esaurimento delle riserve di glicogeno, il corpo aumenta significativamente la lipolisi, ovvero il processo di scissione dei lipidi, e la formazione di corpi chetonici nel fegato, un fenomeno noto come chetogenesi. I corpi chetonici, tra cui acetoacetato, beta-idrossibutirrato (BHB) e acetone, diventano le principali molecole energetiche che sostituiscono il glucosio. Di questi, il BHB è il corpo chetonico primario che circola nel sangue e che può essere facilmente convertito in energia cellulare, equivalente al glucosio, attraverso i processi cellulari nel mitocondrio, il motore energetico delle cellule.

Il passaggio alla chetogenesi non influisce solo sul metabolismo energetico, ma ha anche effetti sistemici su vari aspetti della salute. Per esempio, la chetogenesi ha dimostrato di ridurre i livelli di insulina e aumentare la sensibilità all'insulina, beneficiando così le persone con resistenza all'insulina o diabete di tipo 2. Allo stesso modo, la produzione di corpi chetonici ha effetti anti-infiammatori e antiossidanti, che possono aiutare a gestire o migliorare le condizioni croniche associate a infiammazioni e stress ossidativo.

Oltre agli aspetti metabolici, la dieta chetogenica ha impatti sul controllo dell'appetito e sulla gestione del peso. I corpi chetonici, in particolare il BHB, hanno dimostrato di influenzare positivamente i livelli di ormoni legati alla fame, come la grelina e il colecistochinino, riducendo la sensazione di fame e aumentando la sazietà. Questo effetto può facilitare il mantenimento di un deficit calorico e supportare la perdita di peso a lungo termine.

La transizione verso una dieta chetogenica richiede anche modifiche nella composizione della dieta, non solo nei macro-nutrienti, ma anche nei micronutrienti. Gli alimenti ricchi di grassi che sono comunemente consumati nella dieta chetogenica includono olii di origine vegetale come l'olio di cocco e di oliva, il burro, il lardo, il pesce grasso come il salmone e il tonno, le uova, le noci, e alcuni formaggi a basso contenuto di carboidrati. Oltre ai grassi, è essenziale incorporare una varietà di verdure a basso contenuto di carboidrati per garantire un adeguato apporto di fibre, vitamine e minerali. Questi includono verdure a foglia verde come spinaci e cavoli, broccoli, cavolfiore, zucchine e peperoni, tra gli altri.

In definitiva, la dieta chetogenica non è solo una moda o una soluzione rapida per la perdita di peso, ma una trasformazione profonda delle abitudini alimentari che può avere effetti duraturi e benefici sulla salute metabolica, neurologica e fisica. La scienza dietro la produzione di chetoni e la loro utilizzazione come fonte primaria di energia rappresenta una fascinante rivisitazione delle capacità metaboliche umane, offrendo una nuova prospettiva sulle potenzialità del corpo umano quando adeguatamente nutrito e gestito.

Continuando l'esplorazione della dieta chetogenica, è interessante notare come questa dieta influenzi anche il sistema endocrino. Le modifiche metaboliche indotte dalla chetogenesi hanno un impatto diretto sugli ormoni. Ad esempio, la chetogenesi riduce significativamente i livelli di insulina, un ormone anabolico che regola il metabolismo dei carboidrati e il deposito di grassi. A lungo termine, questa riduzione dell'insulina può migliorare la sensibilità insulinica, contribuendo a ridurre il rischio di sviluppare diabete di tipo 2 e altre malattie metaboliche.

Un'altra dimensione interessante della dieta chetogenica è il suo impatto sulla lezione dell'ormone della crescita (GH) e sui corticosteroidi, che sono coinvolti nella regolazione del metabolismo dei grassi e delle proteine, nonché nella risposta allo stress e nell'infiammazione. Studi hanno mostrato che la dieta chetogenica può influenzare positivamente la secrezione di GH, che ha effetti benefici sul mantenimento della massa muscolare e sul metabolismo del grasso, contribuendo alla composizione corporea ottimale e al rafforzamento delle funzioni immunitarie.

La dieta chetogenica modifica anche il microbioma intestinale. Questi cambiamenti nel microbioma possono avere effetti profondi sulla salute generale, dato che la flora intestinale gioca un ruolo cruciale nella digestione, nella produzione di vitamine e nella protezione contro i patogeni. La riduzione dei carboidrati può diminuire la quantità di certi batteri fermentanti i carboidrati, mentre l'incremento del consumo di grassi può favorire altri tipi di batteri benefici. Queste modifiche possono contribuire a migliorare la permeabilità intestinale e ridurre le condizioni di infiammazione sistemica.

Dal punto di vista neurologico, la dieta chetogenica è stata studiata per i suoi effetti protettivi sul cervello. I corpi chetonici sono neuroprotettivi, riducono lo stress ossidativo e migliorano la funzione dei mitocondri nelle cellule cerebrali. Questo può spiegare perché la dieta chetogenica è efficace non solo nell'epilessia, ma anche in altre condizioni neurologiche come l'Alzheimer e il Parkinson. La ricerca suggerisce che i corpi chetonici possono migliorare la funzione cognitiva e persino rallentare la progressione di alcune malattie neurodegenerative.

Sul fronte della longevità e della prevenzione delle malattie, la dieta chetogenica presenta interessanti implicazioni. La restrizione calorica, che è spesso una conseguenza naturale dell'adozione di una dieta chetogenica a causa della diminuita sensazione di fame e dell'aumentata sazietà provocata dai corpi chetonici, è stata associata in numerosi studi alla longevità e alla riduzione dell'incidenza di malattie croniche. Inoltre, il mantenimento di uno stato di chetosi lieve può ridurre l'infiammazione, un fattore di rischio comune per molte malattie croniche, tra cui le malattie cardiovascolari e il cancro.

L'impatto della dieta chetogenica sul metabolismo lipidico è altrettanto notevole. Mentre i livelli di colesterolo LDL ("cattivo") possono aumentare in alcuni individui, molti sperimentano un aumento del colesterolo HDL ("buono") e una riduzione dei trigliceridi. Questo miglioramento nel profilo lipidico può contribuire a un minor rischio di malattie cardiovascolari. Tuttavia, è importante monitorare questi cambiamenti attraverso regolari controlli medici per assicurarsi che la dieta sia bilanciata e personalizzata in base alle esigenze individuali di salute.

In sintesi, l'approccio multidimensionale della dieta chetogenica nel modulare vari aspetti del metabolismo umano non solo fornisce una via efficace per la perdita di peso e il controllo metabolico, ma offre anche potenziali benefici nel contesto di un'ampia varietà di condizioni patologiche e nella promozione di una maggiore longevità e benessere generale. Le ricerche continuano a esplorare questi effetti, ampliando la comprensione di come le modificazioni dietetiche possono influenzare profondamente la salute umana oltre il semplice bilanciamento calorico.

Proseguendo l'analisi degli effetti della dieta chetogenica, è importante considerare come questa dieta possa influenzare la gestione di alcune condizioni specifiche, come il sindrome dell'ovaio policistico (PCOS). Studi hanno dimostrato che la chetogenesi può migliorare la sensibilità all'insulina, un fattore chiave nella patogenesi del PCOS, riducendo così i sintomi e migliorando la fertilità nelle donne affette. Ciò è dovuto principalmente alla diminuzione dei livelli di insulina che contribuisce a normalizzare i livelli ormonali, riducendo i sintomi come l'irsutismo e la disfunzione ovarica.

Oltre a influenzare le condizioni metaboliche e endocrine, la dieta chetogenica può anche avere implicazioni significative nella gestione dell'infiammazione e delle malattie autoimmuni. Si ritiene che i corpi chetonici abbiano proprietà anti-infiammatorie, in quanto inibiscono vie infiammatorie specifiche e riducono la produzione di citochine infiammatorie. Per esempio, il beta-idrossibutirrato (BHB) ha mostrato di inibire i complessi NLRP3 inflammasome, che sono coinvolti in molte malattie infiammatorie croniche, come l'artrite e l'aterosclerosi.

Per quanto riguarda il sistema immunitario, la dieta chetogenica sembra esercitare effetti complessi. Da una parte, riduce alcuni aspetti dell'infiammazione sistemica, che può essere benefico in condizioni di iperattività immunitaria come le malattie autoimmuni. Dall'altra, la chetosi modula la funzione dei linfociti T, che sono cruciali per la risposta immunitaria adattativa. Questo può avere implicazioni nella resistenza alle infezioni o nella risposta ai vaccini, quindi è essenziale una comprensione approfondita di questi meccanismi per gestire adeguatamente la dieta in individui con specifiche esigenze immunitarie.

La dieta chetogenica influisce anche sulle funzioni cognitive e sull'umore. Alcuni studi suggeriscono che i corpi chetonici possono migliorare la funzionalità cognitiva e ridurre i sintomi di condizioni psichiatriche come l'ansia e la depressione. La teoria è che i corpi chetonici forniscono una fonte di energia più stabile per il cervello, riducendo le fluttuazioni del glucosio che possono influenzare l'umore e le funzioni cognitive.

In ambito sportivo, la dieta chetogenica è stata oggetto di studi per valutare il suo impatto sulle prestazioni atletiche. Sebbene possa esserci una diminuzione delle prestazioni in attività ad alta intensità che dipendono fortemente dai carboidrati come fonte di energia rapida, alcuni atleti di resistenza possono beneficiare di un aumento della capacità di utilizzare i grassi come fonte di energia, potenzialmente migliorando la performance in esercizi di lunga durata.

La sostenibilità a lungo termine della dieta chetogenica è un altro tema di grande interesse. Mentre alcuni individui trovano che una rigorosa aderenza alla dieta chetogenica sia sostenibile e benefica, altri possono incontrare difficoltà nel mantenere un regime così restrittivo nel tempo. Questo porta a considerare varianti più flessibili della dieta, come la dieta cheto-ciclica o la dieta cheto-targetizzata, che permettono un'integrazione periodica di carboidrati per supportare specifiche esigenze, come gli allenamenti intensivi o per migliorare la tollerabilità della dieta.

Con la crescente popolarità della dieta chetogenica, la ricerca continua a espandersi, offrendo nuove prospettive sulle sue potenziali applicazioni terapeutiche e preventive. Esaminando in modo critico sia i benefici che i possibili rischi, si può ottenere un quadro più equilibrato su come questa dieta possa essere adattata e personalizzata per rispondere alle diverse esigenze individuali e promuovere la salute e il benessere a lungo termine. La dieta chetogenica non è solo un fenomeno di perdita di peso, ma un profondo intervento metabolico con ramificazioni che toccano molti aspetti della fisiologia umana.

Approfondendo ulteriormente gli effetti della dieta chetogenica, è fondamentale esplorare come questa influenzi la salute cardiovascolare. Tradizionalmente, c'è stata una certa preoccupazione riguardo all'elevato apporto di grassi saturi e il loro impatto sui livelli di colesterolo nel sangue. Tuttavia, studi recenti suggeriscono che il profilo lipidico può effettivamente migliorare in molti individui che seguono la dieta chetogenica. Si è osservato che, nonostante l'aumento del consumo di grassi saturi, molti seguaci della dieta esperiscono una diminuzione dei trigliceridi e un aumento del colesterolo HDL, conosciuto come il "colesterolo buono". Inoltre, il colesterolo LDL, o "colesterolo cattivo", tende a cambiare dalla forma piccola e densa, che è più aterogenica, a una forma più grande e fluttuante, considerata meno dannosa.

Inoltre, la chetogenesi ha un impatto sul metabolismo degli acidi grassi che può portare a un miglioramento nella funzione mitocondriale. Questo è particolarmente rilevante per il cuore, un organo che richiede grandi quantità di energia e si avvale ampiamente dei mitocondri per soddisfare questo bisogno. Studi hanno indicato che la dieta chetogenica può aumentare il numero di mitocondri per cellula cardiaca, migliorando così la funzionalità cardiaca e potenzialmente proteggendo contro alcune forme di cardiopatia.

L'effetto della dieta chetogenica sulla pressione sanguigna è un altro ambito di interesse. Numerosi partecipanti riportano una riduzione della pressione arteriosa quando aderiscono a un regime chetogenico. Questo può essere parzialmente attribuito alla perdita di peso corporeo, ma anche a una riduzione dell'infiammazione sistemica e a miglioramenti nella sensibilità all'insulina, che sono effetti collaterali comuni della dieta.

Uno degli aspetti meno discussi della dieta chetogenica è il suo potenziale impatto sull'osso. Esistono preoccupazioni che una restrizione prolungata di carboidrati possa portare a una riduzione dell'assorbimento di minerali importanti, come il calcio, aumentando così il rischio di osteoporosi. Tuttavia, la ricerca è ancora inconcludente in questo settore, e alcune evidenze suggeriscono che un'adeguata integrazione e la scelta di fonti alimentari ricche di nutrienti possono mitigare questi rischi.

La questione della sostenibilità ambientale della dieta chetogenica è un'altra considerazione importante. Di solito, una dieta ricca di grassi animali e proteine può avere un impatto ambientale maggiore rispetto a diete più basate su carboidrati e alimenti vegetali. Tuttavia, con l'adozione crescente di fonti di grassi e proteine più sostenibili, come il pesce pescato in modo sostenibile, il pollame allevato a terra e i prodotti lattiero-caseari da fonti responsabili, è possibile seguire una dieta chetogenica con una maggiore consapevolezza ecologica.

La dieta chetogenica può anche influenzare il sistema gastrointestinale. La riduzione del consumo di carboidrati e l'incremento dell'assunzione di grassi possono alterare la motilità intestinale e la composizione della flora intestinale. Alcuni seguaci della dieta possono sperimentare problemi come stitichezza o diarrea nelle fasi iniziali, anche se questi problemi possono spesso essere gestiti con adeguate modifiche dietetiche, come l'aumento dell'assunzione di fibre attraverso verdure a basso contenuto di carboidrati e un adeguato apporto idrico.

Mentre la ricerca continua a evolversi, è chiaro che la dieta chetogenica non è solo un semplice strumento per la perdita di peso, ma una profonda modifica dietetica con vasti effetti metabolici e fisiologici. Le implicazioni a lungo termine di tali cambiamenti richiedono ulteriori studi e un'attenta considerazione clinica, soprattutto quando la dieta è seguita per periodi prolungati o da popolazioni specifiche con esigenze mediche particolari. Con la crescente popolarità e l'accettazione della dieta chetogenica come un potenziale cambiamento dello stile di vita oltre che come un intervento dietetico, è essenziale che sia i professionisti della salute sia gli individui siano informati e consapevoli degli aggiornamenti continui nella ricerca e delle migliori pratiche per implementare questo regime alimentare in modo sicuro ed efficace.

Concludendo l'ampia discussione sulla dieta chetogenica, è essenziale riconoscere che, nonostante i numerosi benefici potenziali e gli effetti positivi documentati, la dieta chetogenica richiede una considerazione attenta e una pianificazione meticolosa per essere implementata in modo sicuro ed efficace.

Questo regime alimentare non è adatto a tutti e può variare significativamente nei suoi effetti da individuo a individuo, richiedendo quindi un approccio personalizzato.

Implicazioni Nutrizionali

La dieta chetogenica limita severamente l'assunzione di carboidrati, che può portare a carenze nutrizionali se non gestita correttamente. Nutrienti essenziali come le fibre, le vitamine e i minerali trovati comunemente in frutta, verdura e cereali integrali possono essere insufficienti in questa dieta. Pertanto, è cruciale includere varietà di alimenti chetogenici che siano ricchi di nutrienti e considerare la supplementazione per prevenire carenze. Questi includono la scelta di verdure a foglia verde, semi e noci, e l'utilizzo di integratori specifici come vitamina D, magnesio e omega-3.

Monitoraggio Medico

Data l'intensa modificazione del macronutriente, il monitoraggio medico è raccomandato, specialmente per coloro con condizioni preesistenti come il diabete di tipo 2, malattie cardiache o disturbi alimentari. La supervisione di un professionista della salute può aiutare a mitigare i rischi potenziali come l'alterazione dei livelli di lipidi nel sangue, l'ipoglicemia, o l'aggravamento di condizioni renali o epatiche.

Effetti a Lungo Termine

Gli effetti a lungo termine della dieta chetogenica rimangono un'area attiva di ricerca. Mentre alcuni studi suggeriscono benefici per la gestione di condizioni come l'epilessia, il diabete e alcune malattie neurodegenerative, i potenziali rischi associati a una restrizione prolungata di carboidrati richiedono ulteriori indagini. È importante valutare i benefici a breve termine in rapporto agli effetti a lungo termine, soprattutto per quanto riguarda la salute ossea, renale e cardiovascolare.

Sostenibilità e Qualità della Vita

La sostenibilità di qualsiasi dieta dipende dalla sua capacità di essere integrata in uno stile di vita a lungo termine. Per molti, la dieta chetogenica può risultare troppo restrittiva, portando a difficoltà nel mantenere l'aderenza nel tempo. Considerazioni sulla qualità della vita, inclusi il piacere del cibo e la gestione sociale dei pasti, sono cruciali. È essenziale che la dieta chetogenica non solo soddisfi le esigenze metaboliche ma anche quelle psicologiche e sociali dell'individuo.

Approccio Personalizzato e Flessibile

Infine, la personalizzazione della dieta chetogenica è fondamentale. Adattamenti come la dieta cheto-ciclica o la dieta cheto-targetizzata possono offrire un equilibrio tra gli effetti benefici della chetosi e la flessibilità alimentare, permettendo agli individui di sperimentare i benefici della chetogenesi senza gli svantaggi di un regime estremamente rigido.

In conclusione, la dieta chetogenica offre un approccio unico e potente alla nutrizione che può avere profondi effetti sulla salute e sul benessere. Tuttavia, deve essere adottata con cautela, guidata dalla conoscenza e dal supporto professionale, e con una chiara comprensione dei propri obiettivi di salute e delle esigenze personali. Con la giusta implementazione, può essere uno strumento trasformativo nel percorso di salute di un individuo, ma deve essere considerato come parte di un approccio olistico al benessere.

2. La Scienza del Dimagrimento Chetogenico: Esaminare come il corpo brucia i grassi invece dei carboidrati e perché questo può portare a una perdita di peso più rapida.

2. La Scienza del Dimagrimento Chetogenico

La dieta chetogenica, con il suo focus sulla limitazione dell'assunzione di carboidrati e sulla promozione del consumo di grassi, induce nel corpo un cambiamento radicale nel modo in cui vengono utilizzate le fonti energetiche, conducendo a una perdita di peso rapida ed efficace. Per comprendere il processo alla base del dimagrimento chetogenico, è essenziale esaminare diversi aspetti biochimici e metabolici.

Passaggio da Carboidrati a Grassi come Principale Fonte di Energia

Il corpo umano normalmente utilizza i carboidrati come sua principale fonte di energia. I carboidrati vengono convertiti in glucosio, il quale viene poi trasportato nel sangue e utilizzato dalle cellule per produrre energia tramite un processo chiamato glicolisi. L'eccesso di glucosio viene immagazzinato sotto forma di glicogeno nei muscoli e nel fegato, o convertito in grasso per essere conservato nei tessuti adiposi.

Quando l'assunzione di carboidrati è drasticamente ridotta, come nella dieta chetogenica, le scorte di glicogeno si esauriscono rapidamente, costringendo il corpo a cercare un'alternativa energetica. In assenza di glucosio sufficiente, il fegato inizia a convertire i grassi in acidi grassi e corpi chetonici, processo noto come chetogenesi. I corpi chetonici servono come fonte alternativa di energia, soprattutto per il cervello, che non può utilizzare direttamente gli acidi grassi come combustibile.

Effetti della Chetogenesi sulla Perdita di Peso

1. **Aumento del Metabolismo dei Grassi**: Quando il corpo entra in chetosi, il tasso al quale i grassi vengono bruciati aumenta significativamente. Gli acidi grassi sono estratti dai depositi di grasso e metabolizzati in corpi chetonici, un processo che richiede più energia rispetto alla semplice conversione dei carboidrati in glucosio. Questo aumento del dispendio energetico contribuisce alla perdita di peso.

2. **Riduzione dell'Appetito**: I corpi chetonici hanno un effetto soppressivo sull'appetito. Studi hanno mostrato che la chetosi modula diversi ormoni che influenzano la fame, inclusi ghrelin e leptin, riducendo la sensazione di fame e aumentando la sensazione di pienezza. Questo può portare a una riduzione spontanea dell'assunzione calorica, facilitando ulteriormente la perdita di peso.

3. **Perdita di Peso Iniziale Rapida**: Nei primi giorni di dieta chetogenica, il peso perso è in gran parte dovuto alla perdita di acqua. Come accennato, il glicogeno legato all'acqua viene utilizzato rapidamente, e l'acqua viene escreta. Questa rapida perdita di peso può essere motivante per coloro che iniziano una dieta.

4. **Efficienza Metabolica**: Alcuni studi suggeriscono che la dieta chetogenica può aumentare la spesa energetica totale, ovvero il numero di calorie bruciate in riposo. Questo fenomeno, sebbene sia soggetto a dibattito scientifico, potrebbe contribuire ulteriormente al deficit calorico e quindi alla perdita di peso.

5. **Preservazione della Massa Muscolare**: A differenza di molte diete a basso contenuto calorico, la dieta chetogenica tende a preservare la massa muscolare magra, in parte a causa dell'effetto anti-catabolico dei corpi chetonici e del moderato apporto di proteine.

Mantenere la massa muscolare è cruciale durante la perdita di peso, poiché il tessuto muscolare brucia più calorie del tessuto grasso, contribuendo a un metabolismo più attivo.

In conclusione, la dieta chetogenica sfrutta una serie di processi metabolici e fisiologici per ridurre il peso corporeo. Attraverso la chetogenesi, la soppressione dell'appetito, l'efficienza energetica migliorata e la preservazione della massa muscolare, questa dieta offre un metodo efficace per la perdita di peso rapida. Tuttavia, è importante notare che, nonostante i suoi benefici, la dieta chetogenica dovrebbe essere seguita sotto la supervisione di professionisti per assicurarsi che sia equilibrata e adatta alle esigenze individuali di salute.

Continuando l'analisi degli effetti della dieta chetogenica sulla perdita di peso, è importante esplorare altri meccanismi attraverso i quali questa dieta può influenzare il metabolismo e il benessere generale, contribuendo ulteriormente al dimagrimento.

Adattamento Metabolico e Uso dei Grassi

Il corpo umano è estremamente adattabile alle diverse fonti di energia disponibili. Quando i carboidrati sono limitati e il corpo entra in chetosi, si verifica un adattamento metabolico nel quale il fegato produce corpi chetonici a un ritmo accelerato. Questo processo non solo fornisce energia ai tessuti che possono utilizzare i chetoni (come il cervello e il cuore) ma aiuta anche a stabilizzare i livelli di glucosio nel sangue mantenendo una bassa secrezione di insulina. Questa bassa attività insulinica è cruciale, in quanto l'insulina è un ormone anabolico che promuove la sintesi dei grassi e impedisce la loro degradazione.

Effetto Termogenico dei Cibi

La dieta chetogenica è anche caratterizzata da un alto consumo di proteine, che hanno un effetto termogenico più elevato rispetto ai carboidrati e ai grassi. Ciò significa che il corpo utilizza più energia per digerire, assorbire e metabolizzare le proteine rispetto agli altri macronutrienti. Questo aumento del dispendio energetico può contribuire ulteriormente al deficit calorico necessario per la perdita di peso.

Riduzione dell'Infiammazione

Gli effetti anti-infiammatori della dieta chetogenica sono un altro fattore che può contribuire al successo della perdita di peso. L'infiammazione cronica è legata a un aumento del rischio di obesità, e ridurre l'infiammazione attraverso la dieta può aiutare a migliorare il metabolismo e la funzione degli adipociti, le cellule del tessuto grasso che immagazzinano energia sotto forma di grasso. Inoltre, la riduzione dell'infiammazione può migliorare la mobilità e ridurre il dolore, rendendo più facile per le persone aumentare l'attività fisica, un altro componente chiave nella perdita di peso.

Miglioramento della Salute Intestinale

Il cambiamento nella composizione della dieta può anche influenzare la salute intestinale. Anche se la riduzione dell'assunzione di fibre può sembrare problematica, alcuni trovano che la dieta chetogenica riduce i sintomi di disturbi gastrointestinali come la sindrome dell'intestino irritabile. Inoltre, il cambiamento nella fermentazione intestinale dovuto alla riduzione dei carboidrati può diminuire la produzione di gas e gonfiore, migliorando la qualità della vita e potenzialmente contribuendo alla percezione di un addome più piatto.

Effetti sulla Retenzione Idrica

La dieta chetogenica favorisce una significativa perdita di acqua corporea. La riduzione dei carboidrati porta alla diminuzione delle riserve di glicogeno, ogni grammo del quale è associato a circa tre grammi di acqua. Questa riduzione del peso dell'acqua può fornire risultati rapidi sulla bilancia, motivando ulteriormente gli individui a continuare la dieta. Benché questa non sia una perdita di massa grassa, può avere effetti psicologici positivi.

Modulazione dell'Asse Ipotalamo-Ipofisi

La dieta chetogenica può anche modulare l'asse ipotalamo-ipofisi, una parte del cervello responsabile della regolazione di molti ormoni nel corpo. Questo può influenzare la produzione di ormoni come il cortisolo e l'ormone della crescita, che hanno un impatto diretto sul metabolismo del corpo, sull'appetito e sulle capacità di recupero e crescita muscolare. La gestione dei livelli di cortisolo, in particolare, può ridurre lo stress e aiutare a prevenire l'accumulo di grasso viscerale, che è spesso stimolato da alti livelli cronici di stress.

In sintesi, la dieta chetogenica non solo cambia la fonte energetica primaria del corpo da carboidrati a grassi, ma interviene anche in numerosi altri processi biologici che possono potenziare la perdita di peso e migliorare la salute complessiva. Tuttavia, è essenziale che questa dieta sia ben pianificata e monitorata per evitare carenze nutrizionali e per assicurare che i benefici superino i possibili rischi associati a un tale regime alimentare.

Proseguendo nell'esplorazione della scienza dietro il dimagrimento chetogenico, ci sono ulteriori aspetti da considerare che influenzano la perdita di peso e il benessere complessivo quando si adotta questa dieta.

Impatto sul Metabolismo Lipidico

La dieta chetogenica trasforma il metabolismo lipidico. Normalmente, i lipidi vengono immagazzinati nel corpo come trigliceridi e utilizzati come fonte secondaria di energia dopo i carboidrati. Tuttavia, in stato di chetosi, i lipidi diventano la principale fonte di energia. Questo processo non solo aiuta a ridurre le riserve di grasso corporeo, ma può anche migliorare i parametri lipidici nel sangue, come la riduzione dei trigliceridi e l'aumento del colesterolo HDL. Alcuni studi suggeriscono che la chetogenesi può anche influenzare la dimensione e la composizione delle particelle di LDL, rendendole meno aterogene.

Riduzione del Carico Glicemico

Un altro vantaggio significativo della dieta chetogenica è la riduzione del carico glicemico, che è la quantità totale di glucosio che entra nel sangue dopo i pasti. Alimenti ricchi di carboidrati elevano rapidamente i livelli di glucosio nel sangue e richiedono una grande secrezione di insulina per facilitare l'assorbimento del glucosio nelle cellule. Riducendo l'ingestione di carboidrati, la dieta chetogenica mantiene i livelli di glucosio nel sangue relativamente bassi e stabili, il che può prevenire picchi e cali di energia e può aiutare a controllare l'appetito.

Miglioramento della Resistenza all'Insulina

La dieta chetogenica può essere particolarmente efficace per le persone con resistenza all'insulina, che è spesso un precursore del diabete tipo 2. Al ridurre l'assunzione di carboidrati, la necessità del corpo di produrre insulina diminuisce, migliorando la sensibilità all'insulina e permettendo al corpo di gestire meglio il glucosio. Questo non solo aiuta nella gestione del peso, ma può anche ridurre il rischio di sviluppare diabete e altre complicazioni metaboliche correlate.

Effetti sul Sistema Nervoso Centrale

La chetosi ha dimostrato di avere effetti benefici anche sul sistema nervoso centrale. I corpi chetonici sono noti per avere proprietà neuroprotettive e possono migliorare la funzione cerebrale. Ciò è particolarmente evidente in condizioni neurologiche come l'epilessia, per la quale la dieta chetogenica è stata originariamente sviluppata. Questi effetti possono anche tradursi in miglioramenti nell'umore e nella cognizione, potenzialmente a causa della riduzione delle fluttuazioni del glucosio nel sangue e dell'effetto stabilizzante sui neurotrasmettitori.

Adattamento Fisiologico a Lungo Termine

Il corpo umano passa attraverso un adattamento fisiologico significativo durante la transizione a una dieta chetogenica. Oltre alla chetosi, il corpo può aumentare l'efficienza nell'assimilazione e nell'utilizzo dei grassi come combustibile. Questo cambiamento può richiedere diverse settimane e durante questo periodo, gli individui possono sperimentare sintomi come stanchezza, mal di testa e irritabilità, comunemente noti come "influenza chetogenica". Tuttavia, una volta che il corpo si adatta, molti riportano un aumento dell'energia e una migliore stabilità dell'umore.

Considerazioni Nutrizionali

Infine, è essenziale mantenere un focus sulle considerazioni nutrizionali quando si segue una dieta chetogenica. Mentre si limitano i carboidrati, è importante garantire un'adeguata assunzione di nutrienti essenziali. Ciò include un adeguato apporto di fibra, che può essere carente in una dieta a basso contenuto di carboidrati. Le verdure a basso contenuto di carboidrati, i semi e alcune noci possono fornire sia fibre che altri nutrienti vitali come vitamine e minerali essenziali. Oltre alla fibra, la dieta chetogenica deve essere bilanciata con un'adeguata assunzione di grassi sani, come quelli provenienti dagli oli di pesce, avocado, e oli vegetali non raffinati, che contribuiscono a una salute ottimale del cuore e riducono l'infiammazione.

Effetti Ormonali della Dieta Chetogenica

La dieta chetogenica influisce anche sugli ormoni oltre all'insulina. Ad esempio, può influenzare il funzionamento degli ormoni tiroidei, che sono cruciali per il metabolismo. Alcuni studi indicano che la dieta chetogenica può ridurre l'attività tiroidea, il che potrebbe rallentare il metabolismo nel tempo. Questa è una delle ragioni per cui la supervisione medica è cruciale quando si segue una dieta chetogenica, specialmente se mantenuta per lunghi periodi.

Riduzione della Risposta Infiammatoria

Gli effetti anti-infiammatori dei corpi chetonici, in particolare del beta-idrossibutirrato, possono giocare un ruolo significativo nel controllo delle condizioni infiammatorie croniche. Ridurre l'infiammazione può non solo aiutare con malattie autoimmuni e condizioni infiammatorie come l'artrite, ma può anche migliorare la funzione generale del metabolismo e ridurre il rischio di malattie metaboliche croniche.

Sostenibilità della Dieta Chetogenica

Mentre la dieta chetogenica può offrire benefici significativi per la perdita di peso e la gestione metabolica, la sua sostenibilità a lungo termine è un argomento di dibattito. Le restrizioni severe sui carboidrati possono rendere difficile mantenere questa dieta per alcuni individui, soprattutto considerando le sfide sociali e pratiche. Adattamenti come la dieta cheto-ciclica, che permette periodi di reintroduzione di carboidrati, possono aiutare a rendere la dieta più gestibile a lungo termine.

Impatto sulla Salute Mentale

La chetogenesi ha mostrato effetti positivi sulla salute mentale in alcuni studi, migliorando sintomi di depressione e ansia. Si ritiene che i corpi chetonici possano migliorare la neuroplasticità del cervello - la capacità delle cellule nervose di adattarsi, che può influenzare positivamente la salute mentale.

Biodisponibilità e Utilizzo di Nutrienti

Importante è anche considerare come la dieta chetogenica possa influenzare la biodisponibilità di certi nutrienti. Ad esempio, la riduzione dell'assunzione di carboidrati può influenzare l'assorbimento del calcio e del magnesio, importanti per la salute ossea e muscolare. La supplementazione e una scelta attenta degli alimenti sono cruciali per prevenire carenze.

Personalizzazione della Dieta

Data la varietà nella risposta individuale alla dieta chetogenica, personalizzare la dieta in base alle esigenze metaboliche, preferenze alimentari, e obiettivi di salute di ogni persona è fondamentale. Un nutrizionista o un medico possono aiutare a adattare la dieta chetogenica per massimizzare i suoi benefici e minimizzare i rischi potenziali.

In ultima analisi, la dieta chetogenica è più di una semplice strategia per la perdita di peso; è un cambiamento complesso nel consumo di energia che può avere ampi effetti sul corpo e sulla mente. Ogni aspetto della dieta deve essere attentamente considerato e monitorato per garantire che gli effetti positivi superino le possibili complicazioni o carenze. Continuando a esplorare e comprendere i meccanismi sottostanti e gli effetti a lungo termine della dieta chetogenica, possiamo ottimizzare il suo uso come strumento per migliorare la salute e il benessere.

Continuando con l'esplorazione approfondita degli effetti e delle implicazioni della dieta chetogenica, è essenziale considerare anche come questa influenzi la regolazione dell'equilibrio elettrolitico nel corpo. A causa della ridotta assunzione di carboidrati e del conseguente esaurimento delle riserve di glicogeno, si verifica una perdita significativa di elettroliti come sodio, potassio e magnesio, che sono essenziali per molte funzioni biologiche, inclusa la regolazione della pressione arteriosa, il funzionamento muscolare e nervoso, e l'equilibrio dei fluidi. Questo può portare a sintomi come crampi, stanchezza e, in casi estremi, disidratazione. Pertanto, chi segue la dieta chetogenica potrebbe aver bisogno di integrare la propria alimentazione con questi elettroliti per mantenere un equilibrio adeguato e prevenire complicazioni.

Impatto sulla Performance Atletica

Un altro aspetto rilevante della dieta chetogenica è il suo impatto sulla performance atletica. Mentre alcuni atleti possono trarre beneficio dall'aumentata capacità di bruciare grassi come fonte di energia, soprattutto in sport di resistenza, altri possono sperimentare una diminuzione delle prestazioni in sport che richiedono esplosività e sprint veloci, a causa della limitata disponibilità di carboidrati, che sono una fonte di energia rapida. È importante per gli atleti che considerano la dieta chetogenica lavorare con professionisti del settore sportivo e della nutrizione per personalizzare il loro regime alimentare in modo da ottimizzare sia il loro apporto di energia sia le loro prestazioni sportive.

Effetti sul Sonno

Inoltre, l'impatto della dieta chetogenica sul sonno è un campo di studio intrigante. Alcuni report suggeriscono che l'adattamento a una dieta a basso contenuto di carboidrati può inizialmente disturbare il sonno, potenzialmente a causa delle alterazioni nei livelli di serotonina e melatonina, che sono regolati dai carboidrati. Tuttavia, una volta che il corpo si adatta, molti riportano un miglioramento nella qualità del sonno, probabilmente dovuto alla stabilizzazione dei livelli di zucchero nel sangue durante la notte.

Potenziale Impatto sul Sistema Immunitario

L'influenza della dieta chetogenica sul sistema immunitario è un altro ambito di ricerca attiva. In alcuni studi, i corpi chetonici hanno mostrato proprietà immunomodulatorie, che possono rafforzare la risposta immunitaria contro le infezioni virali e batteriche. Tuttavia, una restrizione prolungata di carboidrati potrebbe anche sopprimere alcune funzioni immunitarie, quindi è essenziale valutare attentamente come la dieta influisce sul sistema immunitario individuale.

Gestione della Sindrome Metabolica e Altre Malattie Croniche

La dieta chetogenica ha mostrato benefici promettenti nella gestione della sindrome metabolica, un insieme di condizioni che include ipertensione, iperglicemia, eccesso di grasso corporeo intorno alla vita e livelli anormali di colesterolo o trigliceridi. Questi effetti sono principalmente dovuti alla perdita di peso, miglioramento della sensibilità all'insulina e riduzione dei livelli di trigliceridi. Inoltre, i benefici anti-infiammatori dei corpi chetonici possono contribuire a mitigare alcuni aspetti di altre malattie croniche, come le malattie cardiovascolari e il diabete di tipo 2, sebbene la ricerca a lungo termine sia ancora necessaria per capire appieno questi impatti.

Considerazioni Pratiche e Psicologiche

Dal punto di vista pratico e psicologico, adottare e mantenere una dieta chetogenica può essere una sfida significativa. Le restrizioni alimentari possono influenzare le interazioni sociali e la possibilità di godere di pasti in compagnia. Inoltre, la gestione continua del proprio apporto di carboidrati e la necessità di pianificare i pasti possono risultare onerose per alcuni individui. La motivazione, il supporto sociale e l'accesso a risorse educative adeguate sono cruciali per chiunque consideri questa dieta come un'opzione a lungo termine.

La dieta chetogenica continua ad essere un argomento di grande interesse sia nella ricerca scientifica sia nella pratica clinica, con un crescente corpo di letteratura che esplora i suoi effetti e potenziali benefici. Mentre offre possibilità promettenti per la perdita di peso e il controllo di varie condizioni di salute, è fondamentale approcciarsi alla chetogenesi con un piano ben considerato e sotto la guida di professionisti della salute per garantire che sia sicura, efficace e sostenibile per la salute individuale a lungo termine.

Continuando con l'approfondimento sugli effetti e sulle dinamiche della dieta chetogenica, è rilevante considerare ulteriormente come questo stile alimentare influenzi vari aspetti del metabolismo e della salute generale oltre quanto già discusso.

Impatti sulla Salute Cardiovascolare a Lungo Termine

Mentre la dieta chetogenica può offrire miglioramenti immediati nei parametri come i livelli di trigliceridi e colesterolo HDL, la questione degli effetti a lungo termine sulla salute cardiovascolare rimane complessa. Alcuni studi hanno indicato potenziali rischi associati a un aumentato apporto di grassi saturi, che potrebbero influenzare negativamente i livelli di colesterolo LDL e aumentare il rischio di malattie cardiovascolari. Tuttavia, altri ricerche suggeriscono che la dimensione e la densità delle particelle di LDL, che sono più rilevanti per il rischio cardiovascolare, possono migliorare con una dieta chetogenica. La necessità di una valutazione personalizzata diventa pertanto essenziale, considerando il profilo lipidico individuale e altri fattori di rischio cardiovascolare quando si segue una dieta chetogenica.

Interazione con Farmaci

Un altro aspetto importante riguarda l'interazione della dieta chetogenica con vari farmaci, specialmente per coloro che sono trattati per il diabete o per l'ipertensione. La dieta chetogenica può ridurre significativamente il bisogno di certi farmaci ipoglicemizzanti o antipertensivi a causa della sua efficacia nel migliorare la sensibilità all'insulina e abbassare la pressione sanguigna. Questo richiede un attento monitoraggio medico per evitare ipoglicemia o ipotensione, condizioni che possono emergere con cambiamenti rapidi nell'alimentazione e nella gestione farmacologica.

Impatto sulla Longevità

La ricerca sull'impatto della dieta chetogenica sulla longevità è ancora agli inizi, ma alcune teorie suggeriscono che la riduzione dell'infiammazione sistemica e la diminuzione dello stress ossidativo potrebbero contribuire a un allungamento della vita. Gli effetti della chetosi sui meccanismi cellulari come l'autofagia, un processo di pulizia cellulare che rimuove le proteine danneggiate e i detriti cellulari, potrebbero anche giocare un ruolo nella prevenzione delle malattie legate all'età e nel promuovere una maggiore longevità.

Regolazione dell'Equilibrio Ormonale

Approfondendo gli effetti ormonali, la dieta chetogenica può influenzare diversi assi ormonali oltre a quello insulinico. Ad esempio, la regolazione degli ormoni sessuali — estrogeni, progesterone e testosterone — può essere influenzata dalla dieta chetogenica, a volte migliorando condizioni come la sindrome dell'ovaio policistico (PCOS) nelle donne o alterando i livelli di testosterone negli uomini. La comprensione di come la dieta chetogenica modula questi ormoni è fondamentale per prevenire e gestire potenziali effetti collaterali o per ottimizzare gli effetti benefici.

Effetti sulla Composizione Corporea

Oltre alla perdita di peso, la dieta chetogenica può modificare in modo significativo la composizione corporea. Riducendo l'assunzione di carboidrati e aumentando quella di grassi e proteine, il corpo può non solo bruciare più grassi ma anche preservare la massa muscolare magra durante la perdita di peso. Questo è particolarmente vantaggioso per gli anziani o per chiunque desideri evitare la sarcopenia, la perdita di massa muscolare associata all'età.

Considerazioni Psicologiche e Comportamentali

Dal punto di vista psicologico e comportamentale, la dieta chetogenica può influenzare il benessere mentale e le abitudini alimentari. L'adattamento a una dieta così restrittiva può essere difficile per alcuni, potenzialmente portando a sentimenti di isolamento sociale o frustrazione. Allo stesso tempo, altri possono trovare nella chetogenesi una riduzione dell'ansia legata al cibo, poiché i livelli stabili di glucosio possono ridurre le fluttuazioni dell'umore e i comportamenti compulsivi verso il cibo.

Adattamenti per Popolazioni Speciali

Infine, la dieta chetogenica necessita di essere adattata per popolazioni speciali, come i bambini, gli anziani o quelli con condizioni mediche specifiche. Ad esempio, nei bambini, una stretta supervisione è cruciale per garantire un adeguato apporto di nutrienti essenziali per la crescita e lo sviluppo. Negli anziani, l'attenzione si sposta sulla prevenzione della perdita muscolare e sulla mantenimento della funzione cognitiva, mentre per coloro con specifiche condizioni mediche, le modifiche dietetiche devono essere attentamente gestite per evitare complicazioni o per massimizzare i benefici terapeutici.

La dieta chetogenica, quindi, non è semplicemente un metodo per perdere peso, ma un'ampia ristrutturazione dell'alimentazione che tocca ogni aspetto della fisiologia umana, dall'equilibrio metabolico e ormonale alla salute mentale e comportamentale, richiedendo un'approccio olistico e personalizzato per ottenere i migliori risultati possibili.

Concludendo la discussione sulla scienza del dimagrimento chetogenico, possiamo riconoscere che questa dieta non solo cambia il modo in cui il corpo metabolizza i macronutrienti, ma ha anche una vasta gamma di effetti su diverse funzioni corporee, salute complessiva e benessere psicologico.

La dieta chetogenica sposta la principale fonte di energia del corpo dai carboidrati ai grassi, portando all'induzione della chetosi, un processo metabolico in cui il fegato produce corpi chetonici per servire come energia alternativa. Questo cambio radicale nella gestione dell'energia può risultare in una significativa perdita di peso, principalmente attraverso la riduzione dell'appetito, l'aumento del metabolismo dei grassi e la diminuzione del deposito di grasso indotto dall'insulina. La perdita di peso iniziale è spesso accelerata dalla riduzione delle riserve di glicogeno e dalla conseguente perdita di acqua.

I benefici della dieta chetogenica, tuttavia, vanno oltre la semplice riduzione del peso. Include il miglioramento del profilo lipidico, con potenziali aumenti nel colesterolo HDL e modifiche nella composizione delle particelle LDL che possono ridurre il rischio di malattie cardiovascolari. L'impatto sul metabolismo del glucosio aiuta nella gestione del diabete tipo 2, mentre i corpi chetonici hanno dimostrato di possedere proprietà anti-infiammatorie e neuroprotettive, beneficiando condizioni come l'epilessia e potenzialmente influenzando positivamente altre malattie neurodegenerative.

Nonostante questi potenziali benefici, la dieta chetogenica comporta anche delle sfide e dei rischi che non possono essere ignorati. La restrizione severa di carboidrati può portare a carenze nutrizionali, disidratazione ed elettroliti squilibrati se non gestita correttamente. Inoltre, l'alto consumo di grassi, particolarmente se provenienti da fonti non salutari, può avere effetti negativi sulla salute del cuore a lungo termine. La dieta può anche interagire con vari farmaci, richiedendo aggiustamenti e un monitoraggio medico attento.

Inoltre, la sostenibilità a lungo termine della dieta chetogenica è un tema controverso. Molti trovano la dieta difficile da mantenere a causa delle sue restrizioni severe e dell'impatto sulle interazioni sociali e la qualità della vita. La transizione verso un modello di dieta cheto-ciclica o cheto-adattata può offrire una maggiore flessibilità e migliorare la sostenibilità, permettendo agli individui di godere dei benefici della chetosi pur mantenendo un approccio più bilanciato e meno restrittivo al consumo di cibo.

Infine, è essenziale che qualsiasi persona che consideri la dieta chetogenica come opzione per la perdita di peso o per la gestione della salute consulte professionisti della salute qualificati. Questo non solo aiuta a personalizzare l'approccio dietetico in base alle esigenze individuali, ma anche a monitorare e gestire possibili effetti collaterali o complicazioni. In sintesi, mentre la dieta chetogenica offre molte promesse come strumento per la perdita di peso e il miglioramento della salute, deve essere approcciata con una strategia ben informata e cautamente ottimista, con una chiara attenzione alla scienza nutrizionale, alle esigenze personali e alle considerazioni pratiche.

3. Prepararsi al Successo: Consigli su come preparare la mente e la casa per iniziare la dieta chetogenica.

3. Prepararsi al Successo: Consigli per Iniziare la Dieta Chetogenica

Prepararsi adeguatamente per iniziare una dieta chetogenica è essenziale per massimizzare le possibilità di successo e ridurre il rischio di complicazioni. Questa preparazione coinvolge tanto la mente quanto l'ambiente fisico, come la casa. Ecco alcuni passaggi chiave per iniziare:

Preparazione Mentale

1. **Informarsi sulla Dieta Chetogenica**: Prima di iniziare, è cruciale comprendere i principi fondamentali della dieta chetogenica, i benefici attesi e i potenziali rischi. Leggere libri, articoli scientifici e testimonianze

può fornire una base solida di conoscenze e prepararti mentalmente per i cambiamenti alimentari e di stile di vita che seguiranno.

2. **Impostare Obiettivi Realistici**: Stabilire obiettivi chiari e raggiungibili è fondamentale. Questi dovrebbero essere specifici, misurabili, raggiungibili, rilevanti e temporali (SMART). Ad esempio, un obiettivo potrebbe essere perdere 5 kg in un mese o semplicemente completare 30 giorni di dieta chetogenica senza deviazioni.

3. **Mentalità e Motivazione**: Rafforzare la motivazione interna può essere fatto visualizzando i benefici che si spera di ottenere dalla dieta. Inoltre, prepararsi mentalmente per gli ostacoli e pianificare in anticipo come superarli può aiutare a mantenere la dieta quando si presentano sfide.

4. **Supporto Sociale**: Condividere il proprio piano con amici o familiari può fornire una rete di supporto necessaria. Considerare la possibilità di unirsi a gruppi online o comunità locali che seguono la dieta chetogenica può anche offrire supporto, consigli e incoraggiamento.

Preparazione dell'Ambiente Domestico

1. **Ripulire la Dispensa**: Eliminare gli alimenti ricchi di carboidrati, come cereali, pasta, snack dolci e salati, succhi di frutta e bevande zuccherate, può ridurre la tentazione e le possibilità di scivolare fuori dalla dieta. Questo include anche sbarazzarsi di condimenti dolci come ketchup e salse pronte che possono essere ricchi di zuccheri nascosti.

2. **Fare Scorta di Alimenti Chetogenici**: Fare scorta di alimenti ammessi nella dieta chetogenica è essenziale. Questi includono carni, pesce, uova, latticini a basso

contenuto di carboidrati, olio d'oliva e di cocco, avocado, verdure a foglia verde e altre verdure a basso contenuto di carboidrati. Non dimenticare di includere anche alcune erbe e spezie per variare i sapori.

3. **Organizzare il Frigorifero e la Cucina**: Organizzare il frigorifero e i ripiani della cucina per rendere più accessibili gli alimenti chetogenici può facilitare la preparazione dei pasti. Avere a portata di mano strumenti di cucina utili, come una friggitrice ad aria, pentole a cottura lenta o un Instant Pot, può rendere la preparazione dei pasti chetogenici più conveniente e meno dispendiosa in termini di tempo.

4. **Pianificazione dei Pasti**: Creare un piano settimanale di pasti e snack che rispetti i macronutrienti necessari per mantenere la chetosi. Questo aiuta a evitare decisioni alimentari dell'ultimo minuto che potrebbero non essere ideali e supporta una transizione più fluida alla dieta chetogenica.

5. **Strumenti di Monitoraggio**: Considerare l'acquisto di strisce reattive per urine, un misuratore di chetoni nel sangue o nel respiro, per monitorare il proprio stato di chetosi. Questo può aiutare a personalizzare la dieta in base alle proprie esigenze specifiche e a vedere come diversi alimenti influenzano la chetosi.

Con queste preparazioni in mente e in atto, l'inizio della dieta chetogenica può essere meno intimidatorio e più gestibile. Preparare adeguatamente sia la mente che l'ambiente domestico pone le basi per una transizione più fluida e sostenibile verso una dieta chetogenica, aumentando così le probabilità di successo a lungo termine.

Continuando con la preparazione per il successo nella dieta chetogenica, ci sono altre strategie importanti da considerare che possono migliorare l'esperienza e massimizzare i risultati.

Educazione Continua

Man mano che procedi con la dieta chetogenica, è fondamentale continuare ad educarti sulle ultime ricerche e sulle pratiche migliori. Iscriverti a newsletter, seguire esperti di keto su social media, e leggere studi scientifici aggiornati può aiutarti a restare informato sulle nuove scoperte e sulle linee guida nutrizionali che potrebbero influenzare la tua esperienza con la dieta chetogenica.

Strategie di Coping per la Keto-Flu

Una sfida comune per molti all'inizio della dieta chetogenica è la cosiddetta "keto-flu", un gruppo di sintomi che possono includere stanchezza, mal di testa, irritabilità e difficoltà digestive. Essere preparato a gestire questi sintomi è cruciale. Aumentare l'assunzione di liquidi, assicurarti di ottenere abbastanza sodio, potassio e magnesio, e possibilmente ridurre l'intensità dell'esercizio fisico nei primi giorni può aiutare a mitigare questi sintomi.

Gestione delle Aspettative

Impostare aspettative realistiche è vitale per qualsiasi cambiamento dietetico, soprattutto per uno così drastico come la dieta chetogenica. Comprendere che ci possono essere alti e bassi, e che la perdita di peso non sarà lineare, può aiutare a mantenere la motivazione nel tempo. Celebrare piccoli successi e imparare dai contrattempi invece di scoraggiarsi può creare una mentalità più resiliente e sostenibile.

Sperimentazione Culinaria

Adottare la dieta chetogenica non significa rinunciare al piacere di mangiare. Esplorare nuove ricette chetogeniche e sperimentare con sostituti low-carb per i tuoi piatti preferiti possono rendere il percorso più divertente e meno restrittivo. Libri di cucina chetogenica, blog e tutorial video possono essere risorse preziose per mantenere la varietà nel tuo piano alimentare.

Ascolta il Tuo Corpo

Ogni persona è unica, e come tale, la risposta alla dieta chetogenica può variare. È importante ascoltare il proprio corpo e adattare la dieta in base alle proprie reazioni. Se trovi che certi alimenti non ti fanno sentire bene, anche se sono "keto approvati", potrebbe essere necessario modificarli. Allo stesso modo, se ti senti costantemente stanco o hai altri sintomi persistenti, potrebbe essere il momento di riconsiderare la composizione della tua dieta o consultare un professionista della salute.

Gestione Sociale e Emotiva

La dieta chetogenica può influenzare anche la tua vita sociale, poiché le uscite a cena e le occasioni speciali spesso ruotano attorno al cibo. Prepararti a gestire queste situazioni, come controllare i menu dei ristoranti in anticipo, portare i tuoi snack keto quando visiti amici o parenti, o persino offrire di cucinare per gli altri, possono aiutarti a mantenere il tuo regime alimentare senza isolarti socialmente.

Valutazione Continua

È essenziale valutare periodicamente l'efficacia della dieta chetogenica per te. Questo può includere il monitoraggio dei progressi verso i tuoi obiettivi di salute, la valutazione di come ti senti fisicamente e mentalmente, e il controllo regolare con un professionista della salute per assicurarti che la dieta non stia causando problemi non intenzionali. Adattamenti possono essere necessari man mano che il tuo corpo cambia o come risposta ai feedback del tuo sistema.

Incorporare questi elementi nella tua preparazione e mantenimento della dieta chetogenica può non solo aiutare a garantire una transizione più fluida ma anche sostenere la tua aderenza a lungo termine e il successo nella realizzazione dei tuoi obiettivi di salute.

Proseguendo con la preparazione per il successo nella dieta chetogenica, esploriamo ulteriori aspetti che possono influenzare il percorso di chi decide di adottare questo regime alimentare. Un approccio olistico e ben pianificato può facilitare il raggiungimento degli obiettivi desiderati e contribuire a una migliore esperienza complessiva.

Adattamento del Piano Alimentare nel Tempo

Come per qualsiasi dieta, la flessibilità e l'adattabilità sono cruciali nella dieta chetogenica. Col tempo, potrebbe essere necessario aggiustare il rapporto tra grassi, proteine e carboidrati per rispondere ai cambiamenti nel metabolismo, al livello di attività fisica o semplicemente alle preferenze personali. Monitorare i risultati e fare aggiustamenti basati su dati concreti, come misurazioni del corpo, chetoni nel sangue, e livelli di energia, può aiutare a ottimizzare la dieta per il tuo stile di vita e i tuoi obiettivi di salute.

Creazione di un Ambiente Stimolante

L'ambiente in cui vivi può avere un impatto significativo sulla tua capacità di mantenere una dieta chetogenica. Rendere la tua cucina un luogo invitante e ben organizzato, dove sia facile accedere a alimenti compatibili con la dieta chetogenica e dove la preparazione dei pasti possa essere efficiente e piacevole, può fare una grande differenza. Investire in strumenti da cucina che facilitano la preparazione di pasti sani, come blender potenti, taglieri di qualità, e contenitori per la conservazione degli alimenti, può semplificare il processo e rendere la cucina un'attività meno onerosa e più divertente.

Educazione Continua e Supporto Professionale

Mantenere un dialogo aperto con professionisti della nutrizione che comprendono la dieta chetogenica può fornire un supporto cruciale. I nutrizionisti possono non solo aiutare a personalizzare il piano alimentare, ma anche a identificare e correggere eventuali carenze nutrizionali o problemi digestivi che possono emergere. Inoltre, partecipare a workshop, seminari online o gruppi di supporto può offrire nuove idee, motivazione aggiuntiva e consigli pratici per navigare sfide comuni.

Sviluppo di Strategie di Resistenza agli Impulsi

Apprendere tecniche per gestire gli impulsi verso cibi non chetogenici è fondamentale. Tecniche di consapevolezza e di mindfulness possono aiutare a riconoscere la differenza tra fame fisica e voglia emotiva di mangiare. Allo stesso tempo, avere sempre a disposizione alternative chetogeniche gustose può prevenire deviazioni dalla dieta. Ad esempio, preparare in anticipo snack chetogenici come noci, semi, bastoncini di formaggio, o mini frittate può offrire soluzioni rapide quando la fame si fa sentire improvvisamente.

Gestione del Stress e dell'Esercizio Fisico

La gestione dello stress è vitale, dato che lo stress può influenzare negativamente le decisioni alimentari e il metabolismo generale. Tecniche come la meditazione, lo yoga o semplicemente periodi regolari di rilassamento possono migliorare la tua capacità di aderire alla dieta chetogenica. Inoltre, integrare un regolare esercizio fisico che ti piace può non solo aiutare a mantenere la chetosi, ma anche migliorare il benessere mentale e fisico.

Valutazione Continua dell'Impatto sulla Salute

Infine, è essenziale valutare continuamente come la dieta chetogenica influenzi la tua salute complessiva. Oltre alla perdita di peso, monitorare parametri come i livelli di colesterolo, la pressione sanguigna, la composizione corporea e i marker di funzionalità renale ed epatica può fornire una panoramica più completa degli effetti della dieta. Questo monitoraggio dovrebbe idealmente essere fatto in collaborazione con un medico che può aiutare a interpretare i risultati e a decidere se continuare, modificare o cessare la dieta chetogenica.

Prepararsi adeguatamente per il successo con la dieta chetogenica implica un impegno costante, non solo nell'adottare un piano alimentare specifico, ma anche nel curare la propria salute mentale e fisica, nel creare un ambiente di supporto e nell'adattare la dieta alle esigenze e agli obiettivi individuali nel corso del tempo.

Approfondendo ulteriormente le strategie per una preparazione efficace alla dieta chetogenica, consideriamo alcuni aspetti complementari che possono aiutare a rendere questa transizione più gestibile e sostenibile a lungo termine.

Abbracciare un Approccio Flessibile

L'adozione di un approccio flessibile alla dieta chetogenica può aiutare a ridurre la pressione psicologica e a migliorare l'adesione nel tempo. Ad esempio, alcuni potrebbero trovare vantaggioso seguire un regime cheto-ciclico, dove i carboidrati sono reintrodotti a intervalli programmati, permettendo una maggiore varietà dietetica e facilitando il mantenimento sociale e la soddisfazione culinaria. Questo tipo di approccio può essere particolarmente utile per gli atleti che hanno bisogno di carboidrati per rifornire il glicogeno muscolare dopo l'allenamento intenso.

Sviluppare una Mentalità Positiva

Sviluppare e mantenere una mentalità positiva è fondamentale per il successo a lungo termine con la dieta chetogenica. Ciò può includere praticare l'autocompassione, celebrare i piccoli successi lungo il percorso, e imparare a vedere gli eventuali fallimenti come opportunità di apprendimento anziché come colpe. Una mentalità positiva può anche derivare dal riconoscere e apprezzare i benefici per la salute oltre la perdita di peso, come maggiore energia, miglioramento della concentrazione e riduzione dei sintomi di condizioni mediche preesistenti.

Creare un Diario Alimentare e di Benessere

Tenere un diario alimentare e di benessere può essere uno strumento prezioso per monitorare i progressi, le sfide e le reazioni a vari alimenti e attività. Annotare quotidianamente ciò che mangi, come ti senti e qualsiasi sintomo nuovo o cambiamento nel benessere può aiutarti a individuare pattern e a fare aggiustamenti mirati nel tuo piano chetogenico. Questo può essere particolarmente utile nei primi stadi della dieta, quando stai ancora capendo come il tuo corpo reagisce alla chetosi.

Incrementare l'Attività Fisica Gradualmente

Incorporare l'esercizio fisico in modo graduale può aiutare a migliorare l'efficacia della dieta chetogenica e a promuovere una perdita di peso sana. L'attività fisica regolare non solo aiuta a bruciare calorie, ma può anche migliorare l'umore, rafforzare la resistenza e supportare la salute del cuore. Scegliere attività che ti piacciono e che puoi mantenere a lungo termine è essenziale per integrare l'esercizio fisico come parte della tua routine quotidiana.

Utilizzare la Tecnologia per Supportare la Dieta

L'uso di app per la dieta, dispositivi di monitoraggio fitness e altri strumenti tecnologici può rendere più semplice tracciare il tuo apporto calorico, i macronutrienti e il tuo livello di attività fisica. Questi strumenti possono offrire feedback immediato e

analisi dettagliate che possono aiutare a rimanere informati e
motivati.

Costruire una Comunità di Supporto

Costruire o unirsi a una comunità di persone che seguono la
dieta chetogenica può fornire un supporto emotivo e morale,
oltre a consigli pratici e ricette. Che si tratti di gruppi online,
club di salute locali, o amici e familiari, avere una rete di
supporto può essere incredibilmente potente per mantenere la
motivazione e ottenere sostegno durante momenti di sfida.

Prepararsi per le Fluttuazioni Emotive

Riconoscere che le modifiche dietetiche possono influenzare
l'umore e le emozioni è importante. Durante la transizione verso
la chetosi, alcune persone possono sperimentare irritabilità o
cambiamenti dell'umore a causa delle fluttuazioni dei livelli di
zucchero nel sangue e delle modifiche alla dieta. Prepararsi a
gestire queste fluttuazioni con strategie come la meditazione, la
respirazione profonda, o consulenza, può essere cruciale.

Integrare questi elementi nella preparazione per la dieta
chetogenica non solo prepara il terreno per una transizione più
fluida, ma stabilisce anche le basi per un impegno a lungo
termine verso uno stile di vita più sano e sostenibile. Con una
preparazione adeguata, un'attitudine positiva e supporto
continuativo, adottare e mantenere la dieta chetogenica può
diventare un percorso arricchente verso il miglioramento della
salute e del benessere complessivo.

Perseguendo ulteriormente l'approfondimento sulla
preparazione efficace alla dieta chetogenica, ci sono molteplici
aspetti che possono migliorare l'esperienza e il successo di
questo percorso nutrizionale. Approfondire questi aspetti
aiuterà non solo a stabilire una solida base di partenza, ma
anche a mantenere la dieta chetogenica come un cambiamento
sostenibile dello stile di vita a lungo termine.

Approccio Olistico alla Salute

Incorporare un approccio olistico alla salute mentre si segue la dieta chetogenica può fornire benefici che vanno oltre la semplice perdita di peso. Questo include prendersi cura del benessere mentale e emotivo, oltre che fisico. Ad esempio, pratiche come il yoga e la meditazione possono aiutare a gestire lo stress, che a sua volta può influenzare positivamente la compliance alla dieta e l'equilibrio ormonale. Prendere in considerazione la propria salute mentale e cercare consulenza professionale quando necessario può essere cruciale per evitare che lo stress e l'ansia sabotino gli sforzi dietetici.

Personalizzazione Basata su Condizioni di Salute

È essenziale personalizzare la dieta chetogenica basandosi su condizioni di salute specifiche, esigenze nutrizionali e obiettivi personali. Ad esempio, individui con condizioni come il diabete tipo 2 o malattie cardiovascolari possono necessitare di un approccio più cauto e di una stretta supervisione medica per gestire l'apporto di grassi e monitorare gli effetti della dieta sulle loro condizioni. La personalizzazione può includere l'adattamento dei macronutrienti, la selezione di cibi specifici che non solo supportano la chetogenesi ma anche contribuiscono al miglioramento o alla stabilizzazione delle condizioni di salute esistenti.

Integrazione Nutrizionale

Valutare la necessità di integrazioni nutrizionali può giocare un ruolo importante nell'assicurare che non si verifichino carenze mentre si segue la dieta chetogenica. Nutrienti come la vitamina D, il magnesio, il sodio, il potassio e le fibre possono talvolta risultare insufficienti in una dieta a basso contenuto di carboidrati. Consultare un nutrizionista o un medico per determinare quali integratori potrebbero essere necessari per bilanciare la dieta può prevenire complicazioni a lungo termine associate a carenze nutrizionali.

Continua Educazione e Aggiornamento

Mantenere un impegno costante verso l'educazione e l'aggiornamento sulle ultime ricerche e tendenze nella nutrizione chetogenica può aiutare a ottimizzare i benefici e a evitare i rischi. La scienza della nutrizione è in costante evoluzione, e nuove scoperte possono offrire opportunità per migliorare o modificare l'approccio chetogenico per renderlo più efficace o più facile da seguire. Partecipare a seminari, leggere pubblicazioni scientifiche, e restare attivi in comunità online sono modi efficaci per restare informati e motivati.

Pianificazione Anticipata per Eventi Speciali

Prepararsi per eventi sociali o vacanze può richiedere pianificazione aggiuntiva per rimanere in chetosi. Considerare strategie come mangiare prima di partecipare a un evento, portare propri piatti cheto-compatibili a feste, o scegliere ristoranti che offrono opzioni adatte può facilitare il mantenimento della dieta senza isolarsi socialmente. Avere un piano in anticipo può aiutare a ridurre l'ansia legata al cibo e permettere di godersi le occasioni sociali senza stress.

Monitoraggio dei Progressi

Un monitoraggio regolare dei progressi non solo in termini di perdita di peso ma anche di miglioramento dei parametri di salute, livelli di energia, qualità del sonno e benessere generale può fornire feedback prezioso che guida ulteriori personalizzazioni della dieta. Utilizzare strumenti di tracking come app di dieta, diari alimentari o dispositivi wearable che monitorano l'attività fisica e i parametri biometrici può aiutare a tenere traccia di questi progressi in modo oggettivo e motivante.

Adottare questi approcci nella preparazione e mantenimento della dieta chetogenica non solo aiuta a navigare la transizione iniziale con maggiore facilità, ma stabilisce anche le fondamenta per una pratica chetogenica sostenibile che può essere mantenuta come uno stile di vita a lungo termine. Con una preparazione adeguata, supporto professionale e un impegno continuo all'apprendimento e all'adattamento, la dieta chetogenica può diventare un mezzo efficace per migliorare la salute e il benessere complessivi.

Avanzando ulteriormente nella preparazione per la dieta chetogenica, esploriamo altri aspetti che possono facilitare una transizione efficace e sostenibile, garantendo che si mantenga un approccio equilibrato e informato.

Mantenimento della Flessibilità Metabolica

Mentre la dieta chetogenica si focalizza sulla riduzione drastica dei carboidrati per indurre la chetosi, è anche importante considerare la flessibilità metabolica — la capacità del corpo di adattarsi efficacemente all'utilizzo di diverse fonti energetiche. Periodicamente, introdurre giorni in cui si aumentano i carboidrati (conosciuti come giorni di ricarica) può aiutare a mantenere il corpo reattivo sia ai grassi che ai carboidrati, evitando ciò che alcuni esperti chiamano "metabolic rigidity", che potrebbe rendere più difficile mantenere la perdita di peso a lungo termine.

Adattamento delle Ricette Familiari

Per rendere la dieta chetogenica più accettabile e meno restrittiva, adattare le ricette familiari per renderle compatibili con i principi chetogenici può essere un'efficace strategia. Sostituire gli ingredienti ricchi di carboidrati con alternative a basso contenuto di carboidrati, come la farina di mandorle o di cocco al posto della farina di grano, può permettere di godere dei piatti preferiti mentre si rimane entro i limiti della dieta.

Coinvolgimento dei Membri della Famiglia

Coinvolgere i membri della famiglia nel processo di transizione alla dieta chetogenica può non solo fornire supporto aggiuntivo ma anche semplificare la gestione dei pasti domestici. Educare i membri della famiglia sui benefici della dieta e su come possono supportare il processo, sia partecipando attivamente sia rispettando le scelte alimentari, può ridurre i conflitti e aumentare la motivazione.

Sfruttare la Tecnologia per la Pianificazione dei Pasti

Utilizzare strumenti tecnologici come app di pianificazione dei pasti può semplificare significativamente il processo di adesione alla dieta chetogenica. Queste app possono aiutare a tracciare l'assunzione di macronutrienti, suggerire ricette chetogeniche e persino creare liste della spesa personalizzate, rendendo più facile rimanere organizzati e evitare errori alimentari.

Gestione del Ritorno ai Carboidrati

Per coloro che non intendono seguire la dieta chetogenica a vita, è importante pianificare attentamente il ritorno all'assunzione di carboidrati per evitare un rapido recupero del peso perso. Introdurre gradualmente i carboidrati, monitorando la risposta del corpo e regolando l'apporto calorico e l'attività fisica, può aiutare a stabilizzare il peso e a mantenere i benefici metabolici acquisiti.

Apprendimento da Esperienze Altrui

Ascoltare o leggere le esperienze di altre persone che hanno seguito la dieta chetogenica può fornire spunti preziosi e realistici sulle sfide e sui successi. Questi racconti possono offrire ispirazione, strategie pratiche e un senso di comunità che può essere estremamente motivante durante i momenti difficili.

Preparazione per Eventuali Effetti Collaterali

Essere consapevoli e preparati per eventuali effetti collaterali, come il mal di testa, la stanchezza o i disturbi digestivi nei primi giorni, può aiutare a gestirli più efficacemente. Avere rimedi a portata di mano, come integratori elettrolitici e snack chetogenici idonei, può aiutare a minimizzare il disagio e a mantenere la coerenza nella dieta.

Monitoraggio Medico Regolare

Infine, mantenere un monitoraggio medico regolare è fondamentale, specialmente se ci sono preoccupazioni per la salute preesistenti. Controlli regolari possono aiutare a monitorare gli effetti della dieta sul corpo e ad ajustare il piano alimentare per garantire che rimanga sicuro ed efficace nel tempo.

Attraverso questi metodi e strategie, chi segue una dieta chetogenica può non solo facilitare una transizione efficace ma anche creare un ambiente che supporti una pratica sostenibile a lungo termine, massimizzando i benefici per la salute e mantenendo un elevato livello di benessere.

Concludendo, prepararsi adeguatamente per iniziare e mantenere una dieta chetogenica richiede un approccio olistico che considera non solo gli aspetti nutrizionali, ma anche le implicazioni psicologiche, sociali e pratiche. Un'efficace preparazione inizia con un solido fondamento di conoscenza sulla dieta chetogenica, impostazione di obiettivi realistici e un piano ben strutturato che include sia la preparazione mentale che quella dell'ambiente domestico.

Ripulire la dispensa da alimenti ricchi di carboidrati e rifornirla di opzioni compatibili con la dieta chetogenica è un passo pratico cruciale. La personalizzazione del piano alimentare in base alle condizioni di salute preesistenti, l'ascolto del proprio corpo e l'adattamento della dieta in risposta alle sue esigenze uniche sono fondamentali per il successo a lungo termine.

Incorporare l'esercizio fisico, mantenere una flessibilità metabolica, gestire lo stress attraverso tecniche di mindfulness e cercare il supporto di amici, famiglia o gruppi online possono notevolmente aumentare le possibilità di successo. Preparare mentalmente per gestire gli effetti collaterali iniziali, come la keto-flu, e utilizzare strumenti tecnologici per monitorare l'assunzione di nutrienti e pianificare i pasti possono aiutare a rimanere coerenti e motivati.

Infine, il monitoraggio medico regolare e la valutazione continua della dieta assicurano che la dieta rimanga salutare e sostenibile, permettendo di apportare le necessarie modifiche per ottimizzare i benefici per la salute. Adottando queste strategie, chi segue la dieta chetogenica può non solo raggiungere i propri obiettivi di perdita di peso, ma anche godere di un miglioramento complessivo del benessere e della qualità di vita.

4. Pianificazione dei Pasti e Lista della Spesa: Guida alla creazione di piani alimentari settimanali e liste della spesa ottimizzate per la dieta chetogenica.

4. Pianificazione dei Pasti e Lista della Spesa: Ottimizzazione per la Dieta Chetogenica

L'adozione della dieta chetogenica richiede una pianificazione attenta dei pasti e una strategia precisa per la spesa, per garantire che tutti gli alimenti consumati rispettino i requisiti nutrizionali specifici della dieta. Ecco una guida dettagliata per creare piani alimentari settimanali e liste della spesa ottimizzate per una dieta chetogenica efficace e soddisfacente.

Creazione di un Piano Alimentare Settimanale

1. **Definire Macro Nutrienti**: Prima di tutto, stabilire i rapporti di macronutrienti necessari — tipicamente, una dieta chetogenica standard consiste in circa 70-80% di calorie da grassi, 15-20% da proteine e 5-10% da carboidrati. Usare app o calcolatori online può aiutare a

personalizzare questi rapporti in base a età, sesso, livello di attività e obiettivi personali.

2. **Selezione dei Cibi**: Scegliere alimenti ricchi di grassi buoni e poveri di carboidrati. La lista include:

   o Grassi: oli (come olio d'oliva e di cocco), burro, strutto;

   o Proteine: carni (preferibilmente non lavorate), pesce, frutti di mare, uova, formaggi a basso contenuto di carboidrati;

   o Carboidrati: verdure a foglia verde, come spinaci e cavolo, e altre verdure non amidacee come zucchine, peperoni e asparagi.

3. **Pianificazione dei Pasti**: Suddividere i pasti in colazione, pranzo, cena e snack. È utile usare un modello di pianificazione per organizzare i pasti per ogni giorno della settimana. Considerare la varietà per evitare la monotonia alimentare e includere sempre una componente proteica, una fonte di grassi e verdure a basso contenuto di carboidrati.

4. **Preparazione in Anticipo**: Quando possibile, preparare i pasti in anticipo. Cucinare in lotti e utilizzare il congelamento può risparmiare tempo durante la settimana e aiutare a mantenere la dieta.

Creazione della Lista della Spesa

1. **Lista Basata sui Pasti Pianificati**: Creare una lista della spesa che rifletta esattamente gli ingredienti necessari per i pasti pianificati. Questo aiuta a evitare acquisti impulsivi di alimenti non chetogenici.

2. **Organizzazione della Lista per Categorie**: Organizzare la lista della spesa per categorie (proteine, grassi, verdure, condimenti, ecc.) può rendere lo

shopping più efficiente e meno soggetto a distrazioni da prodotti non compatibili con la dieta.

3. **Scegliere Alimenti Integrali**: Preferire alimenti integrali rispetto a quelli lavorati. Alimenti come carne fresca, pesce e verdure fresche sono preferibili ai prodotti pre-confezionati che possono contenere zuccheri nascosti o carboidrati eccessivi.

4. **Controllare le Etichette**: Imparare a leggere le etichette nutrizionali è fondamentale per evitare alimenti che contengono zuccheri aggiunti o carboidrati indesiderati. Anche piccole quantità di zuccheri nascosti possono accumularsi e influire sulla chetosi.

5. **Approvvigionamenti Regolari**: Data la freschezza richiesta per molti alimenti chetogenici, può essere necessario fare la spesa più frequentemente. Investire in buone risorse di conservazione degli alimenti può aiutare a mantenere gli alimenti freschi più a lungo.

Implementando questi passaggi nella pianificazione dei pasti e nella preparazione della lista della spesa, chi segue una dieta chetogenica può assicurarsi di avere sempre a disposizione pasti deliziosi e nutrienti che soddisfano i requisiti della dieta. Questo non solo contribuisce a una transizione più fluida e sostenibile verso uno stile di vita chetogenico, ma anche a mantenere una dieta equilibrata e salutare nel lungo termine.

Proseguendo nella pianificazione efficace dei pasti e della lista della spesa per una dieta chetogenica, è utile considerare ulteriori dettagli che possono facilitare il successo e l'efficienza di questo regime alimentare.

Variazione dei Pasti

Per evitare la monotonia e mantenere l'interesse nella dieta chetogenica, è cruciale variare i pasti regolarmente. Questo non solo previene la noia alimentare, ma aiuta anche a garantire un ampio spettro di nutrienti essenziali. Si può pensare di integrare nuove ricette ogni settimana, sperimentare con diversi tipi di verdure a basso contenuto di carboidrati, o variare le fonti proteiche tra carne, pesce, uova e formaggi. La variazione aiuta anche a identificare quali alimenti funzionano meglio per il tuo corpo e gusti personali.

Utilizzo di Erbe e Spezie

Le erbe e le spezie giocano un ruolo fondamentale nel rendere gustosi i piatti chetogenici senza aggiungere carboidrati inutili. Alcuni esempi includono basilico, coriandolo, rosmarino, curcuma, paprika e pepe nero. Non solo aggiungono sapore senza carboidrati, ma molte erbe e spezie offrono benefici antinfiammatori e antiossidanti che possono migliorare ulteriormente la salute.

Pianificazione dei Snack

I snack chetogenici devono essere pianificati con attenzione per evitare di cadere nella tentazione di cibi non approvati. Opzioni come olive, avocado, noci, semi, formaggio a pasta dura, e fette di salame o prosciutto sono scelte eccellenti. Avere sempre a disposizione snack compatibili con la chetogenesi può aiutare a gestire la fame improvvisa e mantenere i livelli energetici stabili.

Strategie di Acquisto Economico

Seguire una dieta chetogenica può essere costoso, dato l'alto consumo di prodotti animali e altri alimenti a basso contenuto di carboidrati. Tuttavia, ci sono modi per ridurre i costi senza compromettere la qualità. Acquistare in bulk, sfruttare le offerte locali, comprare da mercati degli agricoltori o aderire a gruppi di acquisto possono tutti contribuire a ridurre la spesa. Inoltre, investire in un congelatore, se possibile, permette di acquistare alimenti in grande quantità quando sono in offerta e conservarli per l'uso futuro.

Sfruttare le Tecnologie Alimentari

Utilizzare strumenti tecnologici moderni può semplificare la preparazione dei pasti chetogenici. Ad esempio, friggitrici ad aria, slow cooker e Instant Pots possono essere usati per preparare pasti chetogenici deliziosi con meno fatica e supervisione. Questi strumenti possono aiutare a cucinare in modo più efficiente, mantenendo il gusto e la qualità nutrizionale degli alimenti.

Preparazione di Emergenza

Essere preparati per situazioni inaspettate che potrebbero rendere difficile seguire la dieta chetogenica è un altro aspetto importante. Avere un piano per quando si è fuori casa, in viaggio, o in situazioni di stress può prevenire deviazioni dal piano alimentare. Ciò potrebbe includere la preparazione di pasti pronti da congelare, portare con sé snack chetogenici quando si esce, o anche solo avere una lista di ristoranti che offrono opzioni compatibili con la chetogenesi.

Rivalutazione Periodica del Piano Alimentare

Infine, è importante rivalutare periodicamente il piano alimentare per assicurarsi che continui a soddisfare le tue esigenze nutrizionali, preferenze e obiettivi di salute. Questo può includere l'aggiustamento dei macronutrienti, l'introduzione di nuovi alimenti, o la riduzione di altri. L'adattabilità è cruciale per mantenere una dieta chetogenica efficace e piacevole a lungo termine.

Integrare queste strategie avanzate nella pianificazione dei pasti e della spesa può notevolmente aumentare le possibilità di aderenza e successo a lungo termine con la dieta chetogenica, rendendo il percorso verso il benessere sia gustoso che sostenibile.

Mentre proseguiamo nell'approfondimento sulla pianificazione dei pasti e della lista della spesa per la dieta chetogenica, emergono ulteriori strategie e considerazioni che possono ottimizzare e arricchire l'esperienza dietetica.

Integrazione di Superfoods

Incorporare superfoods chetogenici può aumentare il valore nutrizionale dei pasti mantenendo il corpo in stato di chetosi. Alimenti come l'avocado, ricco di grassi salutari e potassio, il salmone selvatico, fonte di omega-3, e le noci di Macadamia, ricche di grassi monoinsaturi e a basso contenuto di carboidrati, sono tutti esempi di superfoods che si adattano perfettamente alla dieta chetogenica. Essi non solo offrono benefici per la salute a lungo termine, ma anche aiutano a migliorare la sazietà e a stabilizzare i livelli di energia.

Pianificazione dei Pasti Stagionali

Approfittare della disponibilità stagionale di verdure a basso contenuto di carboidrati può variare la dieta e ottimizzare il budget per la spesa. Verdure come zucchine, cavolfiori e asparagi possono essere acquistati in abbondanza durante la loro stagione di picco a un costo inferiore. Questo non solo supporta una dieta variata ma incoraggia anche un consumo più sostenibile e consapevole di risorse locali.

Utilizzo Creativo degli Avanzi

Organizzare i pasti in modo da massimizzare l'uso degli avanzi può ridurre sia lo spreco che il tempo trascorso in cucina. Per esempio, un grosso arrosto di carne può essere utilizzato inizialmente come piatto principale, poi gli avanzi possono essere trasformati in insalate, zuppe o frittate per i pasti successivi. Questa strategia non solo è economica ma anche pratica, facilitando l'adesione alla dieta durante una settimana impegnativa.

Sperimentazione con Sostituti dei Carboidrati

Esplorare e sperimentare con vari sostituti dei carboidrati può rendere la dieta chetogenica più piacevole e meno restrittiva. Ingredienti come la farina di mandorle per la panificazione, il riso di cavolfiore come alternativa al riso tradizionale, e le "zoodles" (zucchine tagliate a spirale come sostituto degli spaghetti) possono aggiungere diversità e creatività ai pasti chetogenici.

Coinvolgimento in Comunità Online

Partecipare a forum online e gruppi di supporto chetogenici può offrire consigli pratici, ricette nuove e supporto emotivo da altri che seguono lo stesso percorso alimentare. Queste comunità possono essere particolarmente utili per condividere esperienze, risolvere dubbi e trovare motivazione.

Preparazione per le Vacanze e Occasioni Speciali

Le vacanze e altre occasioni speciali richiedono una pianificazione extra per mantenere la coerenza con la dieta chetogenica. Pianificare i pasti in anticipo, comunicare le proprie esigenze dietetiche agli ospiti o agli organizzatori degli eventi, e preparare e portare piatti chetogenici possono aiutare a gestire tali situazioni senza stress.

Monitoraggio del Progresso Alimentare

Infine, tenere un diario alimentare dettagliato o utilizzare app di tracking può aiutare a monitorare l'assunzione di macronutrienti e a valutare l'impatto dei diversi alimenti o pasti sulla chetosi. Questo tipo di monitoraggio può essere essenziale per affinare ulteriormente la dieta e assicurare che sia nutritiva, equilibrata e efficace nel raggiungere gli obiettivi di salute e di perdita di peso.

Incorporare queste strategie avanzate e considerazioni nella pianificazione dei pasti e della lista della spesa può notevolmente migliorare l'efficacia e la piacevolezza della dieta chetogenica, aiutando gli individui a navigare con successo il loro percorso verso una salute ottimale e una maggiore benessere.

Proseguendo con la comprensione approfondita della pianificazione dei pasti e della lista della spesa per la dieta chetogenica, esaminiamo altre tecniche e suggerimenti utili per mantenere e rafforzare la dieta nel tempo.

Controllo Qualitativo degli Alimenti

Mantenere un alto standard di qualità negli alimenti consumati può influenzare notevolmente i risultati della dieta chetogenica. Optare per carni allevate al pascolo, prodotti biologici e pesce pescato in modo sostenibile può migliorare non solo l'impatto ambientale del consumo, ma anche la qualità nutrizionale degli alimenti. Alimenti di alta qualità tendono a contenere più nutrienti essenziali e meno additivi nocivi, supportando una salute ottimale.

Valorizzazione delle Fonti di Grassi Salutari

Data l'importanza dei grassi nella dieta chetogenica, selezionare fonti di grassi di alta qualità è cruciale. Integrare una varietà di grassi salutari, come quelli derivati da oli vergini (olio d'oliva, olio di cocco), grassi di origine animale (burro di buona qualità, strutto), e grassi provenienti da frutta come le olive e gli avocado, garantisce che il corpo riceva un mix equilibrato di acidi grassi essenziali.

Abbinamento Nutrizionale Ottimale

Per massimizzare l'assorbimento dei nutrienti, è utile considerare l'abbinamento degli alimenti. Ad esempio, abbinare fonti di grassi con verdure ricche di vitamine liposolubili (come vitamina A, D, E, e K) può migliorare l'assorbimento di questi nutrienti essenziali. Questa strategia nutrizionale non solo ottimizza i benefici per la salute, ma aiuta anche a mantenere il corpo più sazio e soddisfatto.

Strategie per Ridurre gli Sprechi Alimentari

Essere consapevoli di quanto si acquista e si consuma può ridurre significativamente gli sprechi alimentari. Pianificare l'uso di alimenti che potrebbero deperirsi rapidamente, come alcune verdure o prodotti freschi, e conservare correttamente i cibi possono estendere la loro durata e garantire che la dieta rimanga economica ed ecologica.

Uso Creativo delle Avanzate Tecnologie da Cucina

Sfruttare le tecnologie da cucina moderne può trasformare il modo in cui prepari e godi i pasti chetogenici. Strumenti come sous-vide, deidratatori, e blender ad alta potenza possono essere utilizzati per preparare pasti chetogenici in modi innovativi, conservando il sapore e la qualità nutrizionale degli alimenti e diversificando le opzioni alimentari disponibili.

Pianificazione Anticipata per Ristorazione Fuori Casa

Mangiare fuori può presentare sfide per chi segue una dieta chetogenica. Ricercare in anticipo menu e ristoranti che offrono opzioni chetogeniche compatibili, comunicare chiaramente le tue esigenze al personale del ristorante, e decidere in anticipo cosa ordinare può aiutare a evitare scelte alimentari impulsiva e mantenere l'adesione alla dieta.

Valutazione Periodica del Piano Alimentare

Esaminare e valutare periodicamente il piano alimentare è essenziale per assicurare che soddisfi ancora le tue esigenze nutrizionali e di stile di vita. Questo può includere l'aggiustamento dei macronutrienti in risposta a cambiamenti nella routine di esercizio, variazioni del peso corporeo, o altri fattori di salute. Un nutrizionista o un medico può fornire supporto e guida in questo processo di valutazione continua.

Integrare queste strategie avanzate nella tua routine quotidiana può notevolmente migliorare l'efficacia e l'esperienza complessiva della dieta chetogenica. Attraverso un'attenta pianificazione, un'impeccabile esecuzione e una continua valutazione, la dieta chetogenica può diventare non solo un metodo per perdere peso, ma una trasformazione sostenibile verso uno stile di vita più sano e consapevole.

Espandendo ulteriormente le strategie per la pianificazione efficace dei pasti e la creazione di liste della spesa ottimizzate per la dieta chetogenica, possiamo considerare altre tattiche avanzate che supportano una nutritiva e variegata alimentazione chetogenica.

Approfondimento Nutrizionale

Approfondire la comprensione delle proprietà nutrizionali degli alimenti può giocare un ruolo critico nella selezione degli ingredienti per la dieta chetogenica. Ad esempio, capire le differenze tra i tipi di grassi (saturi, monoinsaturi, polinsaturi) e il loro impatto sulla salute può aiutare a fare scelte alimentari più informate. Alimenti come l'olio di oliva e il pesce ricco di omega-3 sono eccellenti per la salute cardiovascolare e dovrebbero essere inclusi regolarmente nel piano alimentare chetogenico.

Integrazione di Alimenti Fermentati

Includere alimenti fermentati nella dieta chetogenica può migliorare la salute intestinale e potenziare il sistema immunitario. Alimenti come il kimchi, il kefir e la sauerkraut sono bassi in carboidrati e ricchi di probiotici, che aiutano a mantenere un microbioma intestinale sano. Questi possono essere integrati nei pasti come contorni o snack per arricchire la dieta senza aggiungere carboidrati significativi.

Ottimizzazione della Lista della Spesa

Per ottimizzare ulteriormente la lista della spesa, può essere utile categorizzare gli alimenti non solo in base ai macro gruppi alimentari ma anche in base alla frequenza di utilizzo. Ad esempio, dividere la lista in "necessari per ogni settimana", "acquisti mensili" e "occasioni speciali" può rendere lo shopping più efficiente e aiutare a gestire il budget. Questo approccio riduce il rischio di acquisti superflui e assicura che gli alimenti base non vengano mai dimenticati.

Pianificazione dei Pasti Intorno agli Allenamenti

Per coloro che sono attivi fisicamente, pianificare i pasti intorno agli allenamenti diventa cruciale. Consumare pasti più ricchi di proteine e grassi sani prima o dopo gli allenamenti può aiutare a ottimizzare il recupero muscolare e la prestazione. Alimenti come petto di pollo, uova, avocado, e noci possono essere distribuiti strategicamente nei pasti per supportare l'esercizio fisico senza compromettere lo stato di chetosi.

Sviluppo di Ricette Modificabili

Sviluppare un repertorio di ricette facilmente modificabili può facilitare l'adattamento alla dieta chetogenica in base ai cambiamenti di stagione, disponibilità di ingredienti o preferenze personali. Questo tipo di flessibilità nella preparazione dei pasti può prevenire la noia alimentare e rendere la dieta più sostenibile e piacevole a lungo termine.

Uso di App di Pianificazione Alimentare

Sfruttare app di pianificazione alimentare che offrono funzionalità specifiche per la dieta chetogenica può semplificare notevolmente il processo di pianificazione dei pasti. Queste app possono aiutare a calcolare i macro nutrienti, suggerire ricette e persino generare liste della spesa personalizzate in base alle preferenze alimentari e ai bisogni nutrizionali.

Risorse per l'Inspirazione Culinaia

Infine, cercare ispirazione da varie fonti, come blog di cucina chetogenica, libri di cucina e canali di cucina su YouTube, può offrire nuove idee e tecniche per mantenere la dieta fresca e interessante. Scoprire nuovi modi per preparare i pasti può contribuire a mantenere alta la motivazione e a sperimentare con piacere la cucina chetogenica.

Continuando a integrare queste pratiche avanzate nella tua routine di pianificazione dei pasti e della spesa, puoi arricchire la tua dieta chetogenica, rendendola non solo più efficace per raggiungere i tuoi obiettivi di salute, ma anche più godibile e sostenibile a lungo termine.

Concludendo, una pianificazione efficace dei pasti e una strategia di spesa ben organizzata sono fondamentali per il successo a lungo termine di una dieta chetogenica. Questa pianificazione non solo assicura che la dieta rimanga varia e nutritivamente bilanciata, ma facilita anche l'adesione costante e sostenibile al regime chetogenico.

Punti Chiave della Pianificazione Alimentare e della Lista della Spesa per la Dieta Chetogenica

1. **Definizione dei Macronutrienti**: Impostare chiari obiettivi per le proporzioni di grassi, proteine e carboidrati basati sui propri obiettivi di salute e sulle esigenze del corpo.

2. **Scelta Intelligente degli Alimenti**: Concentrarsi su alimenti che supportano lo stato di chetosi—grassi di qualità, proteine magre, e verdure a basso contenuto di carboidrati. Preferire sempre alimenti integrali e non trasformati per massimizzare i benefici nutrizionali.

3. **Variazione e Creatività nei Pasti**: Utilizzare erbe, spezie e varietà di alimenti per mantenere i pasti

interessanti e gustosi, riducendo il rischio di monotonia
alimentare.

4. **Preparazione e Conservazione**: Cucinare in grandi
   quantità e utilizzare tecniche di conservazione per
   facilitare la gestione dei pasti durante la settimana,
   risparmiando tempo e energia.

5. **Pianificazione Strategica della Spesa**: Organizzare
   la lista della spesa per categorie e sfruttare le offerte locali
   per gestire il budget senza compromettere la qualità degli
   alimenti.

6. **Uso di Tecnologie e Risorse**: Applicare tecnologie
   come app di pianificazione dei pasti e utilizzare risorse
   online per trovare ispirazione e supporto nella
   preparazione dei pasti.

7. **Gestione dei Pasti in Contesti Sociali e Speciali**:
   Prepararsi per occasioni speciali e situazioni sociali
   pianificando in anticipo può aiutare a mantenere la
   coerenza senza isolarsi o deviare dal piano alimentare.

8. **Monitoraggio e Adattamento**: Valutare
   periodicamente l'efficacia del piano alimentare e fare
   aggiustamenti in base ai risultati di salute, alle risposte
   del corpo e ai cambiamenti nelle routine di vita.

9. **Educazione Continua**: Mantenere un impegno
   costante verso l'apprendimento e l'aggiornamento sulla
   dieta chetogenica e le tendenze nutrizionali per
   ottimizzare continuamente l'approccio e integrare nuove
   scoperte scientifiche.

Incorporando questi elementi dettagliati nella pianificazione dei
pasti e nella preparazione della lista della spesa, chi segue una
dieta chetogenica può navigare con successo il proprio percorso,
mantenendo una dieta che non solo supporta la perdita di peso e
la gestione della salute, ma che è anche piacevole, variata e

sostenibile nel tempo. Questo approccio olistico non solo aiuta a raggiungere gli obiettivi fisici ma supporta anche il benessere generale, contribuendo a una vita più sana e attiva.

5. Alimenti da Mangiare e da Evitare: Un capitolo dettagliato sugli alimenti consentiti nella dieta chetogenica e quelli da evitare.

5. Alimenti da Mangiare e da Evitare: Un Capitolo Dettagliato per la Dieta Chetogenica

Nell'ambito della dieta chetogenica, è fondamentale comprendere quali alimenti sono ammessi e quali sono da evitare per mantenere lo stato di chetosi, il quale è essenziale per il successo della dieta. Ecco una guida dettagliata sugli alimenti da privilegiare e quelli da limitare o eliminare.

Alimenti da Mangiare

1. **Grassi e Oli**: Scegliere fonti di grassi salutari è cruciale. Questi includono:

   - Oli naturali come l'olio d'oliva, olio di cocco e olio di avocado.

   - Burro e ghee.

   - Grassi animali, inclusi strutto e sego.

2. **Proteine**: Le proteine devono essere consumate in moderazione. Le fonti di proteine adatte alla dieta chetogenica includono:

   - Carni come manzo, maiale, agnello, pollame e selvaggina. Preferire tagli più grassi per aumentare l'apporto lipidico.

   - Pesce grasso come salmone, aringhe e sardine.

o   Frutti di mare.

o   Uova.

3. **Verdure a Basso Contenuto di Carboidrati**: Le verdure sono una fonte importante di vitamine, minerali e fibre. Optare per:

o   Verdure a foglia verde come spinaci, cavolo e lattuga.

o   Verdure crucifere come broccoli, cavolfiori e cavoli di Bruxelles.

o   Altre verdure come zucchine, peperoni e asparagi.

4. **Latticini a Basso Contenuto di Carboidrati**: I latticini possono essere inclusi, ma è importante scegliere opzioni a basso contenuto di carboidrati.

o   Formaggi a pasta dura e semidura come cheddar, parmigiano e gouda.

o   Panna e creme dense.

o   Yogurt greco intero o yogurt a basso contenuto di carboidrati.

5. **Noci e Semi**: Sono ottime fonti di grassi, ma dovrebbero essere consumate con moderazione a causa del loro contenuto di carboidrati.

o   Mandorle, noci, noci pecan, macadamia.

o   Semi di chia, semi di lino, semi di zucca.

6. **Condimenti**: Gli condimenti possono aggiungere sapore senza aggiungere carboidrati eccessivi.

o   Erbe e spezie fresche o essiccate.

o   Salse e condimenti fatti in casa privi di zuccheri aggiunti, come maionese e senape.

Alimenti da Evitare

1. **Carboidrati e Zuccheri**: La dieta chetogenica limita severamente l'assunzione di carboidrati.

   o Cereali e derivati come pane, pasta, riso e cereali.

   o Legumi come fagioli e lenticchie.

   o Dolci e prodotti da forno, inclusi dolci, biscotti e altri snack dolci.

   o Frutta dolce come banane, mele, arance e uva.

2. **Verdure Ricche di Carboidrati**: Alcune verdure contengono più carboidrati e dovrebbero essere evitate o limitate.

   o Tuberi come patate, patate dolci e carote.

   o Altre verdure ricche di carboidrati come mais e piselli.

3. **Bevande Zuccherate**: Evitare tutte le bevande che contengono zuccheri aggiunti.

   o Bibite gassate, succhi di frutta, bevande energetiche e sportive.

4. **Alcol**: Molti alcolici contengono carboidrati che possono interferire con la chetosi.

   o Birra, cocktail zuccherati, e liquori dolci come liquori e alcuni vini.

Comprendere chiaramente quali alimenti includere e quali evitare è essenziale per chiunque segua una dieta chetogenica. Mantenere lo stato di chetosi richiede disciplina e attenzione nella scelta degli alimenti, garantendo così che la dieta sia non solo efficace ma anche nutrizionalmente equilibrata. Questa guida dettagliata aiuta a fare scelte alimentari informate, contribuendo al successo a lungo termine della dieta chetogenica.

Proseguendo nella nostra discussione dettagliata sugli alimenti da incorporare e quelli da evitare nella dieta chetogenica, esaminiamo ulteriori sfumature e considerazioni che possono migliorare l'efficacia della dieta e garantire un apporto nutrizionale ottimale.

Alimenti Funzionali e la Loro Importanza

Nella dieta chetogenica, oltre ai macronutrienti principali, è importante considerare il ruolo degli alimenti funzionali che forniscono benefici aggiuntivi per la salute:

- **Alimenti Fermentati**: Prodotti come il kefir e il kimchi, che sono poveri di carboidrati ma ricchi di probiotici, possono aiutare a migliorare la salute intestinale e rafforzare il sistema immunitario.

- **Alghe**: Le alghe sono una fonte eccezionale di iodio e altri minerali, utili, in particolare, per chi segue una dieta chetogenica e può avere una limitata assunzione di altri vegetali ricchi di micronutrienti.

Cibi da Considerare con Cautela

Alcuni cibi che tecnicamente possono rientrare nei limiti di una dieta chetogenica dovrebbero essere consumati con moderazione o cautela:

- **Formaggi e Latticini Grassi**: Sebbene ricchi di grassi, alcuni formaggi possono anche contenere livelli più elevati di proteine o carboidrati latenti, che possono sommarsi nel corso della giornata.

- **Frutti a Guscio e Semi**: Questi sono generalmente alti in grassi e un'ottima scelta per uno snack, ma il loro contenuto calorico è elevato e alcuni frutti a guscio hanno una quota di carboidrati che può accumularsi rapidamente.

Attenzione ai Condimenti e agli Additivi

La scelta dei condimenti può avere un impatto significativo sulla manutenzione dello stato di chetosi:

- **Salse e Condimenti Commerciali**: Molte preparazioni commerciali contengono zuccheri aggiunti e carboidrati nascosti. Leggere attentamente le etichette o preparare condimenti in casa può aiutare a evitare ingredienti indesiderati.

- **Edulcoranti Artificiali**: Anche se non contribuiscono a carboidrati netti, alcuni edulcoranti possono influenzare i livelli di zucchero nel sangue o causare desideri di dolci. La scelta di edulcoranti naturali come stevia o eritritolo è generalmente preferibile.

Bevande Consentite e da Evitare

La selezione delle bevande è altrettanto importante quanto la scelta degli alimenti solidi:

- **Caffè e Tè**: Sono generalmente accettabili senza aggiunte zuccherate; la crema e un dolcificante a basso contenuto di carboidrati possono essere usati per chi li preferisce non amari.

- **Bevande Alcoliche**: Alcuni alcolici come vini secchi e alcuni spiriti puri (senza mixer zuccherati) possono essere consumati con moderazione, ma è essenziale controllare l'impatto personale sulla chetosi.

Gestione Pratica della Dieta Chetogenica

Infine, il successo a lungo termine nella dieta chetogenica dipende anche dalla gestione pratica della dieta nel contesto della vita quotidiana:

- **Preparazione dei Pasti**: Investire tempo nella preparazione dei pasti può semplificare la seguente della dieta durante la settimana lavorativa impegnativa.

- **Educazione Continua**: Mantenersi informati sugli ultimi studi e consigli riguardo alla dieta chetogenica può fornire nuove idee e motivazione.

- **Rete di Supporto**: Costruire una rete di supporto, sia online sia offline, con altre persone che seguono la dieta chetogenica può offrire supporto, scambio di ricette e consigli pratici.

Considerare questi dettagli può aiutare a navigare con successo la dieta chetogenica, garantendo non solo l'adesione ai principi di base della dieta ma anche l'approfondimento nel modo più nutriente e sostenibile possibile.

Approfondendo ulteriormente le strategie per una gestione ottimale degli alimenti nella dieta chetogenica, possiamo esplorare altri aspetti essenziali che influenzano l'efficacia e la sostenibilità della dieta.

Integrazione di Grassi di Qualità Superiore

Una considerazione importante è l'origine e la qualità dei grassi consumati. Grassi di qualità superiore come l'olio di oliva extra vergine, l'olio di cocco vergine e il grasso di avocado possono fornire benefici per la salute oltre alla semplice aderenza ai requisiti di macronutrienti della dieta chetogenica. L'inclusione di grassi Omega-3 provenienti da fonti come i pesci grassi (salmone selvatico, sardine) e integratori di alta qualità può aiutare a bilanciare il rapporto tra Omega-6 e Omega-3 nel corpo, favorendo una migliore salute cardiovascolare e riducendo l'infiammazione.

Variazione Stagionale e Locale degli Alimenti

Incorporare alimenti che sono sia locali sia stagionali può migliorare la sostenibilità della dieta chetogenica e garantire che si consumino prodotti al picco della loro freschezza e valore nutrizionale. Ad esempio, verdure a foglia verde come la bietola e il cavolo possono essere consumati freschi nei mesi più freddi, mentre cetrioli, pomodori e peperoni sono migliori in estate.

Importanza della Qualità Proteica

Le fonti proteiche dovrebbero essere selezionate con cura, preferendo quelle che non solo rispettano i requisiti di basso apporto di carboidrati, ma sono anche sostenibili e eticamente prodotte. Carne proveniente da allevamenti biologici, sostenibili o al pascolo, così come i prodotti ittici certificati MSC (Marine Stewardship Council) per la pesca sostenibile, possono fare una grande differenza nell'impatto ambientale della dieta e nella qualità delle proteine ingerite.

Strategie di Evitamento per gli Alimenti Ad Alto Indice Glicemico

Essere consapevoli degli alimenti che possono causare picchi di zucchero nel sangue è fondamentale, anche per quelli che possono sembrare "chetogenici" per il loro contenuto di grassi. Ad esempio, alcuni prodotti dietetici o a basso contenuto di zuccheri possono contenere alcol zuccherino che, in alcune persone, può elevare i livelli di zucchero nel sangue e quindi interferire con lo stato di chetosi.

Considerazioni Culturali e Personalizzate

Adattare la dieta chetogenica per rispettare le preferenze culturali e personali può aiutare a mantenere questa alimentazione a lungo termine. Integrare piatti tradizionali modificati per essere cheto-compatibili permette di godere di cibi confortevoli e culturalmente significativi senza compromettere gli obiettivi dietetici.

Uso di Supplementi Nutrizionali

Mentre la dieta chetogenica può fornire molti nutrienti
essenziali, alcuni possono essere difficili da ottenere in quantità
sufficienti, come specifiche vitamine, minerali e fibre.
Consultare un nutrizionista o un medico per discutere se sia
necessario integrare la dieta con supplementi nutrizionali può
aiutare a prevenire carenze potenziali e mantenere un corpo
sano.

Monitoraggio Continuo del Corpo

Ascoltare il proprio corpo e monitorare gli effetti della dieta è
vitale. Questo include non solo tracciare la perdita di peso o la
manutenzione, ma anche monitorare altri indicatori di salute
come i livelli di energia, la qualità del sonno, la digestione e il
benessere emotivo. Regolare la dieta in base ai feedback del
proprio corpo può contribuire a una personalizzazione più fine e
a risultati migliori.

Approfondire questi aspetti della dieta chetogenica può non solo
ottimizzare la composizione e il consumo degli alimenti, ma
anche elevare il benessere generale e supportare un approccio
chetogenico più consapevole, personalizzato e sostenibile.

Continuando l'esplorazione approfondita degli alimenti da
includere e da evitare nella dieta chetogenica, esaminiamo
ulteriori aspetti che possono influenzare significativamente la
sua efficacia e sostenibilità.

Valorizzazione della Diversità Nutrizionale

È essenziale mantenere una dieta variegata anche all'interno
delle restrizioni dei carboidrati per garantire un'ampia gamma
di micronutrienti essenziali. Questo include il tentativo di
incorporare una varietà di verdure a basso contenuto di
carboidrati di diversi colori, che possono offrire diversi
fitonutrienti e antiossidanti, come il cavolo rosso, la rucola, i
peperoni verdi e gialli, e le erbe fresche.

Attenzione ai Falsi Amici

Alcuni alimenti possono sembrare compatibili con la dieta chetogenica sulla base del loro contenuto di grassi o proteine, ma in realtà possono nascondere carboidrati o additivi che compromettono lo stato di chetosi. Per esempio, alcuni tipi di salsicce o altri prodotti carnei lavorati possono contenere zuccheri aggiunti o amido come riempitivi. È cruciale leggere attentamente le etichette e preferire alimenti nella loro forma più pura e non elaborata.

Integrazione di Grasso di Qualità in Modo Creativo

Per assicurare un adeguato apporto di grassi salutari, è utile essere creativi nel modo in cui questi vengono integrati nella dieta. L'uso di condimenti come l'olio di oliva o di avocado nelle insalate, l'aggiunta di cocco grattugiato ai frullati, o l'uso di burro di noci come spuntino possono arricchire significativamente l'assunzione di grassi buoni senza aumentare i carboidrati.

Preparazione e Conservazione dei Pasti

Preparare e conservare i pasti in anticipo può facilitare enormemente l'adesione alla dieta chetogenica. Cucinare grandi quantità di cibo chetogenico amichevole e conservarlo in porzioni può aiutare a gestire i tempi di pasto durante una settimana impegnativa, assicurando che ci sia sempre una scelta salutare a portata di mano.

Uso Strategico delle Spezie

Le spezie non solo aggiungono sapore senza aggiungere carboidrati, ma molte hanno anche benefici per la salute, come proprietà anti-infiammatorie e antiossidanti. Spezie come la curcuma, il pepe di Cayenna, e il cumino possono essere integrate per migliorare il gusto e l'interesse culinario dei piatti chetogenici.

Monitoraggio dell'Impatto dei Pasti su Chetosi

Utilizzare strumenti come misuratori di chetoni per monitorare come specifici alimenti influenzano lo stato di chetosi può aiutare a personalizzare la dieta. Questo è particolarmente utile nelle fasi iniziali della dieta chetogenica, quando si sta ancora imparando quali alimenti funzionano meglio per il mantenimento della chetosi.

Sensibilità Personale ai Carboidrati

Riconoscere la propria sensibilità ai carboidrati è fondamentale. Alcune persone possono essere in grado di mantenere la chetosi con un limite leggermente più alto di carboidrati, mentre altre possono richiedere una restrizione più severa. Ascoltare attentamente il proprio corpo e adattare la dieta di conseguenza può ottimizzare sia la salute che i risultati di perdita di peso.

Innovazione e Sperimentazione Culinarie

Sperimentare con nuove ricette e modalità di preparazione degli alimenti può mantenere la dieta chetogenica fresca e interessante. Esplorare cucine internazionali per ispirazione può portare a scoperte di piatti che sono naturalmente bassi in carboidrati o che possono essere facilmente adattati.

Questi approfondimenti offrono strategie per rendere la dieta chetogenica non solo più gestibile e sostenibile, ma anche più piacevole e personalizzata, garantendo che gli individui possano mantenere la chetosi efficacemente pur godendo di un'alimentazione ricca e varia.

Proseguendo nella disamina degli aspetti più sfumati della dieta chetogenica, esploriamo ulteriori dettagli che possono aiutare a ottimizzare la scelta degli alimenti e la loro preparazione, assicurando una maggiore varietà e soddisfazione nel mantenere questo regime alimentare rigoroso.

Abbinamento Nutrizionale Avanzato

Una strategia efficace nella dieta chetogenica può includere
l'abbinamento di alimenti per massimizzare l'assorbimento di
nutrienti. Per esempio, abbinare fonti di grassi con verdure
ricche di vitamine liposolubili come vitamina A, D, E e K può
migliorare notevolmente la biodisponibilità di questi nutrienti.
Consumare insalate con un'abbondante dose di olio d'oliva o di
avocado può aiutare ad assorbire al meglio le vitamine presenti
nelle verdure.

Ottimizzazione dei Processi di Cottura

La modalità di cottura degli alimenti può influenzare
significativamente il loro profilo nutrizionale. Per esempio,
metodi di cottura a bassa temperatura o brevi possono
preservare meglio i nutrienti sensibili al calore rispetto a metodi
di cottura prolungati o ad alta temperatura. Utilizzare metodi
come la cottura a vapore, il sous-vide, o il salto rapido in padella
può aiutare a mantenere il massimo delle proprietà nutritive
degli alimenti.

Attenzione agli Additivi Alimentari

Molti alimenti processati possono contenere additivi che non
solo sono incompatibili con la dieta chetogenica, ma possono
anche essere dannosi per la salute generale. Additivi come
glutammato monosodico, conservanti artificiali, coloranti e
dolcificanti artificiali dovrebbero essere evitati. Leggere
attentamente le etichette e scegliere prodotti con il minor
numero di ingredienti e additivi possibile è una pratica salutare.

Gestione delle Porzioni e del Senso di Sazietà

Nella dieta chetogenica, è fondamentale gestire attentamente le
porzioni per mantenere il bilancio calorico necessario per la
perdita di peso o la manutenzione, senza eccedere con le calorie.
Alimenti ad alta densità calorica come noci, semi e oli possono
rapidamente aumentare l'apporto calorico totale se non gestiti

con attenzione. Utilizzare strumenti come bilance da cucina o misurini può aiutare a mantenere le porzioni sotto controllo.

Sviluppo di Un Piano di Integrazione Sostenibile

Considerare l'integrazione di specifici nutrienti che potrebbero essere carenti in una dieta chetogenica è importante per prevenire carenze nutrizionali. Nutrienti come il magnesio, il potassio e le fibre possono essere più difficili da ottenere in quantità adeguate in una dieta a basso contenuto di carboidrati. Consultare un professionista della nutrizione per sviluppare un piano di integrazione basato sulle esigenze individuali può essere estremamente utile.

Utilizzo di Feedback Biometrico

Monitorare gli effetti della dieta sul corpo attraverso feedback biometrico come la misurazione dei livelli di chetoni, la glucometria, o anche dispositivi indossabili che tracciano parametri come il battito cardiaco o il recupero può offrire intuizioni preziose sul come il corpo sta rispondendo alla dieta. Queste informazioni possono aiutare a personalizzare ulteriormente la dieta per ottimizzare sia la performance che il benessere.

Sperimentazione e Innovazione in Cucina

Mantenere un approccio sperimentale e innovativo in cucina può rendere la dieta chetogenica più piacevole e meno monotona. Esplorare ricette internazionali, sperimentare con sostituti chetogenici in piatti tradizionali, e utilizzare spezie esotiche può aprire nuovi orizzonti culinari e rendere ogni pasto un'occasione per scoprire nuovi sapori e texture.

Approfondendo e integrando queste pratiche avanzate, chi segue una dieta chetogenica può non solo aderire efficacemente al regime alimentare ma anche godere di un'esperienza alimentare più ricca e gratificante, che supporta la salute e il benessere complessivi mentre mantiene il corpo in uno stato ottimale di chetosi.

Continuando ad esplorare strategie avanzate per ottimizzare l'efficacia e il piacere di seguire una dieta chetogenica, ci sono ancora molte dimensioni che possono arricchire l'esperienza dietetica e assicurare che rimanga nutritiva e sostenibile.

Focus sulla Qualità degli Alimenti Integrali

Priorizzare gli alimenti integrali e minimamente processati nella dieta chetogenica è fondamentale per ottenere il massimo dei benefici nutrizionali. Alimenti come verdure fresche, carni di alta qualità e grassi naturali sono più nutrienti dei loro omologhi processati e contengono meno additivi potenzialmente dannosi o disturbi metabolici.

Valorizzazione dei Metodi di Preparazione Tradizionali

Reintegrare metodi di preparazione degli alimenti tradizionali e artigianali, come la fermentazione o l'essiccazione a basse temperature, può non solo migliorare la digeribilità degli alimenti ma anche incrementare la presenza di probiotici, enzimi e altri fattori nutrizionali benefici nella dieta.

Diversificazione delle Fonti di Grasso

Anche all'interno di una dieta chetogenica, è importante variare le fonti di grasso per garantire un ampio spettro di acidi grassi essenziali e limitare il consumo eccessivo di certi tipi di grassi che possono essere meno salubri in grandi quantità. Rotare tra oli di diversi tipi, grassi animali e grassi provenienti da semi e noci può aiutare a mantenere un equilibrio salutare.

Considerazioni Ecologiche ed Etiche

Scegliere fonti di cibo che siano non solo nutrizionalmente adeguate ma anche prodotte in modo sostenibile ed etico può aumentare l'impatto positivo della dieta chetogenica. Questo include preferire prodotti locali, supportare agricoltori e produttori che adottano pratiche sostenibili, e considerare il benessere animale nella scelta dei prodotti di origine animale.

Pianificazione di Pasti Flessibili

Nel contesto di una dieta rigorosa come la chetogenica, mantenere un certo livello di flessibilità nei pasti può aiutare a gestire situazioni sociali e adattarsi a cambiamenti di routine senza compromettere gli obiettivi nutrizionali. Avere opzioni di pasti che possono essere facilmente adattati, modificati o preparati in anticipo può ridurre lo stress e aumentare il piacere di mangiare.

Esplorazione delle Cucine Etniche

Molte cucine etniche offrono piatti che possono essere facilmente adattati ai principi chetogenici o che sono naturalmente bassi in carboidrati. Esplorare ricette da culture diverse può non solo aggiungere varietà alla dieta ma anche esporre a nuovi ingredienti e modi di cucinare che possono arricchire l'esperienza culinaria.

Uso Attento degli Integritori

Mentre gli integratori possono svolgere un ruolo importante nel bilanciare la dieta chetogenica, è essenziale usarli in modo informato e misurato. Integratori di fibre, elettroliti, vitamine specifiche o minerali dovrebbero essere considerati basandosi su un'analisi attenta delle proprie esigenze individuali, preferibilmente con il consiglio di un professionista della salute.

Monitoraggio Continuo e Personalizzazione

Il successo a lungo termine con la dieta chetogenica spesso richiede un monitoraggio continuo e una personalizzazione della dieta. Utilizzare diari alimentari, app di tracking o feedback biometrico può aiutare a identificare quali alimenti funzionano meglio per il proprio corpo e stile di vita, permettendo aggiustamenti che migliorano l'efficacia della dieta e il benessere generale.

Incorporando queste considerazioni avanzate, chi segue una dieta chetogenica può non solo assicurare il rispetto dei principi chetogenici ma anche godere di una dieta ricca, variata e profondamente soddisfacente che supporta una salute ottimale e uno stile di vita sostenibile.

Concludendo, la dieta chetogenica, quando attentamente pianificata e attentamente gestita, può offrire non solo benefici significativi per la perdita di peso e il controllo metabolico, ma anche un'opportunità per arricchire l'alimentazione quotidiana attraverso scelte alimentari consapevoli e sostenibili.

Principi Fondamentali per la Gestione Efficace della Dieta Chetogenica

1. **Qualità degli Alimenti**: Concentrarsi su alimenti integrali e minimamente processati per massimizzare l'assunzione di nutrienti essenziali. Questo include scegliere grassi di alta qualità, proteine complete e verdure a basso contenuto di carboidrati ricche di fibre e micronutrienti.

2. **Diversificazione e Rotazione**: Variare regolarmente le fonti di grassi e proteine per evitare squilibri nutrizionali e aumentare l'apporto di diversi nutrienti essenziali. Incorporare una varietà di verdure a basso contenuto di carboidrati per sfruttare i diversi profili di vitamine e minerali.

3. **Attenzione ai Dettagli Nutrizionali**: Essere meticolosi nella lettura delle etichette per evitare zuccheri nascosti e carboidrati non desiderati in alimenti confezionati. Optare per alimenti con il minor numero di ingredienti artificiali e additivi.

4. **Adattabilità e Flessibilità**: Essere pronti ad adattare il piano alimentare in base alle reazioni del corpo, ai cambiamenti delle esigenze energetiche e alla disponibilità stagionale degli alimenti. Utilizzare metodi di cottura che preservano o migliorano il valore nutrizionale degli alimenti.

5. **Sostenibilità Alimentare**: Preferire prodotti locali, biologici e sostenibili per supportare non solo la propria salute ma anche quella dell'ambiente. Considerare le pratiche etiche nella produzione alimentare, specialmente per quanto riguarda la carne e i prodotti ittici.

6. **Supporto Sociale e Comunitario**: Sfruttare la comunità, sia online che locale, per scambiare ricette, consigli e supporto morale. Questo può aiutare a mantenere alta la motivazione e a condividere le sfide e i successi.

7. **Utilizzo Strategico di Supplementi**: Integrare la dieta con supplementi mirati, come minerali elettroliti o vitamine specifiche, può aiutare a prevenire carenze nutrizionali e supportare una salute ottimale.

8. **Monitoraggio e Valutazione**: Mantenere un diario alimentare e utilizzare strumenti di monitoraggio per valutare l'effetto degli alimenti e delle modifiche dietetiche sul proprio corpo. Ajustare il piano alimentare in base ai feedback per ottimizzare gli effetti benefici della dieta.

9. **Educazione Continua**: Impegnarsi in un'apprendimento continuo sulle ultime ricerche e raccomandazioni nella nutrizione chetogenica. Partecipare a workshop, leggere studi aggiornati e rimanere informati sulle migliori pratiche.

10. **Piacere e Soddisfazione Alimentare**: Ricordarsi che il cibo non è solo nutrimento ma anche piacere. Sperimentare con ricette nuove e sapori diversi per mantenere la dieta sia gratificante che nutritiva.

Adottando questi principi dettagliati, chi segue una dieta chetogenica può non solo aderire efficacemente ai requisiti nutrizionali ma anche godere di un regime alimentare ricco e soddisfacente. Questo approccio olistico non solo facilita il raggiungimento degli obiettivi di salute e benessere ma rende il percorso verso di essi sostenibile e piacevole.

6. Ricette Chetogeniche Facili e Veloci: Fornire ricette semplici per colazione, pranzo, cena e snack che si adattano al piano alimentare chetogenico.

6. Ricette Chetogeniche Facili e Veloci

Per chi segue la dieta chetogenica, avere a disposizione ricette semplici e rapide è fondamentale per mantenere la dieta nel quotidiano senza sacrificare sapore o varietà. Di seguito, troverai ricette per colazione, pranzo, cena e snack, tutte in linea con i principi chetogenici e veloci da preparare.

Colazione: Frittata di Spinaci e Feta

Ingredienti:

- 4 uova
- 1 tazza di spinaci freschi tritati
- 1/4 di tazza di feta sbriciolata
- 2 cucchiai di burro
- Sale e pepe a piacere

Preparazione:

1. In una padella, sciogliere il burro e aggiungere gli spinaci, cuocendo fino a che non si ammorbidiscono.

2. In una ciotola, sbattere le uova con sale e pepe, poi versarle nella padella con gli spinaci.

3. Cospargere la feta sbriciolata sopra le uova.

4. Coprire e cuocere a fuoco medio-basso per 3-5 minuti o fino a quando l'uovo non si è completamente rappreso.

5. Servire calda.

Pranzo: Insalata di Pollo Avocado

Ingredienti:

- 1 petto di pollo grigliato, tagliato a cubetti

- 1 avocado maturo, tagliato a cubetti

- 1/2 cetriolo, tagliato a cubetti

- 1/4 di tazza di mandorle tostate

- Succo di 1 limone

- Olio d'oliva

- Sale e pepe a piacere

Preparazione:

1. In una ciotola grande, combinare il pollo, l'avocado, il cetriolo e le mandorle.

2. Condire con il succo di limone, un generoso giro di olio d'oliva, sale e pepe.

3. Mescolare delicatamente fino a quando gli ingredienti sono ben combinati.

4. Servire fresca.

Cena: Salmone al Forno con Asparagi

Ingredienti:

- 2 filetti di salmone

- 1 mazzo di asparagi, puliti e tagliati

- 2 cucchiai di olio d'oliva

- Sale e pepe a piacere

- Limone per guarnire

Preparazione:

1. Preriscaldare il forno a 200°C.

2. Disporre i filetti di salmone e gli asparagi su una teglia rivestita di carta da forno.

3. Irrorare con olio d'oliva e condire con sale e pepe.

4. Cuocere in forno per 15-20 minuti, fino a quando il salmone è cotto e gli asparagi sono teneri.

5. Servire caldo con spicchi di limone.

Snack: Chips di Cavolo Riccio

Ingredienti:

- 1 mazzo di cavolo riccio, foglie strappate in pezzi grandi e gambi rimossi

- 2 cucchiai di olio di cocco fuso

- Sale a piacere

Preparazione:

1. Preriscaldare il forno a 150°C.

2. In una ciotola grande, mescolare il cavolo riccio con l'olio di cocco e il sale fino a che è ben ricoperto.

3. Disporre il cavolo riccio in un singolo strato su una teglia rivestita di carta da forno.

4. Cuocere per 10-15 minuti, fino a che non diventa croccante.

5. Lasciare raffreddare prima di servire.

Queste ricette non solo sono rapide e facili da preparare, ma offrono anche il perfetto equilibrio di nutrienti richiesti per mantenere uno stato di chetosi, assicurando che si possa godere di pasti deliziosi senza compromettere la dieta chetogenica.

Espandendo ulteriormente il repertorio di ricette chetogeniche semplici e veloci, esploriamo altre idee che possono arricchire il piano alimentare chetogenico, mantenendo la varietà e il gusto senza compromettere l'efficacia della dieta.

Colazione: Smoothie al Burro di Mandorle e Cacao

Ingredienti:

- 1/2 avocado

- 2 cucchiai di burro di mandorle

- 1 cucchiaio di cacao in polvere non zuccherato

- 1 tazza di latte di cocco

- Dolcificante a base di eritritolo a piacere

- Cubetti di ghiaccio

Preparazione:

1. Mettere tutti gli ingredienti nel frullatore, aggiungendo i cubetti di ghiaccio per ultimo.

2. Frullare ad alta velocità fino a ottenere una consistenza liscia e cremosa.

3. Servire immediatamente per una colazione energizzante e nutriente.

Pranzo: Insalata di Tonno e Avocado

Ingredienti:

- 1 lattina di tonno al naturale, sgocciolato

- 1 avocado maturo, tagliato a cubetti

- 1/4 di cipolla rossa, affettata sottilmente

- 2 cucchiai di maionese a basso contenuto di carboidrati

- Succo di 1/2 limone

- Sale e pepe nero a piacere

Preparazione:

1. In una ciotola media, mescolare il tonno, l'avocado e la cipolla rossa.

2. Aggiungere la maionese e il succo di limone, condire con sale e pepe.

3. Mescolare delicatamente fino a combinare bene gli ingredienti.

4. Servire freddo, ideale per un pranzo rinfrescante e saziante.

Cena: Pollo alla Paprika

Ingredienti:

- 4 cosce di pollo disossate

- 2 cucchiai di paprika affumicata

- 1 cucchiaio di olio d'oliva

- 1/2 tazza di panna da cucina

- 1 cucchiaio di erba cipollina tritata

- Sale e pepe a piacere

Preparazione:

1. Preriscaldare il forno a 180°C.

2. Strofinare il pollo con la paprika, il sale e il pepe.

3. Scaldare l'olio d'oliva in una padella adatta al forno e rosolare il pollo su entrambi i lati fino a doratura.

4. Trasferire la padella nel forno e cuocere il pollo per 25 minuti.

5. Rimuovere dal forno, aggiungere la panna e l'erba cipollina, e cuocere per altri 5 minuti fino a che la salsa non si addensa leggermente.

6. Servire caldo con un contorno di verdure a basso contenuto di carboidrati.

Snack: Bocconcini di Formaggio e Olive

Ingredienti:

- Cubetti di formaggio a scelta (ad esempio cheddar o provolone)

- Olive verdi o nere, denocciolate

- Stuzzicadenti

Preparazione:

1. Alternare su uno stuzzicadenti un cubetto di formaggio e un'oliva.

2. Ripetere l'operazione fino a raggiungere la quantità desiderata.

3. Conservare in frigorifero e usare come snack pratici e soddisfacenti.

Queste ricette non solo sono rapide da preparare e adatte alla dieta chetogenica, ma offrono anche il vantaggio di essere facilmente personalizzabili in base ai gusti personali e alla disponibilità stagionale degli ingredienti, garantendo così che la dieta rimanga interessante, variata e piacevole. Questa varietà può aiutare a mantenere l'impegno a lungo termine verso uno stile di vita chetogenico, rendendo il processo di aderenza alla dieta non solo più facile ma anche più gratificante.

Approfondendo ulteriormente la varietà e la creatività nelle ricette chetogeniche, possiamo esplorare ancora più opzioni per arricchire il piano alimentare, introducendo idee che mantengono l'interesse culinario elevato e garantiscono la soddisfazione a ogni pasto.

Colazione: Pancake di Farina di Cocco

Ingredienti:

- 1/2 tazza di farina di cocco
- 1/4 tazza di farina di mandorle
- 4 uova
- 1/2 tazza di latte di mandorla (non zuccherato)
- 1 cucchiaio di eritritolo o altro dolcificante chetogenico
- 1 cucchiaino di estratto di vaniglia
- 1/2 cucchiaino di lievito in polvere
- Un pizzico di sale
- Olio di cocco per la cottura

Preparazione:

1. In una ciotola, mescolare la farina di cocco, la farina di mandorle, il lievito e il sale.

2. In un'altra ciotola, sbattere le uova con il latte di mandorla, il dolcificante e la vaniglia.

3. Unire gli ingredienti umidi a quelli secchi e mescolare fino a ottenere un composto omogeneo.

4. Scaldare una padella a fuoco medio e ungere con olio di cocco.

5. Versare porzioni di impasto nella padella calda e cuocere fino a quando non si formano bolle sulla superficie, poi girare e cuocere dall'altro lato.

6. Servire caldi con burro e un dolcificante chetogenico a piacere.

Pranzo: Zuppa Cremosa di Funghi

Ingredienti:

- 2 tazze di funghi affettati

- 1 cipolla piccola, tritata

- 2 spicchi d'aglio, tritati

- 2 tazze di brodo di pollo o vegetale

- 1 tazza di panna da cucina

- 2 cucchiai di burro

- Sale e pepe nero a piacere

- Prezzemolo tritato per guarnire

Preparazione:

1. In una pentola grande, sciogliere il burro a fuoco medio.

2. Aggiungere la cipolla e l'aglio e soffriggere fino a che non diventano traslucidi.

3. Aggiungere i funghi e cuocere fino a che non sono dorati e tutto il liquido si è evaporato.

4. Versare il brodo e portare a ebollizione, poi ridurre il fuoco e lasciar sobbollire per circa 20 minuti.

5. Utilizzare un frullatore ad immersione per ridurre la zuppa in crema.

6. Aggiungere la panna, salare e pepare a gusto, e riscaldare fino a quando non è ben calda.

7. Servire guarnita di prezzemolo tritato.

Cena: Bistecca ai Ferri con Salsa Chimichurri

Ingredienti:

- 2 bistecca di manzo di alta qualità
- 1 mazzo di prezzemolo fresco
- 4 spicchi d'aglio
- 1/2 tazza di olio d'oliva
- 2 cucchiai di aceto di vino rosso
- 1 cucchiaino di peperoncino rosso tritato
- Sale e pepe a piacere

Preparazione:

1. Per la salsa chimichurri, tritare finemente prezzemolo e aglio e mescolare con olio d'oliva, aceto, peperoncino, sale e pepe.

2. Lasciare riposare la salsa per almeno un'ora per far si che i sapori si fondano.

3. Grigliare le bistecche a piacere, preferibilmente al sangue o al punto giusto.

4. Servire le bistecche con abbondante salsa chimichurri sopra.

Snack: Bastoncini di Sedano con Crema di Formaggio e Erbe

Ingredienti:

- Sedano, tagliato a bastoncini

- Crema di formaggio intero

- Una miscela di erbe fresche tritate (basilico, erba cipollina, prezzemolo)

- Pepe nero macinato fresco

Preparazione:

1. Mescolare la crema di formaggio con le erbe tritate e il pepe nero.

2. Spalmare la miscela nei solchi dei bastoncini di sedano.

3. Servire freschi come uno snack croccante e rinfrescante.

Queste ricette offrono un equilibrio tra semplicità e sapore, garantendo che si possano godere pasti e snack deliziosi senza deviare dai principi nutrizionali della dieta chetogenica. Incorporando queste opzioni nel proprio piano alimentare, si può mantenere una dieta varia e interessante, che facilita l'adesione a lungo termine alla dieta chetogenica.